MAGAZINE

# Tin House

Volume 17, Number 3

*"Whether it is that the faith which creates has dried up in me, or that reality takes shape in memory alone, the flowers I am shown today for the first time do not seem to me to be real flowers."*

—MARCEL PROUST
translated by Lydia Davis

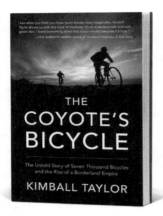

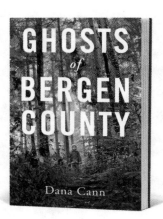

## MONTAUK

a novel by Max Frisch

Translated by Geoffrey Skelton
Introduction by Jonathan Dee

Max Frisch's candid story of a brief love affair illuminates a lifetime of relationships. Casting himself as both subject and observer, Frisch reflects on his marriages, children, friendships, and careers; a holiday weekend in Long Island is a trigger to recount and question events and aspects of his own life, along with creeping fears of mortality. He paints a bittersweet portrait that is sometimes painful and sometimes humorous, but always affecting. Emotionally raw and formally innovative, Frisch's novel collapses the distinction between art and life, but leaves the reader with a richer understanding of both.

"Extremely interesting . . . has an integrity that is original and admirable."

—*The New Yorker*

## GHOSTS OF BERGEN COUNTY

a novel by Dana Cann

Gil and Mary Beth Ferko moved to Bergen County thinking they would lead a typical suburban life. But after a hit-and-run kills their infant daughter, Gil seeks escape through heroin, and Mary Beth finds solace in the companionship of a mysterious girl. Years ago, Jen Yoder witnessed a man fall from a rooftop and chose to walk away. As her quest to rectify that mistake starts to collide with the mystery of the driver who killed Gil and Mary Beth's daughter, all of the characters are forced to face the fine line between fate and happenstance. A literary mystery with supernatural elements, *Ghosts of Bergen County* is a tautly paced and intricately plotted story in which collective burdens manifest into hauntings.

"Elegantly written and sharply observed."

—KIMBERLY MCCREIGHT,
*New York Times* best-selling author of
*Reconstructing Amelia*

**Available April 2016**                    **Available April 2016**

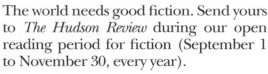

MAGAZINE
# Tin House

EDITOR IN CHIEF / PUBLISHER
Win McCormack

| | |
|---|---|
| EDITOR | Rob Spillman |
| ART DIRECTOR | Diane Chonette |
| MANAGING EDITOR | Cheston Knapp |
| EXECUTIVE EDITOR | Michelle Wildgen |
| POETRY EDITOR | Matthew Dickman |
| EDITOR-AT-LARGE | Elissa Schappell |
| PARIS EDITOR | Heather Hartley |
| ASSOCIATE EDITOR | Emma Komlos-Hrobsky |
| ASSISTANT EDITOR | Lance Cleland |
| EDITORIAL ASSISTANT | Thomas Ross |

CONTRIBUTING EDITORS: Dorothy Allison, Steve Almond, Aimee Bender, Charles D'Ambrosio, Brian DeLeeuw, Anthony Doerr, CJ Evans, Nick Flynn, Matthea Harvey, Jeanne McCulloch, Christopher Merrill, Rick Moody, Whitney Otto, D. A. Powell, Jon Raymond, Rachel Resnick, Helen Schulman, Jim Shepard, Karen Shepard, Bill Wadsworth

DESIGNER: Jakob Vala

INTERNS: Noah Dow, Nicole Flattery, Erin Kaempf, Taylor Lannamann, Boramie Sao, Marie Scarles

READERS: Leslie Marie Aguilar, Stephanie Booth, Susan DeFreitas, Polly Dugan, Selin Gökçesu, Paris Gravley, Todd Gray, Lisa Grgas, Dahlia Grossman-Heinz, Carol Keeley, Louise Wareham Leonard, Su-Yee Lin, Julian Lucas, Ian Nelson, Alyssa Persons, Sean Quinn, Lauren Roberts, Gordon Smith, Jennifer Taylor, JR Toriseva, Lin Woolman, Charlotte Wyatt

| | |
|---|---|
| DEPUTY PUBLISHER | Holly MacArthur |
| CIRCULATION DIRECTOR | Laura Howard |
| DIRECTOR OF PUBLICITY | Nanci McCloskey |
| COMPTROLLER | Janice Carter |

## Tin House Books

EDITORIAL ADVISOR Rob Spillman
EDITORS Meg Storey, Tony Perez, Masie Cochran
ASSISTANT EDITOR Thomas Ross

Tin House Magazine (ISSN 1541-521X) is published quarterly by McCormack Communications LLC, 2601 Northwest Thurman Street, Portland, OR 97210. Vol. 17, No. 3, Spring 2016. Printed by Versa Press, Inc. Send submissions (with SASE) to Tin House, P.O. Box 10500, Portland, OR 97296-0500. ©2014 McCormack Communications LLC. All rights reserved. No part of this publication may be reproduced, stored in a retrieval system, or transmitted in any form or by any means, electronic, mechanical, photocopying, recording, or otherwise, without the prior written permission of McCormack Communications LLC. Visit our Web site at **www.tinhouse.com**.

Basic subscription price: one year, $50.00. For subscription requests, write to P.O. Box 469049, Escondido, CA 92046-9049, or e-mail tinhouse@pcspublink.com, or call 1-800-786-3424. Additional questions, e-mail laura@tinhouse.com.

Periodicals postage paid at Portland, OR 97210 and additional mailing offices.

Postmaster: Send address changes to Tin House Magazine, P.O. Box 469049, Escondido, CA 92046-9049.

Newsstand distribution through Disticor Magazine Distribution Services (disticor.com). If you are a retailer and would like to order Tin House, call 905-619-6565, fax 905-619-2903, or e-mail Melanie Raucci at mraucci@disticor.com. For trade copies, contact W. W. Norton & Company at 800-233-4830.

Samuel Beckett famously ended his novel *The Unnamable* "You must go on. I can't go on. I'll go on." Why? How? Is it faith that drives us onward? And if so, faith in *what*? Writers have struggled with this question since the first hominids started scratching symbols into rocks. Do we put our faith in our survival skills or create a pantheon of deities to guide and protect us? By the Twentieth Century, writers like Beckett put their faith in words. In our time of worldwide upheavals and immanent climate catastrophe, our faith in words is under constant assault. Yet writers do go on. For Joy Williams, a selection of micro-fictions from *99 Stories of God* (soon to be published by Tin House Books) grapples with many of the same themes of her nearly fifty years of writing—the divine and the uncanny. Poet Natalie Diaz writes, "I make my faith in my hands." Alan Lightman puts his faith in the laws of nature, while Pakistani novelist Mohsin Hamid contemplates the fraught nature of writing in a country named after *faith*. President Obama's favorite writer-interview subject, Marilynne Robinson, argues that "*faith* and *religion* are neither synonyms nor antonyms." Mira Ptacin visits Maine in search of the Spiritualists, while Alex Mar examines the life and legacy of Doreen Valiente, the Mother of Modern Witchcraft. Father-and-son authors Jonathan and Adam Wilson discuss their faith in the family seder, the rituals and food that transcend time and space. In his primer on the history of faith, James Carse makes the case for complexity and how not to define religion. We know that there are no simple answers to questions of faith, but after reading this issue perhaps you will be as Plato said, "twice armed if we fight with faith." Our hope is that you are fighting the good fight.

# CONTENTS

ISSUE #67 / FAITH

## Fiction

### Joy Williams

JAIL ............ 16
DEAREST ............ 17
AND YOU ARE . . . ............ 18
GIRAFFE ............ 19
SEE THAT YOU REMEMBER ............ 20
NOT HIS BEST ............ 21
WET ............ 22

### Jamie Quatro

BELIEF ⁃ *Some mornings I wake up a Christian.* ............ 34

### Caoilinn Hughes

SORRY IS THE CHILD ⁃ *One Friday afternoon when they were walking to Heuston Station to be babysat by Auntie Ada, Gael came to know the depth of her brother's conviction.* ............ 42

### Michael Helm

IN THE MASSIF CENTRAL ⁃ *Since the summer Celia turned twelve her father had taken her on expeditions.* ............ 57

### Ramona Ausubel

CLUB ZEUS ⁃ *We choose to commemorate all those gods and goddesses differently— not that we don't have columns. We have plenty.* ............ 110

### Daniel Torday

NATE GERTZMAN DRAWS THE INTERNET - *We didn't have happiness, my wife and I, we didn't have certainty—but we had money for the first time.* ............ 189

## Poetry

### Anne Carson

I WAS THINKING ABOUT HENRY JAMES'S ADVICE TO HIS NEPHEW, BILLY, STRUGGLING TO CLOSE HIS CANVAS BAG FOR THE RETURN JOURNEY FROM LAMB HOUSE, LONDON, TO AMERICA, 1903 ............ 32

### Alicia Jo Rabins

CATHEDRAL ............ 54
WE LEARN TO BE HUMAN ............ 55
THE VAGINA HEALER ............ 56

### Chuang-Tzu

*Translated by Ha Poong Kim*
RAMBLE IN THE VILLAGE OF NOTHINGWHATSOEVER ............ 86

### Sarah V. Schweig

THE TOWER ............ 102

### Maureen N. McLane

R&B ............ 125
AGAINST THE PROMISE OF A VIEW ............ 126

### James Gendron

FROM WEIRDE SISTER ............ 154

### Nate Klug

REV. VALENTINE RATHBURN MEETS THE SHAKERS ............ 160
AUGUSTINE ON TIME ............ 162
GRACE ............ 164

## Marcus Slease

SACRED SPRING ............ 203
BAPTISM ............ 205

## Features

### James Carse

HOW NOT TO DEFINE RELIGION ⊹ *An investigation of one of the world's most beguiling words.* ............ 23

### Mira Ptacin

THE IN-BETWEENS ⊹ *The Spiritualists believed they would live forever, but we only know for sure that their thought has survived.* ............ 130

### Alex Mar

A WITCH IS A WITCH IS A WITCH ⊹ *She held me spellbound in the night / Dancing shadows and firelight / Crazy laughter in another room / And she drove herself to madness with a silver spoon.* ............ 146

### Alexis Knapp

AFTER FORTUNE ⊹ *"The greatest misery in adverse fortune is once to have been happy." Thus spake Boethius.* ............ 165

### Joshua Cohen

DREAM TRANSLATIONS FROM THE EARLY HASIDIC AND ELSEWHERE ⊹ *This world compares to the next world as sleeping does to wakefulness.* ............ 180

## Limits of Faith

### Mohsin Hamid

UNITY, FAITH, DISCIPLINE ............ 39

### Aimee Bender
PORTALS ........... 82

### Alan Lightman
FAITH IN SCIENCE ........... 107

### Natalie Diaz
THE HAND HAS TWENTY-SEVEN BONES ........... 157

### Marilynne Robinson
CONVERSATION WITH THE SACRED ........... 178

### Christian Wiman
NOT EVEN WRONG ........... 199

## Interview

### Louise Erdrich
*The many laureled author communed with Emma Komlos-Hrobsky to rap about kindness, love, and George W. Bush hitchhiking through Syria.* ........... 74

## Lost & Found

### Darcey Steinke
ON FANNY HOWE'S *Indivisible* ⊹ *The most vibrant spiritual lives are often lived outside the traditional church structure.* ........... 88

### Cheston Knapp
ON HAROLD FREDERIC'S *The Damnation of Theron Ware* ⊹ *Faith isn't lost, exactly; it's displaced, redirected. Art stands in for religion.* ........... 91

### Leigh Newman

ON JAYNE ANNE PHILLIPS'S *Sweethearts* – *Most of my thoughts were about my own failures as a person, which clotted up with my failures as a writer.* ............ 94

### Justin Nobel

ON HELMUT TRIBUTSCH'S *When the Snakes Awake* – *Could it be that the animals' super-acute sense of smell warns them of earthquakes?* ............ 97

### Pauls Toutonghi

ON TAHAR BEN JELLOUN'S *This Blinding Absence of Light* – *Those poor men in the desert—buried alive, slowly.* ............ 99

## Readable Feast

### Adam and Jonathan Wilson

PASSOVER, A CONVERSATION – *Father, I want to ask you a question. What up with the Four Questions?* ............ 207

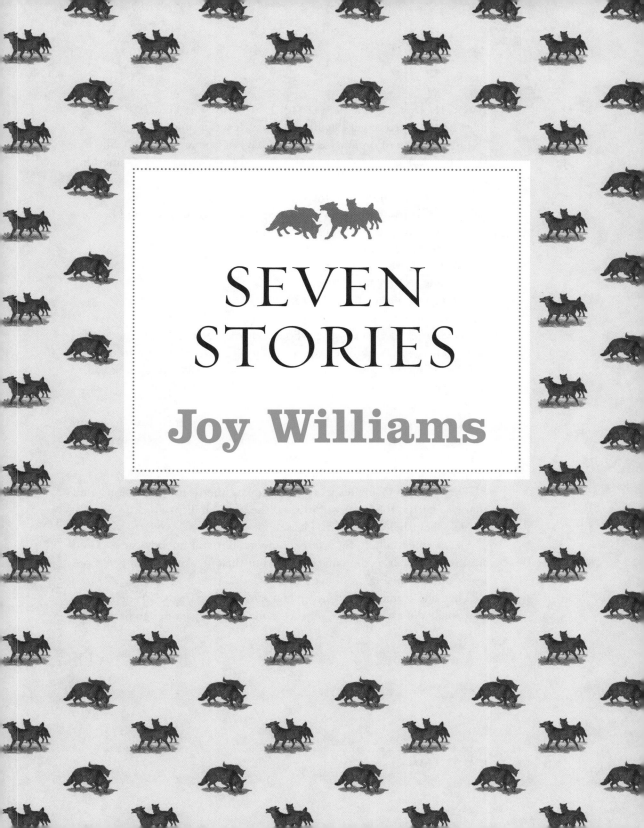

# SEVEN STORIES

## Joy Williams

I WAS IN JAIL FOR SHOPLIFTING. IT WAS SO STUPID. REALLY, I must have wanted to get caught and I was. It was a ring.

But the point of my story is that there was a woman in my cell. She was there before I got there. I was afraid she'd been arrested for something heinous.

Are you acquainted with the Bible? she asked me.

If I had had something to pull over my head like a hoodie and be concealed I would have, but I didn't.

I know the Lord's Prayer, I said.

What about the Book of Q? she asked.

There is no Book of Q, I said.

Vanity, vanity, she said. All is vanity.

Oh yes, I said. That's Ecclesiastes.

Ecclesiastes just means one who assembles. Qoheleth was the assembler. So it is the Book of Q. Most modern scholars use the untranslated Hebrew name of Qoheleth, who was the writer. I bet you think vanity means pride or conceit, I would bet that.

Yes, I said. Sure.

In the original the word means "breath," the merest breath, vapor, something utterly insubstantial and transient. Some translators even suggest the word means futility or absurdity.

Yes, yes. I don't know, I said.

The Book of Q invites us to contemplate the fleeting duration of all that we cherish, the brevity of life and the inexorability of death.

Help, help, help, I thought. Please.

She stopped talking for a few moments. But still nobody came. Then she said, Chrysalis is the same as pupa, but the one word is so much more lovely and promising, wouldn't you say?

Then she seemed to fall asleep and said nothing further. When someone finally did arrive, it was her they came for. They let her go first.

JAIL

PREVIOUS PAGE: ILLUSTRATION BY FRIEDRICH SPECHT

PENNY HAD NEVER LIKED THE HOUSE AND SPENT AS MUCH time as she could away from it. It fit her husband perfectly, however. He loved the open rooms, the little plunge beneath the palm trees, the shelves he had built for his many books, the long table where he and his friends played anagrams and poker. When he died, she accepted a position at a university a considerable distance away and rented out the house.

The new tenants adored it. They paid the rent promptly, planted flowers, and befriended the neighbors far more than Penny ever had. In front of the house they parked their three glorious vehicles—a Harley-Davidson, a Porsche, and a white Toyota Tundra.

They wanted to buy but offered a meager price. Penny's price was fair, everyone said so, but the tenants mentioned the roof, the chipped clawfoot tub, the ailing mahogany tree that would have to be taken down, the foundation. There was frequent mention of the foundation. As well they spoke of the risk they would be taking—the possibility of hurricanes and dengue fever, the continuing poor economy. But they adored the house. This was where they wanted to be.

Penny found them irritating in any number of ways—they were ostentatious, full of self-regard, and cheap. They also did not read. But she knew herself well enough to know that they irritated her because they had found happiness in a simple place where she had not.

A few weeks before their lease was up, they offered to meet her price, but she refused them.

After canceling the insurance, she returned to the vacated house. The rooms were immaculate. Even the glass in the windows sparkled. She went from room to room with a clump of sweet and smoldering sage. She tried to think in the language of blessing. Then, with the assistance of a few gallons of accelerant, she set all that had been the structure on fire.

# DEAREST

WHO WAS THAT OLD GUY AT THE WEDDING? NOBODY KNEW him. He was old and smiling. This was not good. He wore one of those tall, silvery boots that are supposed to assist in the healing of fractured bones. He had long, gray, undistinguished hair.

Finally, one of the groom's brothers went up to him and said, Who are you?

I'm Caradoc, the old man said. Caradoc.

Well, were you invited? You're creeping out the invited guests.

I'm not here to nibble on your fucking salmon, Caradoc said.

Later, the bride said: We should have let him stay. This is not good. What if he were Jesus or something?

The divorce cost seventeen times what the wedding had, and the children didn't turn out all that well either.

# AND YOU ARE . . .

WE WERE IN THE BAR AFTER GOLF AND THIS ACQUAINTANCE of mine says, "My gardener said the damnedest thing to me today."

And I say, "Yeah, well, gardeners."

"He's from Czechoslovakia. He was somehow involved in the shooting of all those giraffes back in the seventies. Forty-nine giraffes. It was the largest captive herd in the world at the time."

What can you possibly say in response to something like that? I said nothing.

"But he's been my gardener for years, and there's nothing he doesn't know about lawns and trees. But he's getting on. The crew he hires to help him are assholes."

"I see," I said.

"So he fires them almost as soon as he hires them, because they're ignorant, they don't want to work, but he works ceaselessly, he never stops moving. It makes me nervous just watching him sometimes."

"Not good," I say.

"So he's working all by himself today, running around, going from one thing to another, and he tells me he feels God at his elbow. All morning he tries to ignore this feeling of God at his elbow, because he knew God had some questions, he knew God wanted to initiate a dialogue with him and he was frightened. But finally he stopped what he was doing and faced God and God said to him, I want to give you something."

End of story.

"That's the damnedest thing," I said, wondering if it would turn out the old guy died on the spot or something.

# GIRAFFE

YOU KNOW THAT DREAM OF TOLSTOY'S WHERE HE'S IN SOME sort of bed contraption suspended between the abyss below and the abyss above? You know that one? Well, I gave it to him, the Lord said.

# SEE THAT YOU REMEMBER

FRANZ KAFKA ONCE CALLED HIS WRITING A FORM OF PRAYER.
He also reprimanded the long-suffering Felice Bauer in a letter: "I did
not say that writing ought to make everything clearer, but instead makes
everything worse; what I said was that writing makes everything clearer
and worse."

He frequently fretted that he was not a human being and that what he
bore on his body was not a human head. Once he dreamt that as he lay in
bed, he began to jump out the open window continuously at quarter-hour
intervals.

"Then trains came and one after another they ran over my body, out-
stretched on the tracks, deepening and widening the two cuts in my neck
and legs."

I didn't give him that one, the Lord said.

## NOT HIS BEST

THE LORD WAS DRINKING SOME WATER OUT OF A GLASS. THERE was nothing wrong with the glass, but the water tasted terrible.

This was in a white building on a vast wasteland. The engineers within wore white uniforms and booties on their shoes and gloves on their hands. The water had traveled many hundreds of miles through wide pipes to be here.

What have you done to my water? the Lord asked. My living water . . .

Oh, they said, we thought that was just a metaphor.

# WET

# HOW NOT TO
# DEFINE RELIGION

## James Carse

*A Primer*

"Religion." Practically ubiquitous nowadays, the word didn't enter popular discourse until roughly the seventeenth century. Enlightenment philosophers and historians, increasingly aware of Eastern religious practices, assumed there must be a common core to the world's religions, one that can be found in a great variety of styles and practices. And while scholars have found the major religions to be more or less incomparable, the presumption continues to the present day. Thus we use one term to encompass many things.

We are all familiar with the usual remarks: "Isn't God, or a form thereof, the main interest in each religion? And don't all religions have a Bible, or at least a sacred literature? How about priests, or rituals of worship, or ideas about death, or moral values, or forms of communal life like monasteries?"

The answer to all of these queries is yes, but only sort of.

• • •

The God question can be easily brushed away. The religions will do it for us, in fact. Let's start with Judaism and Christianity. The God of the Bible is hardly the same in

both traditions. By claiming Jesus was God incarnate, Christians drew an absolute distinction between themselves and Jewish tradition. While the notion of the Messiah is held fondly by many Jews, there is no intimation that he has already come, or that he will resemble Jesus in any way, or that he will be a divine being. Especially on this latter point, there is no possibility of reconciling these two views of the divine. To say that they are the same God worshiped differently has no basis in fact, in language, or in practice.

Disparities are even greater when we turn to the East. It makes no sense to say that Hindus believe in God. They have a multitude of divinities that play a dizzying number of roles in worship, art, politics, personal morality, and public ceremony. It is true that over the centuries, there have been many Hindu thinkers and scholars who have been tempted to construct a grand theology or metaphysical scheme that offers a comprehensive grasp of this array of devas and demons, but the history of these attempts isn't encouraging.

Vedanta, one school of Hindu thought, is the most open to divergent views, and has for several centuries drawn the attention of many Western thinkers. Vedantists have eagerly sought common ground with Western traditions, too. Though the early promise of an inclusive intellectual vision has largely faded, the *Upanishads*,

> Vedantists have eagerly sought common ground with Western traditions, too.

an ancient text of unknown authorship, is regarded as a companion work to Western mysticism, particularly that of the Middle Ages. Its famous phrase, *neti neti*, "not this, not that," has been evoked as confirmation of an overarching oneness that eludes our full understanding of the divine, a point the Christian mystic Meister Eckhart and the Jewish mystic Abulafia often made.

Human intelligence, they claimed, is simply too limited to say that God is *this* or *that*. The divine, they insisted, is beyond all possibility of definition, and remains therefore an ineluctable mystery.

The *Upanishads* often use the term "Brahman" to refer to the highest level of the divine. Brahman, we learn, is not distinct from "Atman," or "soul." This intimate association of that which is most sublime with that which is "closer to us than we are to ourselves" seems an easy fit with Western thought. But this apparent common ground works best at an abstract level. Once it is attached to more concrete and particular texts and contexts, limitations and misleading ideas surface.

Mahatma Gandhi, for example, famously wrote that he found little difference between the Christian Gospels and one of the most revered of all Hindu texts, the *Bhagavad Gita*. The observation is shocking. The *Gita* consists of a wartime conversation between Prince Arjuna and his chariot driver, who happens to be the god Krishna in one of his avatars. Arjuna faces a perplexing decision: for which of the armies should he take up his sword. It is a dilemma because he has friends and close family on both sides. Krishna doesn't hesitate. Arjuna should do his caste duty, he declares, and since the prince is in a warrior caste, he must fight. Which side he fights on doesn't matter at all. Where did the Mahatma find Jesus of the Gospels urging his followers to take up war as a sacred duty? The truth is that, despite any hopefulness, the Christian and Hindu traditions are distinct and irreconcilable. It is quite impossible to imagine even the most ecstatic evangelical Christian worshipers dancing to drunken spiritual excess in the presence of Krishna in any of his poses, much less that of an elephant god.

The notion of God as the defining element of religion crashes most completely in Buddhism. The Buddha made it clear that he had no divine powers, indeed, that no one has divine powers. He was not a performer of miracles, received no messages from on high, and didn't hint at immortality. As he was dying, there was no vision of the Enlightened One ascending to etheric realms, nor were there any promises of his return. With his final instructions to those present, he entirely removed himself from their lives and from all that would follow.

> In short, the Jews do not simply have one sacred text that presents a full idea of their religion.

Buddhism, therefore, is a religion without God, or it is not a religion at all. If the former, the idea of *God* as an essential element of religion is basically useless. If the latter, then the idea of religion can be applied arbitrarily. But the great majority of us refer to Buddhism as one of the world's great religions. Taking this view, we have to conclude that the idea of God will confuse any effort to find the essence of religion.

• • •

What then about sacred texts? Don't all religions have something like a Bible? A good test of this claim is to look at the three major religions in the West—Judaism, Christianity, and Islam—since their adherents are sometimes referred to collectively as "People of the Book." Even more suggestive, they all consider themselves "children of Abraham," as if religiously speaking they were all first cousins. A brief survey of the three will show how little these cousins have in common in their use and understanding of sacred literature.

The Hebrew scriptures, the Christian Old Testament, are an enduring subject of close study for Jews, but they constitute a text that cannot be meaningfully read in a larger literary context. When the Romans destroyed the Second Temple in the year 70 CE, they effectively ended the priesthood and its centralized control over institutional Jewish life. But there had always been noninstitutional, populist movements and sects, mostly rural and independent of the Jerusalem hierarchy, such as the legalistic Sadducees and the monastic Essenes. Among these were a number of itinerant teachers, or rabbis, who were of little interest to the Romans since, having no organization, they posed no political threat to imperial rule. Known collectively as Pharisees (from the Greek word, meaning "to separate"), they continued to teach the law, or Torah, to the people and to live with a demonstrable ritual purity. (Some scholars believe Jesus was himself a Pharisee.)

The Pharisees adopted the popular view that God handed to Moses not one but two Torahs: one written, the other oral. The former is passed on without the slightest alteration. The latter, however, will never be fully known but will be an inexhaustible source of wisdom over the centuries. The Pharisees, having escaped Roman wrath, continued their work declaiming both Torahs, until about the year 200 CE, when they began to write down the body of laws that had so far existed only in memory. Over the next four centuries, the recorded exploration and explanation of Torah grew into the immense works we know as the Palestinian and the Babylonian Talmuds. These comprise a wide range of literary forms, including commentary on the law, reflections on history, speculation, biographies, wisdom, and illuminating tales, all of it rooted in Torah.

In short, the Jews do not simply have one sacred text that presents a full idea of their religion. The only appropriate access to the Torah is through a recorded oral conversation that includes many thousands of learned voices, each refining or correcting the others. The Talmud was closed around 600 CE. Nothing new will be added to it. But the Oral Torah will never close. From the point of view of its sacred text, Judaism looks like nothing so much as an extravagantly rich conversation that cannot end itself.

Christians' traditional understanding of their own sacred literature is remarkably different. Over the centuries, the "Old" Testament was read by Christians primarily as a collection of prophecies fulfilled by the incarnation of God in the person of Jesus. The "New" Testament is the account of that fulfillment. In this way of thinking, the text sacred to Christians brings to its proper end the conversation that is Judaism. What was unknown, or only partly known, to Jews, is now known in full to the followers of Jesus. The Jewish story ends with the birth of the Christ child.

The origin of Islam's sacred text, the Qur'an, places it in a category radically distinct from that of Jews and Christians. The latter two never denied that their scriptures were penned by a number of human hands. All of the human authors were inspired, but the numerous inconsistencies in the text indicate that their natural limitations prevented a completely faultless transcription of the divine voice.

However, Muslims consider the Qur'an a "recitation," that is, a direct quoting of Allah. Muhammad received the text directly from its divine source and, because he was illiterate, precisely recited what was said on any one of his many encounters with the angelic messenger. These were written down, one at a time, by his wife, as well as many others. It was several centuries before these fragments were gathered into a single volume. But since the accuracy of each quotation of the angel was overseen by Allah, the text we have is exactly what was said to Muhammad.

One consequence of this direct communication from the angel is that, since Muhammad was a native Arabic speaker, the Qur'an cannot be properly read in any other language. The sacred text does not translate. It may seem, therefore, that whoever quotes the Qur'an is speaking the words of Allah in all their original authority—since they are, of course, guaranteed to be accurate. But because the angel spoke on so many different occasions over a period of years, the exact order of the recitations cannot be known. In fact, the Qur'an is organized into chapters, or Suras, not according to their content but according to their length. Even an English "translation" will show that the text has the distinct feel of a random gathering of these individual recitations. There is no thematic thread or historical arrangement of the revelations. This may appear to be a disadvantage to the faithful, but Muslims occasionally point out that although the text seems chaotic from a human perspective, from an angelic perspective it is in perfect order and makes utter and final sense. Muslims, by this account, can quote Allah directly, but

they cannot speak the words with divine authority. The final interpretation of their sacred text will forever elude them.

. . .

These last remarks about Islam and the Qur'an might strike an attentive reader as surprising, especially at a time when the news thunders with reports of a turbulent Islam. We read that young warriors justify acts of rape and slavery—even of other Muslims—with passages from the Qur'an. We're all familiar, perhaps overly so, with the idea of jihad. Such justifications and proof-texting are the result of literalist interpretations of the sacred text.

Fundamentalists of this sort are found in all the world's major religions, of course. And we hear so much about them these days that it's easy to forget that fundamentalism is a relatively recent phenomenon. In Christianity, literalism first made its angry appearance in the nineteenth century. Most scholars agree that it was a response to the rise of Darwinism. Suddenly the opening lines of Genesis were taken to be factual accounts, equal in authority to the observations of scientists.

Literalism has also shown up in modern Hinduism, of all places, where it's closely tied to nationalist movements and conflicts with Islam and other religions. We notice it in certain strands of Judaism in Israel, too, where the settler movement and some orthodox groups refer to the Palestinian West Bank as Judea and Samaria. They believe it is God's intention that they should be the exclusive inhabitants of the region.

If we step back and look more closely at the historic use of sacred texts we can see that literalism is essentially cancelled out by the scriptures themselves. The fact that the transcription of the Qur'an and its organization allow multiple interpretations of the same passages reinforces the larger view that only the angels know what the text is really saying. The rest of us live on in partial ignorance.

Because the Hebrew scriptures are to be read only in the larger context of centuries of argument and illumination, to settle on a single historical reference is at best a misreading. Proof-texting Christians should remind themselves that their sacred text—composed by a number of unknown and all-too-human authors—is so full of contradictions and inconsistencies that the best they can hope for is an approximate reading, one always open to correction. Jesus says nothing in opposition to same-sex marriage (it didn't exist), but neither does he condemn slavery (though it was all around him). Deciding what he *might* have said about these issues requires wide study of the cultural setting of his time, and a humble assessment of one's own interpretive skills.

In a phrase, fundamentalism has no place in the living religions. Biblical and Qur'anic literalists display an astonishing

misunderstanding of their most formative literature.

. . .

Now we turn our attention to such phenomena as priestly orders, temples, intentional groups, styles of worship, moralities, theories and practices concerning death, and relationship to surrounding societies. In their efforts to compare one tradition with another, scholars have come to see the essential arbitrariness of such analyses. Why choose to compare, say, a Hindu Brahman with a Muslim imam? Or a Buddhist walking meditation with a Jesuit spiritual retreat? Just because they have some superficial similarity? Such an exercise either shows no real similarity or mirrors back what we were looking for in the first place.

Better then that we look not at how religions compare but at how they differ. These traditions have existed for centuries and, in some cases, millennia. Hinduism can be traced back at least 4,000 years; Judaism as we know it at least 2,000, possibly another two millennia; Buddhism broke from Hinduism about two and a half millennia ago; Islam has been with us for 1,400 years.

What is more, consider the extraordinary fact that Hinduism and Buddhism flourished for a thousand years in the same

> Better then that we look not at how religions compare but at how they differ.

area of India; that Hindus and Buddhists in that region spoke the same languages and deeply influenced each other's art—but never was there a question whether one was a Buddhist or a Hindu. Equally remarkable is the centuries-long overlap of Judaism, Christianity, and Islam in Spain and North Africa, many of their members speaking each other's languages and reading the same literature. There, too, we can be certain that there was no confusion of identities. No one woke up as a Jew, had dinner as a Muslim, and went to bed as a Christian.

The word "identity" is especially useful here. The Latin root for the word (*idem*, or "same") suggests that to have an identity is to be like (or the same as) oneself so completely as never to be another. There may be similarities between you and me: size, age, gender, nationality, vocation, and athletic ability, for example. But no matter how closely we come to sharing these features, neither of us can overlap so completely as to become the other. I may even think the same thoughts as you, but I am not doing your thinking. So it is with religion. There is something in Christianity, say, that cannot identify with anything but itself. The next question would logically be: What exactly *is* that something?

Christians have a ready answer: the person of Jesus. To the disappointment of many inquisitive Christians, but fortunately for Christianity itself, this is an answer that hides a volcanic supply of new questions.

Even during his own lifetime Jesus was confounding to those closest to him.

Immediately following his death there were strongly competing views of the meaning of his life, his teachings, and his ministry. If we were to collect every attempt written over the ensuing two millennia to explain who Jesus *really* was, what he *really* said, and what he *really* did, we would need whole city blocks of towering libraries whose shelves would creak with books in hundreds of languages, not one in full agreement with another. Tens of thousands of Jesuses seemed to have been walking about Galilee. The variety is stunning. In short, Christians are nowhere near an agreement on what they should believe.

On the face of it, this would seem a disadvantage for Christianity, a deficit that counts against its vitality. It has, however, the opposite effect. This deep uncertainty about what it is that makes Christianity Christianity only feeds the desire to settle the matter once and for all, even if the matter won't settle. Of course, individual Christians, and their sects, and their churches, and their denominations, continue to make declarations that have the resonance of certainty, even the authority of dogma. One theologian after another will offer his corrections to what has been declared, often with brilliant and sweeping resolutions, also speaking as with divine authority. If Christians cannot decide what they should believe, they cannot stop trying to close the issue. There is *something* that makes the task impossible and at the same time irresistible. Any claim that this *something* can be isolated and described, however learned or emphatic, just becomes part of the enormous conversation that Christianity is. Christianity, in short, is the unsuccessful two-thousand-year effort to understand what Christianity is about. It is, in other words, an extraordinary failure—which is at the same time its enduring strength.

The same point could be made of the other religions. Given their longevity and the ceaseless struggle to explain themselves, each religion has an identity that sets it off from all others. Like Christianity, each has an enormous literature, its history rife with alternative understandings of itself. Islam may appear to some Americans as a unified block of avid believers, for example, but it is in fact a vast patchwork of sects and schools of interpretation that are often in violent competition with each other. They, too, want to put a cap on the search for that something that constitutes their identity. That they cannot, and that they persist in the effort, gives the religion an astonishing vitality, seen in its expansive growth across the globe.

But religions do die. As any historian of religion knows, there is no guarantee for the timeless survival of any tradition, however vital it may seem over the centuries of its existence. And the reason? In almost every case, the death of a religion comes with its loss of identity—that is, when it allows its identity to shift to something outside itself. A religion can be identified with, for example, a system of thought (as happened to Gnosticism and Manichaeism), a political entity (Mithraism and Shinto), a geographic space (the Incas and the Norse), an ethnicity (Athabascans and pre-Ptolemaic Egyptians), even a distinctive practice (Taoism.)

Will Christianity die? Hinduism? Even Islam? Yes. All of them will. When the elusive identity of each shatters, or shifts to a definable other, the great conversation at the heart of each tradition is over. And then its death is certain to follow. Will other religions take their places? No doubt. But it will take centuries to know whether their replacements have the inner fire that consumes and re-creates itself with sufficient intensity to deserve the tag "religion." 🛡

I WAS THINKING ABOUT HENRY
JAMES'S ADVICE TO HIS NEPHEW,
BILLY, STRUGGLING TO CLOSE HIS
CANVAS BAG FOR THE RETURN
JOURNEY FROM LAMB HOUSE,
LONDON, TO AMERICA, 1903

halfman
halfsodden
halfeaten
halfbearded
halfburnt
halfmangled
half wanting half
halfslave
halffinished
halfboiled
halfgreen
halfgod
halfbroken
half of the inheritance

a semicircle
halfwhite
halfmad
halfwithered
halfdrunk
half a villain
halfdry
containing half as much again
halfass
halfplinth
half pulled down
halfbreathing
of half a stadium
halfsoldier
cut in two
halfshining
halfbald
halfknavish
halflinen
with head dropped to one side

"no captain ever makes port with all the cargo with which he set sail"

FICTION

# Belief

Some mornings I wake up a Christian. On such mornings, upon waking, I feel a precognitive tug of joy in my body, a sense of delight I experienced regularly in childhood—my mind a blank page upon which someone is poised to write a message of bliss. On such mornings I know the tug of joy is a nudge from God, to remind me I am His child, I came to Earth trailing clouds of glory. How blessed, to feel divine approbation in my biological systems, unbidden. Today, out of gratitude, I will strive to please God with my actions. I will be the hands and feet of Christ, spreading love to every soul that crosses my path. I will not do this perfectly—there will be mistakes—but God will forgive. Has already forgiven.

## Jamie Quatro

I get up and brush my teeth. My husband has left the toilet lid up. The cat has vomited on my daughter's comforter. I will have to strip the duvet and wash it and take the comforter to the dry cleaner; as it is made of down, this will be expensive. My neighbor is late for carpool, which means my son will be late to school for a fifth time this semester, which will mean a weekend detention, to which I will have to drive him. At the grocery store a woman I recognize from church says she has read my book and that she would like to sit down with me and talk about it, and about my personal faith, and my stance on Christianity in general. At dinner no one talks except the daughter, who mostly complains. My husband cannot help our son with his calculus homework—the son yells, my husband yells back, I yell at both of them to calm them down. After the children are in bed, I drink wine, too much of it, and Jimmy Fallon says that China has officially surpassed America in economic power, but—good news—America still has the best reality television anywhere. Also rap music. I have always loved Jimmy Fallon but tonight I loathe him. My husband sits down beside me with his glass of wine and I loathe him, too, for finishing off the bottle when I had planned on another glass, for his inability to assist our son with his calculus, for his shortness of temper with the son, and for his persistence in leaving the lid up despite my taping a note above the toilet. I also loathe my son for still requiring help with homework his junior year in high school, and I loathe the cat for always selecting fabric/upholstery on which to vomit. I loathe the woman at the grocery store who thinks my personal faith has anything to do with my art. I especially loathe myself for all this loathing. For the fact that, despite my intention to spread love, I have not only failed to feel love, but I feel only its opposite.

Before getting into bed, I read an essay in a book of essays by a brilliant atheist critic. This critic is someone I have met. He is kind, generous, compassionate, intelligent. He moves among people who are also all of those things. Every person I can think of who is kind, generous, compassionate, and intelligent is atheist or agnostic. None of them have to think about pleasing a divine being, no one is asking them to be grateful for anything, they inhabit a meaningless universe and will cease to exist when they die. Therefore, if they persist in kind, generous, compassionate, and intelligent behaviors, it is heroic. They are free to love, they loathe no one. Glorious. I fall asleep determined that tomorrow I will wake up an atheist.

· · ·

Some mornings I wake up an atheist. On such mornings, upon waking, I do not feel the little tug of joy I used to feel regularly, in childhood. I sense no impending message of happiness. I feel only vacuity, the cold certainty that God is dead and everything I've ever felt of Him is the biological result of hormones, or a bright trigger spot in my brain, or psychology/wishful thinking, or what my parents told me. If I love anyone today, it will be the heroic effort of one tiny pointless accidental creature. There is no one watching, no one to please or displease. No mistakes or the need for forgiveness.

A lightness of spirit enters my being. I have nothing to lose and everything to gain. My daughter cannot find a shoe, and when I locate it beneath the slipcovered couch and bring it to her—though she blames me for losing the shoe, and making her late to school—I sing "Reunited" while she puts the shoes on. This makes her laugh. The woman who drives carpool is late picking up my son but I notice she has her phone to her ear and she is cry-

> Some mornings I wake up an atheist. On such mornings, upon waking, I do not feel the little tug of joy I used to feel regularly, in childhood.

ing. She is recently divorced, her husband left her with three children, but she still keeps up her end of the carpool. The poor woman, I think. To be alone, and lonely, and also a cosmic accident, extinction waiting at the end of all the suffering. I feel a tremendous measure of compassion and gratitude for her. Also, compassion and gratitude for myself, extinction likewise waiting for me, yet here I am, singing, returning a gentle word. At the dry cleaner an elderly man I've seen smoking cigars outside the Mountain Cafe brings in his suits and tells the attendant to please take good care of them, his deceased wife picked them out in 1953 and they're the only suits he's ever owned. The woman in the grocery store asks her question and I want to embrace her, tell her she needn't be so afraid. After dinner I think my son is heroic for trying to do, night after night, what his school requires of him, and I admire my husband for continuing to try to help him, even though he never took calculus himself and has told me, more than once, that calculus in high school is a waste of a year. And here's Jimmy Fallon presiding, making us laugh at ourselves, poor foolish smiling Americans.

Poor serious driven Chinese. Desperate mammals giving life our heartiest effort. How worthy of kindness and generosity and compassion.

Before going to bed, it occurs to me that this all-encompassing compassion for humanity is what Christ taught and embodied. Lost sheep, paralyzed by their fear of death, in need of a shepherd who will enter into, suffer alongside of, die in the stead of. Then rise and overcome the thing they're most afraid of. Give them a fighting chance, something to hope for. The evil things they do en masse are necessarily repugnant to me, a perfectly loving being. The evil things they do cannot help but create a vast divide. But they should not have to bear the blame. It is not their fault. They have simply forgotten who they are. And as I am perfect in justice—all debts must be paid—I am also perfect in mercy, and therefore will become one of them and pay the cost in full. Breach the divide. Treat them as they deserve to be treated: divine beings worthy of love and forgiveness. Glorious.

I get into bed beside my husband, who says he feels like a failure with our son, and that he had a troubling conversation with a client who isn't satisfied with the strategic plan he created and may not renew my husband's retainer. Also that he misses me, physically, as it's been a week since we made love. The loathing for him returns—for the way he uses sex as a panacea—but here is my chance to live out the all-encompassing compassion of Christ. To look not only to my own interests but also to the interests of others.

I pull his hand out from beneath my T-shirt.

I really want to read tonight, I say.

Morning will be better timing, I say.

My husband rolls over. I open my book of essays by the brilliant atheist critic and fall asleep determined that tomorrow, I will wake up a Christian. 📖

# "Unity, Faith, Discipline"

Writing about the subject of faith in a country named for faith, founded upon faith, with *faith* as the central word of its national motto, is, shall we say, a somewhat fraught endeavor. I have for the past six years again lived in Pakistan, where I was born and spent about half of my younger life. Pakistan is the *stan*, the land, of the *pak*, the pure. It was founded as a home for the Muslims of British Imperial India as the British left and partitioned India. Pakistanis learn from our first schoolbook, and see inscribed on signs and posters and sometimes in the form of flowers on the grassy margins of roads, the exhortation "Unity, Faith, Discipline." Unity around faith. Discipline in faith. Unified, disciplined faith.

Even so, I was struck anew upon my return to Pakistan by the degree of coercion and compulsion and indeed violence in matters of faith. When I was a child, restaurants still served food, albeit discretely, during the fasting hours of the month of Ramadan. They do so no longer. When I was a child, I did not know which of my friends were Shia. It did not seem to matter. Now people are not infrequently killed for being Shia, murdered by shadowy assassins. Others are killed for belonging to other sects, or for

## Mohsin Hamid

questioning the nation's blasphemy law, or for defending those who question the nation's blasphemy law.

No, my present home does not seem a particularly auspicious venue for inquiries into faith.

And yet faith takes many forms. There is, of course, the faith one might have in organized religion. And then there is the faith a farmer has when planting a seed purchased with borrowed money that this year the rains will arrive on time, that it is possible to farm and make a living from farming, that a farmer and his family can somehow survive. There is the faith a parent has when sending a child to school that she will return. There is the faith a writer has when sitting down alone, day after day, year after year, that the words will come.

There is also the faith that the place where one lives is indeed a sensible place to call home. In my case, this last item of faith has during the past six years faced a bit of a test.

"Why the hell do you live there?" friends in New York and London have been known to say, a question somehow both mildly offensive and warmingly touching at the same time. My friends say this especially after a recent massacre or bombing or discovery of a terrorist mastermind residing next door to the country's military academy.

My answers turn to family: to the pleasure I get, having grown up in an extended, tri-generational family, to live in a situation where my children can play with their grandparents every morning before the children go to school and the grandparents, who reside next door, go to work. I tell my friends about the importance to me, a storyteller, of feeling I am part of a story, and how I do feel part of a story here. I mention some vague yet not flimsy romantic attachment to Lahore, the way the city moves me.

But I know, have perhaps always known, that the choice to live in Pakistan is at heart a matter of faith: the faith that this land will live up to at least some of its vast potential, that it will stop devouring the dreams of its residents, that its children will grow up with more stability and less potential violence than they face today.

When I first moved back I felt cautiously optimistic. Pakistan had survived so much. Free elections had just transpired. Surely things would begin to improve.

I do not remember the first time I despaired. Perhaps it was brought on by an untimely funeral. Or by schools closing for the holidays prematurely, because of a fear of attacks. Or by glancing at a newspaper one morning. Or by yet another friend finally, after long resisting, packing up and moving abroad.

I have often thought of leaving again myself, but I have not yet left.

My faith in this place has, I will admit, been shaken. But my faith in New York was once shaken, when I lived there. My faith in London was once shaken, when I lived there.

I suppose I have learned to live with intermittent faith in a place. I leap from moments when I think, yes, my home will flourish, to others when I think, no, all that awaits is decline. Maybe this ebb and flow is common. Maybe it has more to do with me. Maybe it is the nature of a fiction writer, some fiction writers, to exist suspended between what is and what we desire there to be, unable, in the end, to pick one over the other, to commit to the life, to reality, or otherwise to the dream. ◈

# Sorry Is the Child

One Friday afternoon when they were walking to Heuston Station to be babysat by Auntie Ada—who was, those days, *relieving* their parents more often than not—Gael came to know the depth of her brother's conviction.

He had become quieter and quieter, as though he believed that each household had a noise equilibrium and that, as long as the total noise amounted to the same decibel sum, he could control the Foess household balance by way of his silence.

## Caoilinn Hughes

Gael handled him like a cloth, rinsing, wringing, twisting, hoping to get something out of him—some grime. She was trying to get him to play "Cursery Rhymes" as they walked. "Just do the next bit. *Mary, Mary quite contrary, how does your garden grow?*"

"I'm *not* changing cockle shells and you can't make me."

Guthrie was pink-cheeked by his sister's resolve to have him grow up at her abnormal rate. Even though nature would hold her to being only sixteen months older than him, with each passing month it seemed as if an extra year of difference were wedging itself between them.

"*Genius*, Guth!" She mouthed versions over and over to herself to perfect it.

"Don't, Gael."

"*With silver bell-ends, cocks, rearends, and pretty maids all in a row!*" She snorted with laughter.

"Stop! Don't. That's disgusting."

"That was all you, Guth."

"No it wasn't."

"Yeah so."

"No it wasn't! I was going to say, *Na-na na-na, na-na na-na. Wouldn't you like to know?*"

"Not bad for a ten-year-old. Less good than mine though. Man, I'd been trying to work in a gardener called José. You know, José uses his hosé to make the garden grow . . . but you beat me by miles. Maybe I don't need to worry about you any longer."

Guthrie had crossed his arms and turned into an open gate to get away from her.

"And now you're trespassing," she said. "*This* is what I'd call progress."

He swiveled around. "I'm *not trespassing*. This is a *park*. Leave me *alone*."

Gael could see he was close to tears, so she left him to it. The gated garden had an exit farther along. She moved slowly toward it, running her fingertips athwart the black railing and relishing the pins and needles produced. She only wanted the best for her brother. It seemed as if he looked up to her—their mother had confirmed as much—so Gael couldn't understand why he wouldn't take her help. He believed everything would go back to normal, soon. Whenever "soon" was, they'd be going to different secondary schools by then because Gael wanted to go to an all-girls school. Girls became fatuous versions of themselves around boys and she didn't want to deal with all that performance. There'd always be lunch breaks for meeting lads and being fingered behind suburban evergreen trees. Whereas Guthrie *wanted* to go to a mixed school, for reasons she couldn't fathom. She did spy pale blue welts on his torso when he stepped out of the shower room in a hand towel once, when the bath towels were all in the wash. That probably had something to do with it. His friends were mostly girls—and too few to make a pack, so they were no use. Their father believed in individual responsibility "to put the civil in civilization": all fights had to be debated into the form of disagreements in an orderly fashion, ideally with an introduction, conclusion, and a moral revelation. It's cool if he's gay, Gael thought, but then he really needs to know how to strike back or, at least, how to survive a beating.

When she reached the far gate, she saw him standing before a bulb-shaped pond that held on its waters a cast bronze statue. It was the figure of a woman reclining, though longer and more still than a human. She had been weathered green from the rippled roots of her hair to her crossed ankles. Mythical art like that—the exalted mother figure—trans-fixed Guthrie. He could have stood there

His friends were mostly girls—and too few to make a pack, so they were no use.

for hours, Gael knew, and she checked her phone to see how long before the next train. Thirty-two minutes. There'd still be time to pick up a chai latte at the kiosk. Auntie Ada made vile tea. Gael reckoned she used hot tap water and mangled four cups' worth out of one teabag.

They were at Croppies Acre Memorial Park. She'd heard of Croppies before and could make sense of that, but she didn't get the Acre bit. This shard of park wasn't an acre, surely. She clicked on the dotted *I* and read from her phone as she ambled pond-ward. The statue was named after a character in James Joyce's *Finnegans Wake*: Anna Livia Plurabelle. Good name. Gael wondered if the "Wake" had something to do with the fact that Anna seemed to be having herself a little lie-down. Females were always sleeping in fables. Sleeping frigid, never snoring. The sculpture was meant to personify the River Liffey, Abhainn na Life, which flows through Dublin Town, Gael read. It had first been part of a fountain in the city center on O'Connell street, but it became a target for litter and graffiti, Fairy liquid squirts that sent the water sudsing over the sidewalks as if she were in heat, and piss probably, if not rides altogether. "Floozie in the Jacuzzi," they called her. The Hoor in the Sewer. Why did Dublin have to be so scuddy? The city council used the excuse of street renovations to extract her from the mobs, and she spent a grim decade recovering inside a crate in a yard at St Anne's Park in Raheny in the Northside, far as you like from her proud river.

Gael would have told Guthrie an embellished version of this tale; only, just then, he needed to be told something very different.

"*Don't.* Guthrie!"

But it was too late.

He had stepped out onto the water, toward the mother sublime, as if the thin film of scum might hold his weight. One wouldn't have needed to know how to swim in that pond, it was so shallow, and Guthrie did know how, but even so he gasped and flailed, his schoolbag still on his back and loading with water. It tugged him the wrong way and down, and his cheap moccasin shoes couldn't get a grip on the pond's slimed base, so his arms and chin were the only parts of him above water. The gulping sounds were what disturbed them more than anything. "You sounded like a donkey getting off," she told him afterward. But in fact, it had sounded of something new to them both: it had sounded of the will to survive, falling short.

> His face was translucent white and unfamiliar to her— as if the experience had made an only child of him.

It was her first scare, dragging her brother from the pond. His face was translucent white and unfamiliar to her—as if the experience had made an only child of him. His eyes were unblinking, like astonished fish eyes beholding the sky for the first time. They shimmered. The sun was breaking through, so Gael emptied his bag and laid all his books out to dry—an illustrated Bible among them—then she peeled off his clothes, piece by piece, and wrung them out as well as she could, trying to grasp what he'd meant by it. She couldn't have upset him that much. "What's going on?" she pleaded, her wrists aching as she dressed him again, but the only sound that came from him was of teeth chattering. His arms were widest at the elbow. Gael's touchscreen kept failing to register her damp thumb clicking Contacts - Dad (Irish#) - Call. *Call.* When she finally managed, she could hear the curl of his close-shaven lip. "I'm in the middle of a meeting, Gael. What is it?"

While they waited, Gael rubbed circles on her brother's back, around and around, trying to imprint them into him like the growth rings of a tree.

Gael eavesdropped from the hallway when Guthrie's voice returned to him late that night. With heroic restraint, he asked his father why he couldn't walk across the water. He had as much faith as anyone he knew, he said, quietly. He really believed his faith was so strong that he could walk across the pond, and the Virgin Mother had been there in the middle and she had told him to come to her. The alarm clock on his bedside table measured the long pause like a metronome.

"Why couldn't I, Dad? Why wasn't my faith strong enough to hold me?"

"Because believing something will work doesn't make it work," Jarleth said. Then he clicked his tongue, exhaled with mild disgust. "The Lord Jesus walking on water was a miracle."

"But my faith's as strong as Jesus's. It *is*. So why couldn't *I* make a miracle?"

The bedside light switched off. The clacking sound was Jarleth wrenching the triple-A batteries out of the alarm clock. He tossed them under the bed, where they spun fitful nonsense orbits like moths.

"There are no more miracles."

. . .

How long now had the kitchen floor of the Foess household been tiled with eggshells, its walls papered with prescriptions, none of whose medicines lessened their mother's hurt? Months. Years. As if to censor the contrast between their mood and hers, the children barely spoke. They became fluent in the language of shoulders. They learned to move light-footed in the kitchen; Guthrie reveling all the while in this courtesy of woe, as if other states of being were lesser, insincere. He was Melpomene— tragic mask at the ready like a handkerchief. Gael played along, to a point. She held her tongue while non-stop noise played through her headphones: a hunger striker hooked up to an IV line beneath her clothes. She had long-since replaced the alarm clock batteries. How does one expedite a coma?

They were advised by relatives to make themselves scarce: To Give Yer Mother a Wide Berth. To Be Loving and Supportive and Patient but Not to Expect Much in the Way of Parenting. Sure That One Never Molly-coddled, Even When She'd a Husband to Impress. That *Might* Have Had *Something* to Do with It. Aren't Ye Very Self-Sufficient Now? We Were Working Ourselves at Sixteen and Aren't You Seventeen Now, Gael, and the Leaving Cert Just around the Corner, and Guthrie Only a Year Behind. No One Would Be Surprised if Ye Grow Up Quick. Ye Might Be Wise to Do the Same.

Sive's will to live now seemed gossamer-sheer, fickle as a whim. She had become a muted rendition of herself. It's true; she had always been what busybody misogynists bitterly described as a "hard woman," the very oxymoron embodied. But that's the problem with gossips: they have no register for nuance. There's refusing to applaud when a Ryanair plane lands and there's refusing to congratulate your son for coming Highly Commended in the regional watercolor championships for under fifteens. (If he had been ten, Sive might have patted the crown of his head, but at just months shy of sixteen, to acknowledge the crown of his head would have been a stretch too far.) Not all coldnesses are equivalent: a person's spirit can freeze at almost any temperature.

In the worst months—when Gael took up residence on friends' couches, leaving Guthrie to ensure no razors or ropes or Sibelius records lay within reach—their mother would neglect to open the curtains or to switch on the central heating or to eat or to visit her eighty-nine-year-old father after he had suffered another minor stroke in the Mystery Rose Residence, as if the fact that he wouldn't know her from Eve had suddenly become relevant. She began to resemble a bass clef, arched and draped in a wide black shawl. Her fingers were willowy wands, but she had forgotten the motions to get them to work. She changed her clothes only when her son delivered half-ironed piles of laundry to the foot of her bed. Guthrie's homeopathic method was to heap all the clothes in a tower, vaguely folded, and to press the iron down on the upper item, hoping the whiff of heat from above would flatten out the whole stack. She refused to even open a score. She was on temporary leave from the orchestra. Guthrie was worried dizzy she'd be elbowed out of her job.

"What if she's not ready to go back for the summer round? What if the stand-in conductor gets to do the tour? What if he gets good reviews and the players prefer him and they make some kind of petition to the musical director and—"

"Stop it, Guth. The guy's a breathing metronome. Mum's a composers' necromancer," Gael said.

"A *what*?"

When they gently knocked at her door to see if she was alive, she would say:

"Never underestimate what can be slept off. Pull the blinds and leave me be."

Gael imagined her mother's heart to be caked in kettle limescale grunge, and was fairly confident that some solution would scour her right again, this year or the next. There was that bottle of red—Settlesoul—on the mantelpiece, still unopened, which Gael had bought for her, for its name. Well, she had stolen it from Tesco but it served them right. Gael foresaw her mother letting her dead locks devastate and pong, ears wax traffic sounds to pasture, letting her limbs succumb to cobwebs like a dust-stuck tuning fork.

She observed her mother one day: standing at the living room bay window, one hand bracing the sill, the other pressing a Maldives travel brochure, sopping with weather, against her thigh. She had been out wandering in a downpour and hadn't bothered to towel herself off. It seemed to mark a new phase: a willingness to go out, to look outward, Gael had hoped. Though, the pane of glass returned a self-portrait in a crestfallen mirror. A sneeze. When Gael said, *Bless you*, Sive turned suddenly. She had the darkest shade of blond hair, which appeared as a whitewashed black, and it had ashed further with age. She usually wore it in a graceful loose French twist, but most of it had fallen down behind her ears and it dripped like a convent faucet.

> Not all coldnesses are equivalent: a person's spirit can freeze at almost any temperature.

"You frightened me," she said. "Why aren't you at school?"

"I don't really go anymore."

"Oh." She stared blearily at Gael's chest, as though there were something written there. "Will they let you do the exams?"

Gael nodded.

"But you'll fail?"

"No."

Sive wiped her nose red with her damp shawl. She was nearly six foot, though one would have wanted measuring tape just now to prove it. "If you say so, Gael. Only, don't have me visited by social services. This custodial is bad enough."

Her mother turned window-ward again and, after a long while, said that she had been trying to convince herself that the rainwater wasn't laboring down the panes. That it was the other way around: gravity working to draw everything down, angling for its loot. She could hardly bear to watch it. "Just get it over with." It's a dreadful torture to remember that nature is there, permitting us to play some trifling part, as if it mattered, she said. A second-cornet part. The third violin section droning two-four tonic. "You'd rather just be a mechanism altogether, rid of the *idea* that we perceive anything or participate in some culture. Meaning. Do you believe in anything, Gael? Any organized idea?"

"No." She felt how dry her lips were. This weather. "No idée fixe," she added, but her mother didn't hear.

"Not even in family?"

The strangest sensation pulsed through Gael's center at this rare communication. She felt that her mother was sizing her up, as a species, that she might suddenly announce a figure she had come to: See? What use is that? It's nothing personal. Gael wondered if either of them had ever heard *just* what the other had intended to say. "Not really," Gael said. "Not in the way you mean."

> Gael knew it hadn't been cheating. Cheating implies a thing gotten away with.

"Not even in markets, then?"

Gael sighed and looked down at her Taiwanese knock-off Converse trainers. "Sometimes Grafton Street looks like one giant closing-down sale." She picked off her stolen silver nail polish with her thumb and let it fall to the floor as sarcastic confetti. Her mother's teeth clacked and her breath was distantly visible. The exhaust pipe of an idling car. She hadn't paid the gas bill.

"Gael, I can't be responsible for you."

"I know."

"You don't know. I feel that I should be. And it's exhausting me." She said this in a low and pragmatic voice, though there was barely any will behind it. "Every day the thought of it, another . . ."

Gael shifted her weight, searching for a body part that would put up with it. Her mother turned toward her, eyes dimmed with the dissociative pain of the past months, and looked at the wall to the left of Gael, at the spot where a family portrait might have hung. "You can go and live with him," Sive said, at length. "You may, I mean. You have the choice. I won't hold it against you and I won't love you . . . any less."

The last two words were grace notes. Gael saw her mother's skin goosepimple so piercingly it might have been for good, as though her thoughts were cold enough to dictate their environment. Being let down by the one person you had ever trusted, had entrusted some twenty years and the very pith of your being to, involved a pain unlike anything Gael recognized. Gael knew it hadn't been cheating. Cheating implies a thing gotten away with. There is something very fun, very blithe, about cheating. Whatever it was though, the way to keep living through it was to move and move headlong, the way a shark can breathe only by conveying water through its body—all the time advancing, even if that movement is in circles.

"I'm moving to England?"

"What did you say?" Sive turned fast, her shawl sloughed off one shoulder to reveal limbs, ribs, damages as defined as cast-iron railings. The impulse was to run one's fingers across her to hear her thrum.

"I'm going to move to England, for college. But I won't, if you need me to stay."

"No. When? I hadn't, realized, you were, there already, at that stage."

"It's nearly May, Mum. It's been . . ." Gael said, stopped herself and allowed time for a response. "I'd only get in somewhere useless in Ireland, but England only counts three grades, so I could—"

"Go. Of course. Go! Live your life. I'll have your brother to keep this place lit, unless he chooses Jarleth."

"Stop, Mum. He won't."

"He'd be entitled to."

"Stoppit."

"Don't tell me to stop. Your father dotes on him." She lifted the travel brochure and held it before her for a long time like a treasured photograph. Then, she slowly wrung it out on the sill. It dripped an unrealistic blue.

"You could take him away with you?" Sive didn't look up, appalled at the truth of what she wanted. It had stopped raining, and everything smelled of what it had been before. The front lawn. The letter box. Electricity cables. The corridor. Dried lavender stuffed in hessian sacs as cheap moth deterrents. Ash in the hearth.

"Mum?"

"What is it, Gael?"

"Is this rock bottom, do you think?"

Sive burst into a coughing fit at being asked this by her daughter. She tried to disguise it as surprised laughter, but it ended up causing her to choke on the unswallowable substance that was this moment of her life. As her mother tried to catch her breath, Gael looked to the oak parquet flooring, which was buckled all over—especially by the fireside, where clarinet lessons had dribbled through the floorboards and down the drain—and soon, by the bay window, where Maldivian fluorescent heavens were seeping in wrongly. At last, her mother replied, and it was with a question.

"How would I know?"

. . .

Sive refused Gael's pleas to drive to the Fitzwilliam Casino & Card Club that night to gamble whatever lay in the balance of Jarleth and her soon-to-be-disjointed account in order to occasion rock bottom and catharsis all in one. Instead, she consigned to lying back on the easy chair, taking as a blanket the pearl-and-plain black-gray scarf Guthrie had knit her in home economics (adamant that if his mother was going to wear mourning clothes, they should at least be made to measure). When every whisper of resistance had been wearied out of her, finally, she resigned to helping Gael draft an obituary.

*Obittery: A Loath Story*

On Wednesday, April 1st 2015, Jarleth Moeder Falker Foess, of 24 Amersfort Way, County Dublin, failed to pass the ECG-SE exam of why he should remain plugged in. The IV league of afterlives wouldn't take him, on account of too much vain. Jarleth was a small man with a large heart attack and a malicious malignant egosarcoma. He deceived experts with his apparent good nature/health. What were initially believed to be scruples were in fact scabies. Jarleth was a families man, borne by his children, liked by his wife, prayed for by his mother, and dearly preyed on by his girlfriend. He will be sorely miffed.

For her every surge of weepy laughter, her mother sank a measure farther into the chair as if into long-denied submission. She reclined crosswise so her legs hung over the arm. Gael lay on the warped oak flooring and blinked large cracks in the ceiling plaster into view. What would they be invoiced to restore the home's structural integrity? She read the final farewell aloud seven times, each more conclusively. The words vibrated between her rib cage and the floor and her mother said she had always been a cello being sandpapered by the skilled hand of time into her final form and that, before long, Gael's complex timbre would be listened to and danced for and pored over, and when that day came she should refuse every follower, accompaniment, every offer of rest most certainly, everything she was bidden, and live only to satisfy her own ear. That is what she would have to sleep on for the rest of her life. Gael didn't want to say anything contrary that might coil her mother back into herself. Surely she knew that the worst time to impart wisdom was when you had been humiliated to the point of psychosis?

She had been dozing, imagining closing a Velcro strap around her mother's upper arm and listening for a little hiss of pressure releasing, when clattering keys brought her to. Guthrie stood, loose-mouthed, at the open front door in the hallway, all manner of draft pursuing him. That instant, he let his satchel fall from his shoulder, worked his shoes off at the heel with the toes of each foot, and took his place on his back on the living room floor, all too readily. The span of his grin made Gael want to spit something vicious at him, to spare her brother of an optimism that could only ever be briefly lived.

Though his eyes and heart were still wide open, Guthrie couldn't see from where he lay—though Gael saw well enough for the both of them—that their mother was dreaming of the life she could have lived without Jarleth; rid of the desperation he elicited, innocent of the assertion of his body upon hers and the pain of its lifting away. Reclining like that personification of a river, confined to a pond, she dreamed a life free of his soldering. The welded join holding her in place, to the ground. Ever the child who walks toward her.

# CATHEDRAL

I type the wrong year
I hold the amethyst in my mouth
Like a sharp purple tongue
I bleed on the chair by mistake
So much blood
I make raspberry leaf tea
I make mistakes
I get a little droopy here and there
We agree on an earthquake meet-up location
We plan to stay married
I cry for the third child I don't want
And won't have
So much I could not have understood
Before turning into an asshole
So much I failed to do
When I rang the bell to the cathedral
And left my heart on the steps
Wrapped in its swaddling clothes
We were all so helpless once
The house would slide right off
Its foundations
The ground became water
It buckled like your hand
We are still telling the story
Even though we are
Temporarily strong
With our electric companies
And our faucets

# WE LEARN TO BE HUMAN

I attended the online seminar on shame
it helped for a minute
more importantly I've been loving
the goddess for a long time and these
hiccups in my groin are a sign
she'll be there when it's time
it could be next week it could be
a month you started as a seed
and now in a white t shirt
you go to bed I'll meet you
when I'm done we learn to go to bed
to put on eyeliner we learn to be human
when we don't get what we want
you too started as a seed my son and now
I feel your fingers curling against my
center from the inside
like a fern dear son I want every flower
you ever plant to blossom

# THE VAGINA HEALER

The vagina healer had a vision

With her gloved hand inside me

She saw my water break

Not in a magnetic field of hospital white

But under the apple tree

Between the garden boxes

"Energetic birth" she called it

And said I could rewrite the script

So here is the new script

I am a fruit geode

My midwife's name is Mary

I give birth in a garden

To a grandfather

Vernix

Light

Apples

# In the
# Massif Central

## Michael Helm

Since the summer Celia turned twelve her father had taken her on expeditions. He led teams of interchangeable members, opening plague pits in London, coring ice in Siberia, hose-blasting perma-frost in the far north to find perfectly intact, extinct creatures, while some grad student who'd pulled the duty to look after her demonstrated the care involved in brushing and screening soil for the tiny bones of long-gone lizards and birds. Three Junes ago they revived the practice for the first time since she left for university. Now he was summering in France, living alone in the Cévennes. A team had come and gone. Once a week he visited friends in a lab ninety minutes away in Montpellier, but most days he spent in the mountains, on foot.

She'd been fifteen hours in transit from Vancouver, had slept maybe two. In final approach she looked down at morning in Paris, bright city, oddly flat. The Eiffel Tower, so small in person, like a male movie star. The high-rises of La Défense seemed like just the beginning of a vision, dream interrupted, sketched out and half realized at a safe distance to the west of the old realities, the beautiful districts, proportioned, ornate, storied in the richer sense.

On the TGV she fell asleep at three hundred kilometers an hour. He met her at the train station in Montpellier. The smile, a little bow, the avid blue eyes. He was lit with a kind of chemiluminescence. Something just below the skin held differently. "You look good, Dad. Great pigmenta-tion." He said he had something exciting to tell her. They drove through a landscape of hard plains, rock outcroppings, sudden sheer faces. His hands cupped the steering wheel, left wrist curled at eleven o'clock, right at three,

From the novel *After James*, forthcoming from Tin House in September 2016 then to the stick shift and back. As he spoke he glanced at her repeatedly. His long jaw worked the lines. He said he had a map of the unexplored cliffs and he'd been investigating as he could. The hikes were physically hard—was she in shape?—but his joints liked the climate. He could still balance on a foothold, still scramble on loose ground. Several days ago for three hours he'd cut a path across the least accessible of the promising rock faces and emerged above a tree line. After a minute along a barely navigable ledge, he came to a deep, uncrossable crevice, and there on the other side, a cave mouth.

"There seems to be no research on this cave. And it's perfectly protected. If it opens up, if it doesn't just run to a full stop in the dark, there could be thousands of years of artifacts inside. Tens of thousands. Neanderthals and humans lived around here at the same time. I've been waiting for you. Tomorrow we'll climb with a ladder."

He looked at her and the car drifted to the shoulder, corrected.

"Okay, sure. Exciting."

Her body thought it was still in Vancouver. She used to trust her body, its distant early warnings and blunt reminders, but lately it had struck its own secret agenda and lost its sense of humor. It would arrive properly rested in a day or two. Until then she'd have to float around on her own, a hovering face, talking and smiling, waiting to close its eyes.

> She'd imagined her arrival, an embrace, an almost wordless greeting, and a slow gathering of the moment.

"They died off very suddenly, the Neanderthals. Twenty-five thousand years ago, in Gibraltar, staring at the sea. They weren't crossers of oceans. Leaps of faith didn't occur to them. Whereas Homo sapiens, well, here we are."

Here they were. She'd imagined her arrival, an embrace, an almost wordless greeting, and a slow gathering of the moment. Now she was here and there'd been no arrival. He might have waited to tell her about the cave. Maybe he was afraid of recognizing her, or of failing to—she was aging, changing, about to enter important years for a childless single woman with a career—and so he'd put something between them that they'd have to pass back and forth. Now she'd wait a day before getting around to life updates, a brief romance come and gone, a health scare come and gone. She supposed she wouldn't tell him about an unwanted pregnancy come and gone.

Or at least a surprise pregnancy, and given the precautions a bit of a mystery one. It seemed to have come and gone on its own, as if it had nothing to do with her, or as if she had failed a test of grace. Not that she believed in grace or even really understood what it pretended to be.

The next day after breakfast they tied an aluminum ladder to the roof of his Suzuki Swift and set off into the mountains. She followed their route on a map covered with his printed additions and notes as they drove on the edge of La Vallée du Terrieu. He'd marked the names of each peak— Montagne d'Hortus, Pic Saint-Loup—each perched chateau, but as they climbed on ever narrower roads the names fell off until finally the doubtful path disappeared from the map and became only a track through a field that ended in trees. Above them the forest climbed steeply to the base of an immense, white vertical rock face. He studied the approach routes. From the trunk he took their supplies, shrugged into a small backpack. He gave her a coil of rope. He untied the ladder, put it over his shoulder, and led the way into the trees. There was little underbrush but the climb was steep, improvised, awkward, and soon they were too spent to speak, though they had said very little that morning anyway, and before long Celia was sweating in her unbreathing layers. Four times at intervals of thirty or forty minutes they stopped to rest. At one point, bent over with her hands on her knees, she looked up to find him resting the ladder vertically, taking her in through the rungs.

> The crevice meant business. There was no telling its depth but the noon light disappeared at about thirty feet.

Something in the elevation brought him to ask about her "career." He viewed her work in the Lifestyle Drugs Division of a pharma giant as a misuse of her talents, if not an outright repudiation of his life in the pure sciences.

"Nothing to report."

"Private companies. They feed on secrecy clauses and blood oaths."

"Whatever moves the ball down the field, as one of my team leaders says. Apparently the ball is knowledge."

"The ball is profit. It's not even pigskin. It's boner pills."

In time they broke above the tree line and rested once more and ate their packed lunches while looking out at the valley and the distant Mediterranean, a seam on the horizon. By the set of his face he seemed fixed in some reverie. She let it run and in time he said he was trying to imagine the view of fifty thousand years ago. A colder climate. The trees would not be oak, as now, but pine and beech, species adapted to the cold. In the valley, deer and sanglier, and European megafauna, mammoths and giant elk. And humans and protohumans. Glaciers had pushed Neanderthals this far south, and Homo sapiens had migrated here from Africa. They overlapped for maybe forty thousand years.

"They must have recognized their difference from one another." His voice was sure. He caught his breath faster than she did. "The genetic record says they interbred. We still have Neanderthal in us. The fossil record gives no evidence of war, though it does of murder. Bones showing evidence of tool scarring, as if they'd been de-fleshed."

"News of the day."

"We still behave this way, yes. But they were much closer to the originating moment, whatever that was. No amount of science will recover it. If we clone them—ancient humans—we'll just be closer to the end moment. Ours, I mean."

He was a genetic anthropologist, extinction branch. His comments tended to take certain turns.

Their path became a ledge that ran above a sharp drop. Navigating it required him to balance the ladder on a forearm held away from the rock face, so that from her position behind him the ladder seemed a floating incongruity, a surrealist object juxtaposed against the stone sublime. The face curved away from them for a time and then the ledge widened to a large table of rock. There was the cave mouth, across a wide cut. He extended the ladder and timbered it across the gap, and squatted to rest, letting his arms hang limp. The crevice meant business. There was no telling its depth but the noon light disappeared at about thirty feet. It was maybe fifteen feet across, too far for anyone to jump, with too short a run up and no safe place to land. Maybe the cave really was unexplored.

She held the ladder firm on one side as he walked across it rung to rung with steady, deliberate steps. If one of them fell, even if they survived the fall, there'd be no way out. What exactly would the other do?

"We're being careless," she said, after he'd crossed. "This is pretty stupid."

"Don't cross if you're not committed. I'll go and report back."

She threw the rope coil to him and told him to hold the ladder and crossed over on her hands and knees, looking forward. He pulled the ladder clear and laid it by the side of the cave mouth. From his backpack he produced two flashlights and a truffle pick for digging out artifacts. There was no threat in the sky, unless it was behind the mountain. No one knew they were up here.

They approached the entrance, ducked under a pediment ledge, and stood in quiet light. Only a short distance ahead the rock ceiling above them curved down to form a back wall. The space was certain and empty. It led nowhere. He said nothing, kept still. She walked in, letting him have his moment of disappointment. Near the back wall she crouched lower, turned and sat on the cave floor and looked out at him silhouetted against the blue sky.

"It could still be your cave. Grotte du Dad."

"I feel something. Do you feel it back there?"

In fact she did feel it, a draft. She shone her light into the corners and saw that the floor opened about twenty feet to her left. She scuttled over on her ass. The walls of the hole formed the first revolution of a kind of curved well that seemed to open into a space beneath them.

She had no time to speak before he was with her, shining his light into the hole.

"Holy Christ," he said.

"Okay."

They were silent. She wanted to stop him from thinking but it was too late.

"I wonder if they named it, the first humans," he said.

"Maybe they called it *the hole in the floor*."

"It's got a real come hither to it. I'm going down."

"That's too stupid even for you. It might just drop you half a mile inside the mountain."

"That's why we have the rope."

"Oh, come on. A cave. We thought we'd walk in, walk out. Nobody said anything about going down holes."

"We're prepared."

"We are definitely not prepared. We should have a team. With radio communication, helmets, gloves, water, first aid, harnesses, those mountain-climbing spiky things, and at least one person who knows what they're doing."

"Humans explore. It's what we do."

She saw how it set up in his mind. He tied the rope to a stone anchor, a kind of newel post at the top of the opening. The rope was just something he'd found along with the ladder in the storage room under the rented house. It was thick, but old and dry, and would fray easily. He tied the other end in a loop under his arms and braced his hands against the smooth wall of the hole mouth.

"Jesus, Dad. If I got hysterical would you stay?"

"You're not the kind. Now, if I get in far enough you won't be able to hear me through the rock. Give me thirty minutes. If I'm not back, then don't—do not—come after me. There's no cell reception so you'll need to go down to the car and drive it to town." He leaned to one side, extracted the car keys from his pocket, and tossed them to her. "Go back to the village, to the police. Take the map so you can tell them how to get here. I'll be fine, likely just stuck with my head in a prehistoric honey jar. I'll have a sleep while you lead them up."

"Let me go instead. I'm lighter and thinner and my joints work better."

"Nonsense. I won't have it. Much too dangerous." He suppressed a smile, clamped the flashlight in his mouth, and started down.

**The space was certain and empty. It led nowhere. He said nothing, kept still.**

There'd been days like this in grad school, up before dawn getting ready for an outing. Back then they'd all loaded into a minivan too small for them and their four tents and propane grill and hiking boots and at least two secreted thesis chapters to be edited by lantern light, headed north for eleven hours, and there they gathered, around a fire, seven students and their mentor, Erik Bouma. The yearly weekend in bear country was unstated mandatory. Research money was siphoned off to fund it. Erik joked in all seriousness that it was "teamship-building," getting the word wrong, but on the third trip Celia wanted the days for silence, or at least talklessness. Erik liked to induce in them a shared dream portending applications for their knowledge that no one could yet imagine, and then he tried to steer the dream and imagine for them. He told stories of disease therapies and reversals, of antiaging, memory enhancement. In their off time, he said, they could sell their genetic science expertise in every direction. Already he'd been offered huge sums to speak to Mounties and G-Men, play the expert at drug piracy trials, authenticate unsigned de Koonings. Not all of these jobs he'd said yes to. A captain of Japanese industry had set before him a briefcase full of money to entice him to clone the long-extinct, thirty-five-hundred-pound South American short-faced bear. The briefcase, the short-faced bear, half of the dreams and their contents were stolen from movies, though they were also real, or possible.

In the pause after Erik said, "The future is in front of us," she said, "No shit," and he added, "and so is the past." He could take some ribbing, could Erik, but he wouldn't stop with the pithy sayings. "We serve the living, the dead, and the unborn." The unborn came up a lot. Celia found she couldn't picture them except as newborns or futuristic adults of very pale skin wearing spaceship uniforms with stirruped pant legs. The real unborn, as they could be conceived of now, in their current state, were more like shapeless energies inside the living. If she followed the thought long enough they became, basically, the sexual impulse. Complicated, to be struggled with or surrendered to. Even when joyful, unstable.

Or so she had imagined then. Now the unborn was someone specific. His name was James. He would be seven months old.

She stayed with the wolves for some duration, until at last she could no longer hear them.

She'd left them at the campfire and gone to pee and then walked farther into the woods until the voices were gone. She hadn't brought a flashlight but the moon was bright. She sat on a fallen tree, felt the bark and guessed cedar, and closed her eyes and listened into the silence. In a centering practice she'd used in city parks, she pictured an ever deeper auditory penetration of the darkness. Smaller sounds could take form. Others might trail the end of a breeze. At first you had to let the sound be sound, and not try to assign it to animals, birds, jet planes, water. She found a state of nonthought and the silence took its place. It seemed she was there a long time, small wind, its empty wake. With nothing to hold on to she heard echoes from the day, mostly voices, Erik's Swiss-German English, making great claims. At one of the highway stops he had looked over at her, standing slightly apart, and she saw a sympathy, or at least a sad acknowledgment of her. She was not the most talented or ambitious of his students, not the easiest to direct. She expanded discussions into strange territories, beset by a kind of speculative ethics. Not just, What are the dangers in bringing extinct viruses back to life? but What does it *mean* to play God or, as she'd always thought of God, Nature? He probably expected her to become a teacher at a minor university or a science journalist, maybe even an enemy of the cause. She was learning about herself through his view of her, as she imagined it.

She tried again to quiet the thoughts. The silence was a presence in itself. When the wind came up she heard something inside it, and let it be, one tree rubbing against another in the distance. The sound hadn't been there before. The wind had changed. Now it was gone but something else was there, then wasn't, then there it was again. On the edge of her perception, miles away, a wolf was howling. She tucked inside the furrowed note and it ran with her and died. Then the same note grew forth again and, in a higher register, a second howl joined the first. Soon there were many overlapping voices, calling and answering, it seemed. Asserting the only shared truth. Blood bone I am.

She stayed with the wolves for some duration, until at last she could no longer hear them. Then came the greater absence, and then even the absence attenuated to nothing. How lucky not to have been with the group. They'd have talked of wolf studies, certainly, the meaning of howls, of pitches and amplitudes, the human measures of animal territories. Maybe someone would have brought up Tchaikovsky or Red Riding Hood, or Lon Chaney versus every wolf man since. Whatever the subject, they would certainly have talked. Briefly she succeeded in banishing the thought of them and now, in the aftermath, came something low, in approach. The underbrush took animal weight. She tried to measure distance with sound. She listened for a kind of breath, the huff of a black bear or grizzly, but the thing in approach was gone and then no it was behind her and she turned and saw the flashlight beam. For a moment her voice wouldn't come, and then she said, "I'm here."

"Oh thank god." It was Chandra. "Erik and Jeremy are out here somewhere looking for you, too."

Chandra was the only other woman in the group, the new student, a hard pragmatism just starting to take up in her dark baby face. She was smart and ambitious. Presumably she understood what it meant that the future and the past were before her. She knew she was in a world of boys and their toys, and she had shared a joke or two with Celia. In the end, though, Celia understood, if it came to it, Chandra would always side with the boys.

"No bears. Just the wolves."

Chandra hadn't heard the wolves. When they returned to the fire, the group, Celia learned that no one had heard them. Erik asked her how far, what direction, how many distinct howls. He didn't ask her to describe the feeling of hearing them, a question she wanted but wouldn't have been able to answer. It intrigued the hapless Jeremy to suggest that she was probably just trying to scare them. He wanted to sleep with her but hadn't puzzled out a method.

Erik was sitting across the fire from her. He turned his head this way and that to address the group, the sternocleidomastoids popping grotesquely in his neck.

"Celia's not the type to cry wolf, Jeremy. It's no game to her. She believes the wolves are out there. Even if they aren't." He looked into her face. The rest of them kept their eyes forward, into the fire. "We need a few Celias in any population. They imagine just enough to keep us honest."

Her story had no defenders but she didn't care—she'd graduate in months and Erik had already written her strong enough letters of support—and yet the pronouncement seemed to render the wolves imaginary, even for her. She found she couldn't call them back to mind, and didn't until the end of the weekend. In the years since, she had never doubted them. The wolves became more certain with time. She didn't think of them as past or as hers alone. Their offspring were still out there somewhere. She tried to let them be nothing other than they were. She tried not to assign meaning to them, not to read portents or to assume they'd been sounding a warning. They were wolves, not harbingers. The harbingers were elsewhere, in numbers and graphs, infection and transmission rates. They had a different pull and cast, and they grew ever closer. Soon everyone would know them. A great wing would appear in the sky and the talking would stop all at once.

She'd been waiting twelve minutes. He'd been in voice contact for about eight. He'd barely disappeared when she heard his first exclamation. Right below her the ground leveled out and opened into a chamber. "I can stand up," he said. After a few seconds he said, "No artifacts or remains but . . . hold on." She stared into the hole. "There's a shelf, sort of recessed in the stone. It's full of seashells." She saw flashes of light come out of the hole and remembered he had a camera in his vest. He said there was a narrow passage ahead. His voice was fainter now. "I'll investigate." She asked him to describe the space and he said, "It's pretty small." "How small?" There was no answer. Four minutes later the rope went slack.

What had he said about the cave on the way up? Nothing useful now. He said certain caves were places of deep solitude, that it wasn't just fear or necessity that would make people gather out of the killing elements, but something inward that needed to be acknowledged to others around a fire. "These were the first stirrings of religion, the deepest parts of ourselves made social. A collective of souls, staving off fear, hunger, loneliness, if not doubt."

She reasoned that he'd come to the end of his rope but not the end of his time. He'd untied himself and kept exploring. Near the thirty-minute mark she'd feel the tension back on the line. She'd hear him, he'd emerge. She tried to have faith in this idea and the faith or tending there opened a space inside her where the dim figure she made out was herself.

The rim of the hole was the only smooth surface, worn by thousands of years of hands and bodies. On the pocked wall above it she tried to detect the smallest movement of the stippled shadows. In its simplest form time was light, nothing more. Our sense of it changed from being with others. Others marked it, were marked by it, set it at variable speeds in the social flux. But isolated, removed from other presences, time was light and non-light in perpetual bend and stretch. The shadows had notched along without detectable movement. The sun leaned on the mountain faces opposite, the distant fields and vineyards far below. From where she sat the superstitious mind would see the god in all things moving each day on the shadow line, left to right, up to down, changing its slant with the seasons. From such a prospect, at an earned altitude, in your very body you felt meanings were arrayed before you, you could look and know yourself. The trouble was in trying to say them, the things you came to know. She would say them only this way. Left to right and up to down.

> The wolves became more certain with time. She didn't think of them as past or as hers alone.

It had been forty-two minutes. No sound for thirty-four. Something was wrong but she hadn't yet moved, weighted in place against the whirl of her thoughts. If she left the cave he'd be alone up here inside the mountain for five or six hours, too long if he was injured or in danger. The rope lay slack against the wall. The first chamber was safe, the one he'd called from, with the shells. It would make sense to lower herself into it and call to him through the next opening. If she couldn't hear him she'd have to keep calm and crawl out and start down the mountain. She had to bring help before dark or she wouldn't know how to find her way back up. Assuming she could do so by day. She hadn't paid attention on the climb, only following his lead in slight variation, as she'd done much of her life.

She imagined sitting with him on a patio somewhere, beginning the story of what they'd done wrong today. It had been a mistake not to tell anyone. Was it from vanity or cool, delicious hope that he wanted this for the two of them alone? Another error, not to have planned for emergency. Were there earlier mistakes? He should have told her of the cave before she left Canada. She would have researched what to bring, planned for contingencies. How far back could they go? What were their mistakes, through the years, and how had they contributed to this last miscalculation?

It wasn't yet panic she felt, as if panic were a stable marker. She wasn't hysterical. Her heartbeat was getting up there but she'd experienced nothing to cause real fear, only a duration of silence. She told herself that her father was simply late. He was often late, he lost track of the hour, though admittedly given the directions she expected him to know it had been forty-four minutes, fourteen overdue, or six if he was counting from the last voice contact. On the imagined patio she told him her calculations. A small delight held on his face. It would all have worked out, of course, so he was enjoying the story. She looked for the slightest sign that the enjoyment went only so far, but unless you knew him, by his face you'd think nothing much had ever happened to him. You'd guess he'd lived a safe and lucky life, that he felt fear only as mock fear, fright, a tingling on the skin, a shiver along the neck. Never as drops of blackness spreading in the blood, thickening the tongue, numbing the light. But he understood as she did that the world divided between those who knew and those who didn't.

> If he was hurt, in trouble, time was short. She did not want to enter the tunnel.

She would need both her hands, so how to carry the flashlight? If she put it in her mouth like on TV she'd gag. It was too thick to fit into a belt loop but she had a belt, pretty much decorative, so she took it off and cinched it around the base and then tied a knot and looped the flashlight around her neck so that it nodded and swayed, catching random shapes in the illuminations as she took the rope in hand and felt along the smooth rock wall and lowered herself into the hole. She found level ground almost immediately and stepped forward before taking hold of the light and looking around. She'd stopped herself all of six inches before a spur in the rock that would have brained her. Another mistake, a lucky break. She ducked and moved forward and stood again. The light now caught all of the small chamber. The ledge with the shells, about a dozen, was at eye level. At its highest point the ceiling was maybe eight feet. The rope ran straight across the floor and into a small opening in the opposite wall, five or six strides ahead. She could not see how anyone could fit through it.

She kneeled at the opening and listened, nothing. Even the light draft she'd felt above was absent. She shone the beam into the passage and up came a wall forty or more feet ahead, but she couldn't tell the dimensions of the space. The rock was smooth, water worn. She called, "Dad. Can you hear me?" and her voice seemed to wreck in the passageway. The rope— how long was it?—ran true along the shadowed ground. Maybe he'd seen a safe way forward beyond the end of his tether. Even if there was no chamber, even if what she was seeing was forty feet of tunnel, there must be a curve or drop or else she'd be able to see him. All she saw now was a frayed rope lying along a rock shaft.

She checked the time. Forty-six minutes, no contact. He was just ahead somewhere. If he was hurt, in trouble, time was short. She did not want to enter the tunnel. She could not go down the mountain, go to the village and get help, come up again in the dark. Already she was sixteen minutes behind in whatever action she would take.

She said fuck it and sat and started in, feet first. With the flashlight resting on her chest, she pulled herself along with her hands. The top side of the passage was inches from her face and she felt her short breaths burst back upon her. Her knees could barely bend but little by little she went forward, telling herself that her father had made it through so there had to be room for her. After several seconds she opened her feet and looked down along the beam. A penumbra had formed around the light on the wall ahead and so she knew that the shaft widened, though by how much she couldn't tell. She seemed to be moving on a slight downward grade. The thought to be suppressed was that she might not be able to reverse her direction. It made no difference to close her eyes so she closed them and kept moving and only when the air and the sound of her motion changed did she open them to see that she'd come out into a large chamber. She sat up, shone the beam around. The rope ran to its end midfloor. She checked her watch. Inching through the shaft had taken less than two minutes.

The chamber looked fifteen or twenty feet high. She stood, breathed. There was something very different about the space, the way it held her imagining. Against this deeper silence even her breath sounded different, muted. If she were here alone she'd panic but knowing her father was ahead somewhere allowed her to keep it together. She crossed the chamber and saw the passageway to her left. Up ahead, through another narrow space, she saw the moving beam.

As he must have seen hers. She could have wept with relief but instead felt a wave of unsteadiness, an inability to speak. She came forward. The opening to the next chamber was narrow but vertical. She crouched and stepped through.

But he hadn't seen her light. Only now did he notice the concentration spot next to his own on the omphalos of rock that hung from the ceiling, huge, rose-colored. The rock was conical, rounded at the bottom, as if shaped by intention, and she saw, felt, immediately why he hadn't been able to leave it. At some point—time was hard to reckon now—he registered the second beam and turned quickly and they trained their lights on each other. His face looked strange, as if she'd woken him from a sleepwalk.

"You didn't come back," she said. She dropped her light to his chest. He did the same. He said nothing. "Are you all right?"

He turned his light back on the hanging rock. It was smooth, vegetable, sparkling. She came forward and stood with him. He walked her around the perimeter. The rock seemed suspended, floating three or four feet from the floor. She felt something larger than fear, though it had the same intensity. It was awe, strickenness, a shiver of beholding, as on first seeing a vast canyon, maybe, or walking into a great cathedral. But here the measurelessness was directly before them, with dimensions perceived all at once. The rock's hovering shape and coloring were hard to account for, but more so its proportions in relation to the rest of the chamber. It hung exactly midspace and though its curving surface was uneven, from anywhere on the cave floor, itself irregular, it seemed to face her.

She stopped walking. He continued. She shone her light up to the dome, then down, and clipped her eyes to him as he was about to round out of sight.

"Stop."

"Quiet, dear."

She came to him, held him at the elbow, shone the light on the back of his head. His hair was matted in blood that had run behind his left ear and down his neck, under his shirt collar.

"What happened?"

"I don't know. I got dizzy. Bumped my head when I fell. It's all part of it."

"Part of what? You fell?"

A short laugh escaped him. He held his hand up to ask her patience as he reached into his pocket and produced a packet of matches. He struck one. It flared and went out immediately. He did it again, there and gone.

"There's not enough oxygen," he said. "This is how they died."

He turned the light into the recesses. He led her forward. At their feet she saw where he'd chipped away at the sediment. There were bones in the floor. Femur staves. Calcified splinters and broken osseous plates. Beyond, ribs breached the surface.

"Human," he said. "Or protohuma—" He didn't quite finish the word or she didn't hear him.

She took him by the arm and drew him away and as they passed by the hanging rock he turned and shone his light and looked at it a last time. She watched him, gauged his movements, as they stooped into the next chamber and crossed it. He was lurching, unsteady. Should she go first

> She felt something larger than fear, though it had the same intensity.

or second? She couldn't reason it through. She was breathing fast. If he went first and passed out she'd be unable to move him. She had him sit near the narrow opening. She looped the rope around his chest, under his arms, and he followed her hands vaguely with his eyes, as if drunk.

"You come in right after me," she said. "Keep your head close to my feet."

She rounded her shoulders and started in on her back, headfirst, with the rope running along her right side so she could tug it as a signal, if nothing else. As she'd feared, the inclined grade was harder to move along in the confined space. She used the heels of her hands and feet to get what traction she could. When her palm touched a smoothness she thought of water, rushing water, filling the passage. He followed well enough but midway he stopped and she said, "Keep coming" and her voice died inches from her face. She tugged the rope and he started again. It seemed to be taking longer than it should have, and then was certainly taking too long, and the despair was in realizing that somehow she'd taken them into the wrong opening. But no, the rope had run to this one, so on she went, her hands bleeding now, her knees banged up, and then the blackness stood higher and she knew they'd made it.

At the mouth of the first entrance they stood in pain, crouched over, breathing hard, and now she was weeping for the air, at the daylight visible above. He went first, climbing and pulling on the rope as she boosted him. Then he reached down and helped her up. They walked out of the cave and stood looking at La Vallée du Terrieu, miles of green and sunlight.

She examined his scalp, the short, deep gash, still bleeding. With a paring knife they'd used at lunch she cut away the sleeve of his shirt and wrapped it tightly around his head, under his jaw.

"Can't open my mouth," he tried to say.

"Perfect, then. Let's go."

They crossed the crevice and left the ladder and walked down, saying nothing.

The part she would never tell anyone, not even herself, she decided, was that the place they'd been didn't exist, not in the way the rest of the world did. Or it existed in space but not time. You could see time from the entrance but the place inside the mountain was outside of time, as if it had absorbed tens of thousands of years of human wonderment and held it, imprisoned it, and to enter the chamber was to enter the imaginings of the dead. It was a trap they'd escaped that others had not, lured by promise, filled with disorienting visions, then weakening, suffocating. The self-deceiving mind could so easily imagine a design there to hold them. You couldn't see the rock's symmetry and color and not imagine it as the shaping of an engineer, a force, a god with aspirants among humans. Some inherited groove in the brain caused people to believe that all order is intended, that balanced wholes can't form by chance and natural circumstance. They can't see that none of the received names, the names cursed or called out in worship, could really attach to an ordering force. Over time, she would likely come to think of the cave visit as a misadventure, a lucky escape that had sparked thoughts of a Maker, thoughts she was already putting in their place. Yet on some future nights to come—how did she already know this?—the sparks would reappear.

And then, a last idea, one she couldn't suppress. It was that she was still inside the cave. She had fallen out of time, even as she descended through the woods as present in the world as she always had been. In thought, memory, body, she was nearly exactly herself. The feeling began to fade, to seem fanciful, at lower altitude, as her blood became better oxygenated, but she understood that it would never entirely leave her. It was somehow familiar, the idea that she was two places at once, or one place in two overlapping times. She must have read it in a junk novel, seen it in movies, things that everyone consumed without really remembering and that she found it harder and harder even to pretend to believe.

She'd been trotting and was too far ahead now. She stopped and looked back, waiting for him to appear through the trees. ⬙

# ORDINARY
# REDEMPTION

## Emma Komlos-Hrobsky

*A Conversation with Louise Erdrich*

Few if any writers can claim a body of work as capacious and as universally *good* as Louise Erdrich's. Her tremendous oeuvre sweeps from poetry to children's literature to short stories and novels. She has been awarded the National Book Award (*The Round House*) and the National Book Critics Circle Award (*Love Medicine*) and was a finalist for the Pulitzer Prize (*The Plague of Doves*). This September she received the Library of Congress Prize for American Fiction, an honor and obligation she, with typical humility, neglected to mention when I contacted her to arrange this conversation. (When I wrote to her that I felt as if I were chucking a rock up onto Mount Olympus whenever I

bothered her with a query, Erdrich reported back that Mount Olympus looks a lot like a sliding wall of white papers.)

Across her thirty-year career, crowned this May by her fifteenth book, *LaRose*, Erdrich's writing has always been as humane as it is deft, incisive, sharp. She describes herself as a perfectionist. Her drive and rigor translate to the most perfectly honed sentences, and to the ever-unfurling tessellation of families that populates her fiction. A dip into this world feels a bit like teleportation. The cans of grape Shasta in the cooler at Whitey's gas station, the glint of the gold tooth of the woman waiting outside, seem to exist inevitably, ours to peek in on as Erdrich chooses to lift the veil. She is the kind of storyteller you'd want riding with you on long nights on the road, keeping your mind spinning, your heart's door ajar, her characters all but real in the seats behind you.

Erdrich's own childhood religious experience was inflected by both Ojibwe tradition and Catholic faith. Both threads run through almost all of her work. Still, her eye is always on the mortal rather than the divine. Erdrich's fiction fulfills the essential promise of storytelling to show us to ourselves, and what she finds in that examination can be bleak, to say the least. Her latest novels circle incidents of racial and sexual aggression, injustice, murder, and revenge. Yet despite the anguish Erdrich sees in the world, she seems to believe in it even so.

At the extraordinary ending of *The Round House*, perhaps Erdrich's masterwork to date, thirteen-year-old Joe Coutts takes it upon himself to realign his family's cosmos, disordered by the violent rape of his mother, after all other measures have failed. Except that Joe does not in fact take this burden on alone. A friend is there in secret, literally watching Joe's back. When I first read this scene, I was moved to tears with delighted surprise—but I should've always known that he would be there. This is quintessential Erdrich. Her vision of the designs of our hearts is as clear-eyed as it is generous. It is her trust in her characters to do good that makes her mythic North Dakota, for all its darkness, a world in which I want to dwell. There is perhaps no authorial voice that is more of a comfort,

and a compass, to me. It was an honor to speak with her about her writing, and the ways humanity might be its own salvation.

**EMMA KOMLOS-HROBSKY:** You grew up in Wahpeton, North Dakota, and were raised around the Catholic Church. What was your experience of religion as a child? Would you have described yourself as Catholic?

**LOUISE ERDRICH:** I was baptized, raised, and confirmed in the Catholic Church. So yes, I was a Catholic. This led to playing the pipe organ at Mass, a fascination with painted blood on the plaster crucifix, memories of the mothball-and-sweat smell of the black woolen clothing nuns and priests wore in those days, the swoony sopranos of Carmelite nuns singing behind a screen, the need that I still have to make shrines to the Blessed Virgin in my house— the iconography still marks me.

My mother's family, from the Turtle Mountains, are mission Catholics but my grandfather practiced his Ojibwe religion along with going to Mass. The Benedictine priests who served there at the time were ecumenical. When I understood more about traditional Ojibwe religion I adopted some practices because I like them—most are about being outside or about appreciating the wild world.

My religion, if I've got one, is being outside, near water if possible. I had an outside childhood. Outdoors was where we played and lived out our thoughts. As my children grew up, I tried to get outside

# My religion, if I've got one, is being outside, near water if possible. I had an outside childhood.

with them as much as possible and on Sunday mornings we went on hikes for a religious experience. Church was the woods.

**EKH:** What stories were important to you growing up?

**LE:** Old Testament stories were important to me because they were about magic. I wanted to experience a stick turning into a snake, or a burning, talking bush. As I grew older and nothing of the sort occurred around me, I felt that I'd been hoodwinked. So I turned to the usual—I adored fairy tales—and then my parents saved Green Stamps. We drove to Fargo to redeem the stamps, and they got a record player. They belonged to a record club, and bought *King Lear*. I had a bedroom all to myself in the basement of our house, and I played *King Lear* over and over. We bought a television in a pink-and-tan plastic case. We were hardly allowed to watch it, but we did tune in for *The Age of Kings* (Shakespeare's history plays), which enthralled me. I've still got the public television paperback edition of the plays; it must have come with a donation or subscription.

Both sides of my family were storytellers, not in a formal sense where they retold traditional tales, but they were natural storytellers. They would make sense of experience by making things that happened into stories. The best ones had an edge of sad humor. My father's stories of his childhood have a mythic quality, an enlarged sense of fate. His mother died when he was quite young. His wonder is always laced with sorrow, with irony.

**EKH:** Faith and justice seem so bound up in each other in the world of your writing. What's the relationship you see between the two?

**LE:** No relationship. If God were just, then George W. Bush would be hitchhiking through Syria this afternoon. As for faith, it seems to me that spiritual faith is about longing. We all want to find out who or what made us and why. People have a need to find meaning in a God who fits their version of the divine. Beyond that, faith is commonplace. Everyone has faith in something, even if it is not God, even if it is not good, it may even be faith in something reprehensible. Faith is how we move from day to day.

Justice has to do with attempting to make sure that people don't follow their worst inclinations. Justice is the necessary

I never did think that being good was a matter of following rules. That, at least, I learned through enduring infuriating religious dicta.

underpinning of society; it is all about being human. Justice should never be dictated by religious faith, obviously. But this happens constantly—people brutalize those who don't keep the "right" religious laws. There is today a terrifying rise in the fanatical notion that one's beliefs give one the right to dispense justice. But that is false justice. It is a way to justify blood violence.

**EKH**: The most horrific things can happen within the worlds of your books, and you write without any sentiment, and yet there's a often a redeeming sweetness, even a tenderness, in the way your characters treat each other when faced with the worst. Do you see this as true beyond the bounds of your writing? Do we as a species tip, on the whole, toward human kindness?

**LE**: We have to believe in kindness, goodness, and mercy, because the alternative is to believe in hatefulness, evil, and cruelty. It isn't that hard to write dark stories that just get darker and meaner until everybody slides away in a slick of grease. Humor in the midst of despair—that's difficult. Or to make an act of kindness or bravery as shocking as an act of violence. I don't often

get to that point in my work—and redemption isn't my thing. I avoid redemption—it's very difficult to write into a book without becoming trite or sentimental. I am always fighting my maternal instincts. I try not to redeem my characters, unless it happens in a fit of irony. Moreover, redemption is too often the stamp we put on violence so that it can be sold as a palatable commodity.

What is redemption, real redemption? It is sometimes ordinary. It is my parents saving Green Stamps so that their daughter, raised in a little North Dakota town, can listen to *King Lear* every night as she falls asleep.

**EKH**: In *The Round House*, Joe is conscious of the way his reputation for being a good kid gives him a certain leverage with adults. By the end of the book he's acted in ways that compromise that reputation. Perhaps more to the point, though, it seems to me that he's grown into a more complicated relationship with what it might mean to be just or do the right thing, and that maybe this is the very nature of his growing up. Does this resonate at all with your own experience? Has your own sense of what it might mean to be good shifted over time?

**LE:** Joe gets pushed into a corner because there is no justice that can keep his mother safe. He sees his parents as annoying mortals whom he desperately loves even as they become real—weak, striving, sometimes heroic—but unable to lift the curse of violence. He should not have to resort to violence himself in order to protect his mother, but because of racist laws, he does.

Everyone's experience of what it means to be good shifts over time. Perhaps at one time I thought it was good to try to change people. Now I think that leaving them alone is better. Perhaps at one time I thought animals should be left alone. Now I think they need help in order to survive this peopled world. I never did think that being good was a matter of following rules. That, at least, I learned through enduring infuriating religious dicta.

To me there is only one true law and it seems simple—love—but of course to love well—whomever or whatever you love—isn't easy over time and often requires not only a sense of humor but also heroic self-discipline. I have seen this in my own parents, married over sixty years, and in the efforts of my brothers and sisters and my children who work in Native education and in the Indian Health Service. They are all truly devoted and excellent people. For a writer this is devastating—they are much too good to make interesting characters. I hang around them all the time, hoping they will reveal fiction-ready flaws. But they never do. I get no material whatsoever and have to resort to making things up.

**EKH:** You've said that you "hate religious rules. They are usually about controlling women." Do you think this is a universal problem with religion or a particularly Western or Catholic or Christian one?

**LE:** Universal. There seems no end to the viciousness of fundamentalism when it comes to women.

**EKH:** You write some of my favorite female characters, women I love precisely because they are so self-possessed, so exclusively in control of themselves. I come back often to the scene in *Love Medicine* when June finds herself trapped in the front seat of a truck, stuck under the weight of a sleeping man. Without waking him, June manages to pop out from the truck, straighten herself, and set off down however many miles of dark, snowy road—truck door still ajar, heat blasting, man, I imagine, drooling. I admire her so much for this. I imagine you must, too? What do you make of the women of your work?

**LE:** Well, June did walk off into a lethal blizzard. Yet the female characters I've written have often been strong, ferocious, and in some ways they have come to my rescue. For a time I needed to learn to command my own strength (Fleur). At another time I needed to learn to live in disguise (Agnes/Father Damian) or to be a roving acrobat (Delphine) or to stop living on the edge of things (Antelope Woman). All are aspects of being a mother.

**EKH:** The operating rules of *The Round House* allow for characters' direct engagement with the otherworldly; it's not just that we're in a reality where magical or mystical things might happen, but we might be a part of them. In one scene in the book, Joe spots a ghost watching him from the bushes of his family's backyard. The ghost may be there to bear some kind of warning. Joe is spooked—as he says to his dad, "The last thing I want to know is something that a ghost wants to tell me"— but there's also something terrific to me in Joe's sense that its presence is negotiable. I love when Joe realizes, "Dad, it's just a ghost. We can get rid of it." Is this capacity to engage with the superhuman something that you think exists in the everyday?

**LE:** People often absorb confounding experiences into their lives, including contact with supernatural entities. Or animals. For instance, there is a rescue by dolphins cited in *The Round House*. I was in a group and mentioned this, and two people in the group had family members who were rescued at sea by dolphins. I have asked people sitting around a table whether they experienced prophetic dreams or ghosts. Nearly everyone spoke of an experience.

**EKH:** Your novels are so intricately built. Perhaps this makes too much of what's really a coincidence, but I noticed that in *The Round House*, the turning point of the book falls exactly at the middle of the book's pages. What's the planning process like for your novels? How do you think about their structuring?

**LE:** I usually plan them out thoroughly, and even draw their shapes, but there are always surprises in the actual writing. Scenes with dialogue, especially, may shift or reveal something I didn't count on in the structure.

**EKH:** It's heartening to know how much you revise even published work. I like the way this suggests a story as one rendering of a squirming, changing thing, rather than a singular, definitive expression. It also reassures me as someone who can't imagine ever completely liking something I've written. That said, I wonder what the moments are in your body of work, big or small, where you feel like you've satisfied your ambitions? And I wonder, too, given how interconnected your writings are, how the effects of this revising then ripples out through the rest of your work?

**LE:** This makes me laugh because I've just finished copy editing my next novel, *LaRose*, which will be published in May 2016. As always I was a wreck. Even now I'm very upset about leaving some lines in the book that I will excise at the last moment, in page proofs. No amount of tinkering is ever enough—so the answer is no. I am not satisfied with anything that I have written. Only exhaustion keeps me from rewriting.

**EKH:** What does it take to build and write about such a complex constellation of families? How do you organize yourself? How extensively have you worked out the shape of this community and its life beyond what we get to see on the page?

**LE:** I have my friend and tormentor, my copy editor Trent Duffy, to thank for keeping that world logically coherent. Once I write the book, he tells me whether the times, places, descriptions, habits, and so forth work with the other books. Sometimes I have long dossiers on the characters, sometimes very little. Often I have a stack of objects and clippings, books and even a pair of shoes or a hat that I think would belong to a character. I keep these things near in a little pile while writing that person.

**EKH:** What are the texts that are touchstones for your own life? Is there a *Star Trek: The Next Generation* to your Cappy and Angus and Joe?

**LE:** *The Lathe of Heaven* and *The Left Hand of Darkness* and *Always Coming Home* by Ursula K. Le Guin, Frank Herbert's the *Dune* trilogy, and *Mockingbird* by Walter Tevis are a few old favorites. My favorite contemporary work of speculative fiction is Kazuo Ishiguro's *Never Let Me Go*.

**EKH:** Has what motivates you to write changed over the arc of your career? Has that impulse, or what you hope to make through following it, altered at all?

**LE:** Nothing has changed except the need for more coffee. I have the same obsession.

**EKH:** It's so personal that I almost hate to ask it, but what are the things or ideas or people in which you'd say you place faith?

**LE:** My family, of course, my friends. Also, perhaps obviously, books.

**EKH:** I hear that your bookstore, Birchbark Books, has a salvaged confessional now living and working as a forgiveness booth. The rumor is that you've collaged the interior with images of your sins and that the booth dispenses "random absolution." Anything particularly juicy you want to fess to? Is your own feeling that absolution is dispensed randomly? And why the move from confessing to forgiving?

**LE:** Crouching in a little closet and whispering made-up sins to a deeply bored priest—what could be more hilarious? It was unbearable. I never told my real sins to the priest, of course, and still resent the veil of shame that the church tried eagerly to lower upon girls. Especially girls. Impure thoughts! Perhaps I kept them bottled up and put them into my books. Anyway, I decided that the confessional should have a second life as a pleasantly impersonal forgiveness booth. Being forgiven by another human is awkward and doesn't help because it means you're *guilty*, and the other person is *soooo good*, but being forgiven by an old beaten-up carved confessional might feel all right. 🕎

# Portals

Shannon called God "the Universe. "I will let the Universe tell me what I should do." "The Universe will guide me." "I put my faith in the Universe." "I'm trying to listen to the Universe."

"Why don't you just call it God?" I asked, one brunch when we were meeting up to talk about our various relationship failures. We'd decided to try out a new restaurant that served brown rice with an egg on top, something I was a hundred percent capable of making at home but still seemed out of reach.

"God is such a loaded word," she said, settling into her chair.

"But it's the same thing, isn't it?" I said. "You're dodging."

The waiter came and took our order. Shannon also ordered a cleanse: lemon, cayenne, honey. She had explained on the walk over that she was fasting and eating at the same time. She said it was weirdly effective, though I did not ask for what.

"The Universe is not the same," she said. "It's everything, it's the whole thing, you know? The grand mystery. It's more connected to science."

Shannon was an actor. Other than writers, the art people I knew best were theater types and I had quite a few friends working in Hollywood in film and on stage and the majority of them spoke of "the Universe" in

## Aimee Bender

this way. It had started around 1998. At that time, I was volunteering with a theater improv group doing outreach in schools and hospitals and suddenly everyone was talking with a great earnestness about the Universe like it could do things for them, like it was a real consciousness they could pray to. It took me by surprise, as if they had all woken up and decided together. No one mentioned God, though no one had talked about God in the first place anyway. I would say that God might be the word least used among my peer group, except in "Oh God" or "Oh my fucking God" or "God, that sucks."

Our food came. I asked for hot sauce. Shannon broke her yolk and began stirring it into the rice.

"And another cleanse, please," she asked the waiter, whom we'd already confirmed we recognized from a car commercial.

I liked the word God but I didn't feel safe telling anyone. I liked it a lot. I maybe even loved it. I liked how it looked alone on the page, decontextualized, capitalized, and I liked how, if I whispered it to myself, it contained a majesty. I did not feel the word itself was responsible for atrocities—that was people, that was corruption. I did not feel the word pointed only to the oft-mentioned old man with a beard. I wasn't sure if I believed in God, but if I did it surely was not a God on a throne high above with bushy eyebrows and a plan. Far worse than the Universe believers were the people I knew who would nod their heads sagely during hard times—mine or their own or the world's—and say everything happened for a reason. I held a very particular prickly rage for them; it is a mantra with a sneaky way of victimizing victims—and anyone, really, who is down on their luck. In fact, to think that all things happen for a reason entirely sidesteps luck, and I had come to believe that luck is a very real force in the world, unpredictable, baffling, and one of the scarier concepts I can imagine. It is not a force with exclusive authority, but still.

"I like the word God," I said to Shannon, stirring my rice.

"You like God?"

"No," I said, carefully. "I didn't say that." My food was fine, easy to eat. The hot sauce tasted good on the rice. "I just like the word."

She laughed. "Well, that's a dodge too," she said. "The word means something."

"What does it mean?"

"I don't know," she said, leaning back in her chair. She peered out the window into the day. "Obviously, it's a hard word to define."

"But can you define the Universe?"

"Way easier," she said. "Right? Everything in outer space, and inner space, quantum and infinite, operating under its own logic."

I shifted in my seat. The chairs at the restaurant were notably uncomfortable. "So, you're asking a galaxy to guide your life?"

"Maybe," she shrugged. "A galaxy has its own internal wisdom, doesn't it? Also, you know that Christians say God is word, right?"

"Yeah."

"So there you go. Liking the word is kind of the same thing."

"For Christians," I said.

"'In the beginning was the word . . .'"

"To me, the word is the word," I said. "I don't know why I like it so much."

"Jesus was word incarnate."

"I don't believe in Jesus," I said. "And does a galaxy really have internal wisdom?"

"It has beauty," she said. "It has form."

I shook my head at her. Shannon was now leaning in very intently with wide eyes the way she did when she was making a point that meant something to her.

"Well," I said. "It's not for me."

She relaxed back in her seat again. "No worries," she said. "No Universe evangelists here."

We made the laughing gestures that can signal the close of a topic and then talked about the dating scene for a while.

Afterward, on the sidewalk outside, she clapped a hand on my shoulder like an uncle might. "You always tell me words are portals, right? Just go through the portal."

She blew a kiss and walked the other way. She lived north of Fountain and I was near Sweetzer and Melrose so we split by Barney's Beanery. On the walk home, through streets messy and gorgeous with jacaranda blossoms, for some reason I found myself remembering the first play I'd seen her in, in college, in a tiny black box of a theater that doubled as a boxing ring. She played the boy orphan who always ate the unusually named mayonnaise. She'd cut her hair short, and she made everyone in the audience cry, even then, even at nineteen. I had felt such awe, watching her. I did not understand how she could be a vessel like that. After, when I went backstage to congratulate her, she was her usual self, glowing from all the compliments, but it was like watching a genie siphon back into the bottle. "I bow to *you*," I said, lowering my head. "Why on earth do they have you bow to us?" and she laughed and hugged me and only in the hug did I feel how incredibly delicate she was right then, and how all the compliments were like fishing lines serving to retrieve her from wherever she had gone to find that boy. "Amazing," I said, "fantastic," and she kept firming up, little by little, and then, with a few other cast members, we went out to get pizza and beer. 🏰

**Chuang-Tzu**
translated by Ha Poong Kim

# RAMBLE IN THE VILLAGE OF NOTHINGWHATSOEVER

*from the* Chuang-Tzu, *Chapter One*

Hui-tzu said to Chuang-tzu:
"I have a huge tree,
People call it a *shu*.
Its trunk is full of knots and bumps so that you cannot apply a measuring
    line to it.
Its branches are so twisted and crooked that you can use neither a
    compass nor a square on them.
Were I to put the tree by the roadside,
No carpenter would stop to look at it.
Now, your talk is big and useless.
So everybody alike turns away from it."
        Chuang-tzu said:
"Apparently, you've never seen a wildcat or a weasel.
It crouches down and hides, waiting for its prey to drift by.

It leaps around east and west, venturing high and low.

Then it gets caught in a trap and dies in a net.

Then again, there is the yak as big as a cloud covering the sky.

No doubt, it has the ability to become big, but can't catch even a mouse.

      "Now you have a huge tree,

And you are worried that it's useless.

Why don't you plant it in the Village of Nothingwhatsoever, the field of
    boundless void,

And lie back by its side, doing nothing?

Or doze off idly in its shade?

        Axes will not cut your life short,

        Nothing will harm you.

        When you are of no use,

        What misfortune will come your way?"

# TENDERER MERCIES

## ON FANNY HOWE'S
### Indivisible

**DARCEY STEINKE**

At my nephew's recent first Communion, the only part of the service that moved me was when the priest carried the huge Bible from the altar to the pulpit to read from the Gospels. As he held the book in its gold cover high over his head, I remembered how my own father, a Lutheran minister, carried his worn New American Standard Bible from altar to pulpit. His was less grand but, to my little-girl mind, still deeply holy.

A book, Bible or otherwise, is a sacred object, filled with stories of human struggle and the unknown movement of God. A few times in my life I've felt a woosh of divinity, but never do I sense the invisible world more strongly than I do in one of my favorite novels.

Unfortunately, in our secular world, authentic novels of faith are hard to come by. Evangelical writers leaves me cold, as do the new atheists. There is the added problem that writing about God is nearly impossible, as ephemeral as cigarette smoke and equally hard to describe. The books that thrill me are not preachy or moralistic, but engaged with a raw and volatile divinity. The very best of this genre are George Bernanos's *Diary of a Country Priest*, *Go Tell It On the Mountain* by James Baldwin, Clarice Lispector's *The Passion According to G. H.*, and, my favorite, *Indivisible* by Fanny Howe.

Howe is a poet and lyric essayist who, in the 1980s, over a single weekend, wrote a long prose work she broke into three novels. *Indivisible* is the most aphoristic of the trilogy. In it we follow Henny, a failed filmmaker and foster mother, as she moves simultaneously through both domestic and spiritual spheres, deciding if she should take on another foster child and dealing with the betrayal of her childhood friend Libby, as well as complications from her charged marriage. When the novel opens, she has locked her husband in a closet so she can more completely connect with the Godhead. Henny needs a break from the pressures of matrimony. She is interested in coauthoring an intimate story with God, a tale "that glides along under everything else . . . [that] jumps out into the light like a silver fish when it wants to see where it lives in relation to everything else."

All of Henny's relationships center on the search for divinity, even when she also hopes for romantic or physical love. Her personal theology is anti-intuitive, and deeply eccentric: "The resurrection is erotic. An erection busting up out of the dirt, all red, fertile." She feels prisons, instead of woodlands, are the sacred groves of our time, and it's in a prison waiting room that she meets Tom, a tall, thin monkish man, and his charge, a small blind boy. Tom brings the child each Saturday to visit his mother, an incarcerated '60s radical, possibly a member of The Weathermen.

Henny feels as if two little darts are lodged in her and Tom's flesh in exactly the same spot and that "they moved in relation to each other like charged needles that seek a thread." Though Henny longs for romantic love she is also ambivalent. It was in mothering that she first felt the movement of the spirit. Through raising others' children, she's learned that people are interchangeable: "Why should you want to be a single individual once you have realized that you are already everything."

Henny, like an Old Testament prophet, rages at God. She's angry that her life never quite coalesces and that she is often lonely and afraid. She takes in the blind child, though Tom remains aloof. Her other love interest, Lewis, an African American man in a wheelchair, is not attracted to her physically. He tells her life's meaning lies in "the 4th chapter of *Bambi*, the 12th chapter of the Gita" and Fellini's film *La Strada*. She struggles to find a coherent sense of self and divinity, asking if a woman is built "to be solitary, thoughtful, maternal, hard working, hateful and God-crazy all at the same time?" Her most enriching adult relationship is with Lewis's mother, Mimi. The two take long walks in the zoo talking about the Upanishads, Polonius, Dionysus, Weil, Dostoyevsky, and Tolstoy. It is Mimi's testimony that is central to the theme of this novel. She tells Henny that only when she understood that she was not getting, after hard work, what she deserved, did she realize God was finally taking her seriously. God's absence, Henny sees through Mimi, is even more important then God's presence. Or as St. John of the Cross suggests: "The most goodly knowing of God is that which is known by unknowing."

I'm convinced that the most vibrant spiritual lives are often lived outside the traditional church structure. Like Simone Weil before her, Howe is a radical-renegade Christian, her theology by turns lucid and surreal. Reading *Indivisible* moves me into the version of myself I most cherish: girl copying down favorite lines in her notebook:

A movie moves in place like certain minds when they are thinking.

Weak desires protect you from disappointment but nothing keeps you safer then being a visible ruin.

All encounters in dreams are indications that relationships travel without their people.

At its best the point of the word "mother" is that it is a quality, not a condition or situation. So let's say "motherer" instead of mother.

Motherers, Henny concludes, have to learn to want nothing, to die for others. She speculates that these qualities could lead to revolution; they are the essence of liberation because they are the opposite of what society wants. It's the practice and theology of mothering that Henny comes to find most sustaining. She takes in the blind child, who is another manifestation of God.

Like all good mystics, Howe is self-critical, frustrated by God talk. Even the word *God* is so stuffed with meaning it makes her sick. As the novel ends, Henny swears not to talk holy talk ever again; still, "the dead have taken off in search of deep time" and religion is like "garbage come alive." It's Howe's spiritual flexibility, intimate engagement, and fierce desire that make this book holy. I'd gladly carry it, like a Bible, high over my head.

ON HAROLD FREDERIC'S

# The Damnation of Theron Ware

CHESTON KNAPP

It was an experiment in Christian community, eleven young adults living together for the summer on Martha's Vineyard. In the house were nine college students—five girls, four boys—and a midtwenties married couple, our chaperones and counselors, leaders mostly by example. Imagine *The Real World*, only ditch the drunken antics for daily quiet times, swap the routine roomie diddling for weekly Bible studies. With an eye to evangelizing, we all worked jobs on the island. As a clerk at Brickman's department store in Vineyard Haven, I sold a sweater to Ted Danson and some beach amusements to Marty McFly, but wussed out when it came time to invite them to our weekly small group. Every evening a couple was responsible for dinner and another for clean up and all together

we occasionally helped administer camps for middle and high schoolers at our host organization's HQ. The Study Center, a compound of bunks and offices and assorted sanctuaries on a wooded knoll in West Tisbury. Christians love them a ponderous handle and our program was no exception. It was called, simply, Cornerstone. *Was* because it no longer exists. And all irony aside, I was surprised to discover how much it disturbed me, learning Cornerstone had been pulled. Its total absence on the organization's website suggested an erasure of a deeper and more metaphorical sort. Which is of course to say that it suggested an absence or erasure in me.

Time has since proven that summer to be a high point in my spiritual whatever. I'd grown up in the church, as the saying goes, had done youth groups and Young Life, prayer breakfasts and "retreats." I once attended a happening called Promise Keepers—tens of thousands of men gathered in a stadium in Philly to pray and sing worship songs and wave their arms together like reefs of sea anemones and weep and embrace one another homosocially. We got hats. But for all this activity, all these events, I'd never had what I conceived of as "an experience," which is to say that a Whitmanesque God had never peeled back the corner of the universe to make moon eyes at me. I understood this to be my failure and, good Protestant that I was, chalked it up to never having been sufficiently *serious* about my faith and, thus convicted, figured I'd give it the old college try.

But if my time on the island was an effort to redeem or resuscitate my religiospiritual past, it was also part of an awakening to other possible experiences of significance and meaning. This was the summer after my sophomore year, during which I'd started to read deliberately, with intent. And I rode this new passion on into the summer. Our morning quiet times were supposed to be given over to reading the Bible and praying, and the journal I kept shows I was doing some of that, but it also shows that I was just as often thinking about Camus and Rilke and Eliot. Before heading down the road to work, Chris, the male half of the married couple, would give me a notecard scribbled on either side with quotes he'd come across in his reading as a grad student in philosophy, lines plucked from folks like Coleridge, Hegel, and Arendt. I'd spend my downtime at the store studying them and later that night, sitting on the house's big front porch and smoking, no shit, pipes, we'd discuss them. When later that summer I suffered a bit of dental trauma (tennis racket, front teeth), a few members of the house went to the annual book sale at the West Tisbury Library and came back with boxes and boxes of books for me. I'd been depressed, literally toothless, and their kindness caught me off guard. Never before had I felt so cared for by people who were not my family.

Given how well it maps onto my experience both at and after Cornerstone, I'm tempted to write that it was in one of those boxes that I found my copy of Harold Frederic's *The Damnation of Theron Ware*.

But it'd be another five years before Chris started pushing the book on me, another six before I got myself a copy.

First published in 1896, the book is often praised as a "minor classic" of American realism. Meet Theron, a young and talented (and ambitious) Methodist minister. At the end of an annual conference—what sounds like an old-fashioned, no-holds-barred preach-off—church brass announces where ministers will serve the coming year. They assign Theron to Octavius, a small town in upstate New York based on Utica. He thinks his preaching should've earned him a better, more distinguished post, but he and his wife head off, comforting themselves with the thought that it's just one year.

Theron's troubles begin more or less upon his arrival, when he meets the church's trustees. Turns out they're not interested in his sensitive and nuanced sermons, in the craft he's worked so hard to hone: "What we want here, sir, is straight-out, flat-footed hell,—the burnin' lake o' fire an' brimstone. Pour it into 'em, hot an' strong."

He finds fellowship instead with a handful of local Irish Catholics, who traffic in ideas, in art. They're literary, philosophical, listen to and play fine music—they're nothing, prejudices being what they were, like what he expected from the Irish. It's under their considerable influence, particularly that of the beautiful and lapsed Celia Madden, a self-proclaimed pagan and "out-and-out Greek," that he begins to turn away from the religion he's been brought to preach.

"Do great works of art, the big achievements of the big artists, appeal to you, stir you up?" Celia asks, but Theron doesn't have a satisfying answer. He goes so far as to claim he's never seen a good painting in his life.

"Evidently there was an intellectual world, a world of culture and grace . . . where men asked one another, not 'Is your soul saved?' but 'Is your mind well furnished?' Theron had the sensation of having been invited to become a citizen of this world."

But he can't become a citizen of this world, of course, at least not a fully naturalized one. What his new acquaintances prize in him (his simplicity, his ideals, what might be called his "authenticity") are the very things that they end up corrupting. On his temporary visa, Theron grows to disdain his job, his parishioners, even his wife. He falls hard for Celia, so hard that he follows her to New York without her knowing. And after she confronts him and tells him she'd been charmed with who he was, not who he's become, Theron suffers a breakdown.

Frederic isn't bent on moralizing or judging, though, and navigates Theron's crisis with a deft ironic distance. Theron is a kissing cousin, in this way, of Emma Bovary. And though he leaves the church and moves west, to Seattle, with his wife, it'd be a mistake to say this is a novel about a minister losing his faith. It's more complicated and knotty than that. Faith isn't lost, exactly; it's displaced, redirected. Art stands in for religion. And if Theron's punished for anything, it's for being inauthentic.

Critics will tell you this shift was culture-wide, a revolution of sorts. There's a deep history here, but since about 1800 we've lionized our artists, have granted them the status of prophets and visionaries. In short, we've come to expect them to provide the spiritual substance of life, that is, to bring us into deeper contact with ourselves, with what Rousseau called "the sentiment of existence." We now have faith in inner depth and individuality, and nobly strive for authentic experience.

By the time I read the book, I'd also moved across the country, to Portland, and was working in earnest for this magazine. And I'd also begun to understand that I'd made a miscalculation of sorts. Books, no matter how many I read, no matter how good, wouldn't succeed where I thought religion had failed. My experiences with them would never completely fill the absence hunkered in the deep seat of me. That absence, in a sense, and the restless desire to fill it, *was* me. Authentically. And every now and again, I imagine Theron in Seattle, sitting inside of a rainy evening, warming himself by a fire, snifter in hand. The excitement of the move has since worn off and I like to think of the peculiar mix of dread and joy he must've experienced when he realized he'd never get fully clear of his former self, no matter how far or fast he ran. When he finally understood that you don't live down your past, you live with it, even into it, now and forever.

## ON JAYNE ANNE PHILLIPS'S
# Sweethearts

LEIGH NEWMAN

Fourteen years ago, I bought my copy of *Sweethearts* in a used-books store in Massachusetts, not because I knew anything about the author or had read the hypnotic first line ("Day of the slaughter they were all of them / the men tensed up") but because I loved the cover. I still love it. The design is simple: a beige background, the title and Jayne Anne Phillips's name in a 1970s-era font that evokes the Allman Brothers more than disco. Even then, in that luxurious split second in which I realized I was about to plunk down money for something I knew nothing of, I felt I understood this book, as if I had seen it before, as if I had studied it the way I'd done with my parents' album covers, listening to the music unspool in the living room.

And yet, at the center of that same cover, outlined in black, is a photograph that so clearly dates back to another time, the late 1940s. A young postwar couple stands in their wedding finery—glove, suits, padded shoulders—in front of a stark Protestant cross. Easter lilies flare behind them on the altar like heavy white stars. The wife holds a bouquet you can just barely make out. The husband wears a tie clip, a corsage, his shiny new ring. Both look off to the right, his face tired, strained, hers unreadable save for a flash-blinded smile.

Nowhere does it say that the photo is of Phillips's parents on their wedding day (though the second piece in the collection, "Wedding Picture," makes you believe it must be). Nowhere does it define the collection as a book of flash fiction, poetry, or plain old fiction or nonfiction. Inside, there is no table of contents and there are no page numbers. Each piece is two pages or shorter. The publishing house that put it out—Truck Press in Minneapolis—originally printed four hundred copies of the book in 1976, then six hundred more in 1978, when it cost a reader a cool $3.95. I paid fifteen bucks for it, which, at the time, felt steep. Now it feels as though I cheated somebody in an almost biblical way, so great is the debt I owe the bookseller who let me have it.

About a year after my purchase, Phillips came to my grad school to do a reading. I stood in line—having not yet read *Black Tickets* or *Machine Dreams*, unlike the far better prepared students ahead of me, but entirely versant in *Sweethearts*. Phillips sat at the table in a cool, velvety tunic. When I presented her the book, she sighed. "I haven't seen this for a long, long time," she said and gave it a pat, as if putting it to bed.

I think I'd expected more. That more included something akin to her declaring: "You found my long lost work of genius!" The two of us would sweep off to a café to celebrate her spot-on choice of titles for the book's two sections—Sweethearts and Slaves—and debate the inclusion of "Swimming" in the latter, a one-paragraph-long story about a girl's shame-tinged fascination with her best friend, Jancey.

I will admit that it was a lonely time in my life. I was separated from my husband; I was living in a garage. I spent more time than was healthy thinking along to the words on the pages of the books I read instead of reading. Most of my thoughts were about my own failures as a person, which clotted up with my failures as a writer.

*Sweethearts* blitzed right through that commentary. My intellect could not keep up and neither could the rest of me. Each story has an almost spooky authority that sweeps aside anything other than the rules of its own world—rules I didn't know and rules I couldn't predict, but rules I was going to follow without thought or question because I believed from the first word.

Reading it, at times, was like watching a slideshow in a neighbor's dark basement—not just the images changing with a click of the carousel, but also the voice of the narrator changing, the shape of her or his or its shadow at the back of the room changing. Sometimes what stood there was what Phillips calls a "monstruro," sometimes it was a stripper working a jukebox.

My least favorite pieces stunned me with my most favorite lines ("My sugar is a panic that melts on your tongue and leaves a tiny hole in what you taste.") and my most favorite pieces contained whole passages and progressions I couldn't understand, except in some joyful animal way, like a dog rolling with glee in deer shit. "Toads" is the best example of this, a story about some kids who find a toad on their enclosed porch: "Twigs tapped in a pattern . . . he danced for us. Someone slipped and the creature bled from its sheltered belly." The way the story is told you swerve from the perspective of the we of the kids to the toad to that we again to the I of a girl who digs up the dead toad to its golden eyes. Somewhere in between all that you run into these two gorgeous sentences: "The funeral took place on a sandpile. Topping the mound with a blue bucket, my cousin exclaimed I gave it a sky!"

Years later, I read *Black Tickets*. Eight of the *Sweethearts* pieces also appear in that later, now classic, collection of stories—either incorporated into longer, more traditionally structured stories or sliced in between them. "Toads" didn't make it. "Cheers"—the story of a seamstress who sews cheerleading outfits for all you girls who are "bout the same'"—did. I used to wonder if *Black Tickets* had been the goal, if the writing of *Sweethearts* was like the drawings old masters made before painting the masterpiece.

Or did the transfer happen the way most things happen with creative people: Phillips made something, then used it to make something else? The *Sweethearts* pieces serve as a contrast, a link to the newer stories. The two talk to each other. "The Wedding Picture" (*Sweethearts*), in which her mother's "heart makes a sound that no one hears," is followed by a story called "Home" (*Black Tickets*), in which an adult daughter goes home to live with her divorced mother. That latter story is also interesting when I think about the 1970s look of the cover of *Sweethearts* with its 1940s photo: the characters are a postwar mother, who divorced despite her traditional values, and a Vietnam-Watergate-era daughter who sleeps with her lover, a vet, in her childhood bedroom.

I recently saw in the back of *Sweethearts* that Phillips, along with Bull City Studios and Truck Press, is credited with the layout and design of the book. In "Home," the daughter takes her lover to the Rainbow, "a bar and grill on Main Street," where they "hold hands, play country songs on the jukebox and drink a lot of salted beer." In *Sweethearts*, there's another photograph that appears after the title page, printed in white and royal blue, so it looks almost like an illustration. The photograph is of a small-town street. The cars are fishtailed beauties; the signs advertise a bank, a fire and auto insurance agency, something called Monongahela Power. Two men talk to each other, one in a straw business hat, the other a farmer, under a sign that reads *Rainbow Restaurant*.

That said, I have zero interest in finding out what these overlaps have to do with the facts of Phillips's own life. I just like how the world of one book bleeds over into the next. I like how *Sweethearts* is not discrete. I get to keep going. I get to go back. I don't really have to wake up at the end of the book. "Some people have the notion that you read the story and then climb out of it into the meaning," writes Flannery O'Connor in *Mystery and Manners*, "but for the fiction writer himself the whole story is the meaning, because it is an experience, not an abstraction." That is true for the fiction reader too, especially while inside the kinds of stories in which, as Phillips describes her process in the front matter of *Black Tickets*, the characters and voices that "began in what is real . . . became, in fact, dreams."

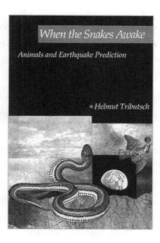

ON HELMUT TRIBUTSCH'S

# When the Snakes Awake

JUSTIN NOBEL

When the earthquake struck San Leopoldo, a small town in the rugged mountains of northeastern Italy, Helmut Tributsch was half a world away, working as an engineer in the Peruvian Andes. It was May 6, 1976. Tributsch returned to his native village and found it in ruins. Peasants huddled in makeshift tents and hay sheds, fearful of aftershocks. To Tributsch, a budding young scientist and anointed man of reason, they told their earthquake stories, many of which shared a particular theme: in the days, hours, and minutes before the quake, animals had acted very strangely.

Stray cats disappeared. House cats carried kittens into vegetable gardens. Chickens refused to enter their coops. Chained cattle tore at their chains. Caged canaries flapped their wings energetically and raced about their cages. A certain parakeet drank

a lot of water. Herds of deer fled the mountains for the fields. Starting about twenty minutes before the quake, dogs of various breeds sprinted in circles, howling. A few minutes prior to the shock, woods and fields erupted in birdsong, even though it was nine at night. And prior to each aftershock, roosters made the following noise: "Krrr . . . Krrr . . . Krrr . . . Krrr . . ."

Tributsch listened attentively. His countrymen's observations deserved scientific examination. And yet, "earthquake premonition by animals does not fit into the rational world of science," Tributsch writes in *When the Snakes Awake*, published in 1982 by MIT Press. "It has become too hot to handle without ever having been seriously tested scientifically." His work was laid out for him. Using folklore, literature, obscure scientific treatises, and the entire earth as his oyster, he would gather evidence of animal earthquake-predictive behavior, then shape a theory that could explain the phenomenon to dismissive, and square, modern scientists.

China proved to be fertile ground. There, the idea that animals can predict earthquakes is well accepted and goes back three thousand years. In 1974, based on careful examination of the region's 2,200-year earthquake history, authorities in Liaoning province forecast a major quake. Peasants, teachers, students, telephone operators, weather-service employees, and animal caretakers were mobilized to monitor warning signs, namely, the clouding up of well waters and unusual animal behavior. By early February 1975, anomalies had indeed begun to pour in: gas bubbles in ponds, foamy well water, madly barking dogs, rats that appeared to be drunk, snakes that slithered out of their burrows and froze to death in the snow. On February 4, residents of Haicheng were evacuated to emergency shelters, and shown outdoor movies. At 7:36 PM, the anticipated earthquake arrived, a devastating 7.3 on the Richter scale.

Brash with the success, that same year the Geological Bureau of Peking put out an informational book that addressed animal earthquake-warning signs via a sort of ditty:

*Pigs do not eat, and dogs bark madly.*
*Ducks do not enter water and stay on shore.*
*Chickens fly up in trees and scream loudly.*
*Snakes come out of burrows in freezing sky*
*  and ground.*
*Big cats pick up little ones and run . . .*

Unfortunately, the following year, seemingly without warning, a catastrophic earthquake struck Tangshan, in northeastern China. As many as 655,000 people died.

"Did the animals' senses fail," wonders Tributsch, "or was it a failure of human organization?"

Tributsch appears to be rooting for the animals, and as he analyzes the possible means by which they sense earthquakes, one starts to see the shortcomings of our own hapless form.

Could the animals be sensing magnetic fields? Although bees, carrier pigeons, and even bacteria have been shown to respond to minute magnetic field changes, Tributsch decides it's unlikely that this is the main instigator. Animals face a daily barrage of magnetic field variations, as they migrate across terrain and also in the daily movements of the sun and moon— any earthquake magnetic signal would be weak, and lost in this complex soup of already palpable magnetic signals.

(Although, two remarkable magnetic asides: About two hours before the 1855 Edo earthquake, a foot-long horseshoe-shaped magnet with nails and iron bits clinging to it that was hanging in the shop window of a Japanese optician suddenly relinquished all of its magnetic attachments. And in the Great Lisbon earthquake of 1755, one of the strongest and deadliest earthquakes to strike Europe in recorded history, the German philosopher Immanuel Kant observed that "the magnets . . . threw off their load and that magnetic needles were brought into disorder.")

Could it be that the animals' super-acute sense of smell warns them of earthquakes? Despite the fact that some salmon can smell their native creeks across a thousand miles of ocean, and the fulmar can apparently smell the fat of marine mammals, and turkey vultures in the American West have been known to sniff out breaks in oil pipelines, Tributsch concludes that smell, although likely playing a role in some instances, is not the main cause. Both electromagnetic radiation and electrical currents are also raised as potential suspects, but duly dismissed. What then?

The answer comes to Tributsch in a eureka moment inspired by a visit to Rudi Zuder, an old man living in a woodshed in San Leopoldo. Zuder is a retired precision mechanic, and just before the quake struck he happened to have been assembling a small wristwatch, a job that required him to put a thin stainless-steel plate into place. But the tiny plate kept repelling itself from its intended place and "jumping off." Zuder attempted the task several times and repeatedly failed. Bewildered, he went outside to check the weather, and the quake struck. At last, Tributsch has found what he believes to be the culprit: electrostatically charged particles that somehow arise from within the earth.

If you're confused as to just what these particles are and how they differ from the already dismissed possible culprits of electricity and magnetism, so am I. But then again, one must remember that if Tributsch had truly solved this riddle, he would probably have won a Nobel Prize and had several institutes named after him. What Tributsch did was lay out a roadmap for persevering future earthquake enthusiasts to follow, a call to arms for seismologists, biologists, magnetologists, meteorologists, physicists, geologists, and everyday observers.

And as the reader reads on, and examples of earthquake perception from the animal world keep coming—penguins, grizzlies, catfish, eels, sea urchins, bonito, carp, lobster, sardines, giant squid, mackerel, crab, plankton—our own eureka moment emerges: humans too are of this biologic kingdom, and although we have adapted to living in a glossy whirring world of explosive stimuli, we may have silenced a set of senses much more ancient, and one must truly wonder just what it is we are missing.

ON TAHAR BEN JELLOUN'S

## This Blinding Absence of Light

**PAULS TOUTONGHI**

In the medina of Fez, Morocco—near the Bab Boujloud, the Blue Gate—past the *one-dirham* donut vendors who fry your donut in a vat of corn oil as you wait, and then hand it to you hot, with a dusting of crunchy sugar granules—past the open-air butchers' shops where the cats congregate, hoping to snag chicken gizzards or intestines or even beaks—past the leather artisan who will make your belt for you while you stand at his stall—past the men listening to the slow, mournful melody of solo-voiced Qur'anic recitation and using chisels to carve Islamic gravestones in travertine or marble—there is a small, mixed-language bookstore. It has some Arabic books. It has some French books. And then it has a wall of novels in English—a wall of English translations of the work of North African writers.

I spent five months in Morocco at the beginning of 2015. For much of the time I was there, I taught creative writing within the context of a study abroad program for a small liberal arts college. My students left campus with me; we all traveled to Marrakech and Fez to study Derija, the Moroccan dialect of Arabic. I also led them in a hybrid creative writing/literature class—for which we read Edward Said's *Orientalism*, Amin Maalouf's *On Identity*, and Tahar Ben Jelloun's novel *This Blinding Absence of Light*.

I'd bought my copy of *This Blinding Absence of Light* the previous year in that bookstore in the medina. Ben Jelloun's novel is a blistering indictment of the government of Hassan II, Morocco's king from 1961 to 1999—and the father of the current king, Mohammed VI. Hassan's rule, known in Morocco as "The Years of Lead," featured some of the worst human rights abuses the world has ever seen. For over twenty years, from the 1960s to the 1980s, Hassan imprisoned his political enemies in filthy underground jails in the most remote parts of the Moroccan desert. These "jails" were actually just pits in the sand; unlit, overrun with roaches and scorpions, they lacked plumbing or heat or even space for the prisoners to stand up. Importantly, purposefully—they also lacked running water; the men were unable to perform the ablutions necessary to clean themselves, and thus to enter into a formal state of Islamic prayer.

The novel follows the story of one of these men. Its narrator, Aziz, is a young military cadet—new to the army—who gets swept up in an attempted coup against Hassan. The coup fails; he is apprehended; at first, he's sentenced to detention in a regular jail but—one day, without warning, he's hooded and bound and loaded into a van and taken to Tazmamart Prison.

There are twenty-two other men who enter Tazmamart with him. Eighteen years later, only four emerge—the survivors of an almost unimaginable physical and psychological torture. Ben Jelloun details this process with excruciating exactitude—cataloguing all the ways a human being can die under these conditions. Men are devoured by scorpions, killed by chronic constipation, by loneliness, by scurvy. They go mad. The deprivations of the mind are almost worse than the deprivations of the body.

The novel—published in 2000—has long presented a dilemma for Moroccan censors. It is certainly fiction. Its vocabulary—which privileges imagistic detail and formal literary tropes—feels like something entirely apart from natural storytelling. It is a built narrative. But it is also deeply true, insofar as any work of art can be true; nearly all of the facts in the novel have been corroborated by multiple sources. And while the current king, Mohammed VI, isn't implicated in the same kinds of human rights abuses as his dad—the things his father did are certainly persuasive arguments against the concentration of all civic power into the hands of a single authority, no matter how "benevolent" it may seem.

What further complicates things is this: Ben Jelloun's narrator finds his only solace in his belief: "I invoked God by His many names . . . I thought once again about the Sura of Light and heard myself repeat the verse: *You see how powerful is the darkness of this light. Stretch out your hand and you will not even see it.*" In order to cope with the terror of his daily existence, he turns to Islam, to its words and its rituals. The spiritual journey of Aziz—his transformation—is one of the most important parts of the text. It also makes *This Blinding Absence of Light* a hard book to ban, in the context of a predominantly Muslim society.

If the storyteller's goal is to extend our understanding of empathy—and of the ways that a human being can come to rely on faith in a crisis—then this book stands for me as one of the most successful I've ever read. Aziz develops the ability—in his mind—to travel throughout the world, to make the pilgrimage to Mecca, to the Masjid Al-Haram: "That is how I found myself, at night, alone in the deserted square of the Kaaba, facing the black stone. I approached it slowly. I caressed it. I felt as though I had been transported several centuries into the past, and at the same time wafted into a radiant future." He is free. It is unreal; but he is free.

Like Ben Jelloun, my father was born in an Arabic-speaking North African nation and educated, there, in French schools. Like him—he turned to French as his principal language of self-expression. And like him, he felt a weight of disapprobation—possibly internal, but nonetheless real—for this choice. After I read *This Blinding Absence of Light* in English, I bought the French version. I made my way, slowly, through its text. The music of the language was a recognizable music. It was familiar—French with an Arabic inflection, a tonal shading that was subtle and difficult to pinpoint, but nonetheless real. And this made me even sadder. Those poor men in the desert—buried alive, slowly. Light's absence. The absence of mercy and justice. Our violent world; a pit in the ground turned into a prison; a kind of brutality almost impossible to understand. 🪨

**Sarah V. Schweig**

# THE TOWER

There was a tower of stone in a field of stone.
And the field of stone was the city.
And the Tower was built to sway in the breeze.
And we attended vocational universities,
where we learned to put our lives in a vise
and work them. At the top of the field,
we wear crinoline. This is why we were built.
This is why the Tower was built.

We knew what was possible by what our Director
announced through the speakers. We turned
our attention up toward the little silver sprinklers.
I often wonder what counts. I had my vise
work on my wounds until the wounds ate their way
into my prayers. It wasn't a competition *per se*
but I had a kind of game going with Christina.
It was called Whichever One of Us Loses.

She had issues with gluten, and I turned
my face up like a coin toward silver at the first
static sputter of speakers. And when Christina
labored her eyes dry like raisins away from her lit
monitor, I wondered whether she was considered
more valuable in the eyes of the company.
Shoeless, she works slowly in her swivel,
while I pay for my pumps to shine sole to heel.

Out by the Tower of stone, on the Avenue,
I sit in the throne of the shoeshine chair,
and the shoeshine man, he calls me *ma'am*,
he soothes my black patent leather.
Every morning is identical to every other
as if the first morning had gone viral forever.
The afternoons are similar. I zip up my sheath
to cover my scabs and look in the mirror.

The Tower was built to weather the weather.
The sun had come into its own and settled.
The sun had accepted its fixed trajectory
of motion, also known as a dead-end position.
I ran a stick of color over my cheeks whenever
the sun came up, a meme. Backward facing,
I crossed my legs and rode trains into the city,
fitted neatly into my sheath. Fall settled in fields.

But in the stone city, the elderly sit on benches
losing memories. Once stone-men, they invested
themselves in the Tower. They sat on a throne
tended by a shoeshine man and tongue-in-cheek
called him *Jeeves*. So the women of our stone city
work to replace the elderly, and our Director grants
the women of the Tower a few months of leave.
This was the advent of the ballooning women.

Our Director, heir to the field, attended an ivy.
From him we learned that to beget the industry
that creates more industries, some authority first hath
beget the word *beget*. It is similar with the population.
Fall comes and the breeze changes and the Tower
fills and empties, swaying. My office comes and goes
through the tunnel, singing the mission statement
of our company. I come home to unzip my sheath.

I come home to my wounds and work them
to heal. I unwind with a glass of wine and release
my life from the vise for the length of a sleep.
Honest, our Director thinks of the office as family.
And after the baby bumps popped out of the other side
of something like it was nothing whatsoever,
the ballooning women came back donning pictures
of the outcomes. The women, they encourage me,

but my skin crawls on the scar of my body.
It won't commit *per se* to such clotting. I wore
my sheath, like a sword, and the weapon was me.
The Director mistakenly called me Christina.
(I think when he said *family* he meant nothing by it.)
Still, the shoeshine man took my sole in his hands,
on the Avenue of stone, on his knees, and gently.
The morning came all viral and it came time

to dismantle the Tower. Through speakers
came the voice of our Director and the staff
sang and beat on monitors led by Christina.
I held my hand up to the sun and saw light work
through it, and while we dismantled our lives,
the pristine blue Director lorded over us was just
an effect of light cast on nothingness. I think
when he said *industry* he meant our obedience.

After the Tower, I settled down with a meat-
and-potatoes man who invested himself in me.
I called him Strawman because of how smoothly
he assembled the bales. I called him Scarecrow
because of how the look of him scattered the crows.
And so we retired my heels, and solid spud and I,
we ate from a bowl of meat at the table's center.
And Tater, he'd undress me after dinner.

Still I failed to work my nothing wounds,
yet felt the coin of my face was worth something.
But the weeks piled, and my sheath gripped
my body tighter. And when Nothing-Spud
undressed my body, who was he
to pronounce me a heathen? *Hare Krishna*,
chanted Spud, to gain us admission to heaven.
He turned his coin heavenward: *Praise God*.

I hadn't thought he was forward thinking.
(It wasn't working for me.) And when I asked him
his dreams, and he answered with nothing,
I shook him open like a box of instant
and mashed him in with the meat. Fall came.
The field emptied itself and crows settled
on a pile of bones. I took care of my balloon
with a hanger. (This is why there are hangers.)

The field of leaves is the world now,
and that blankness of boulders is chief.
My soul is a tool in the shed by which the scab
of my body lives. And I put the vise in the center
like a consulate. Still, I remember the Tower
swaying in the breeze of the city. Yes, I remember
the gentle hands of the shiner, and his skin
distressed as worn leather, almost beautiful.

I'd forgotten about beauty. In the field,
I take a scythe to the leaves like I took care
of my balloon with a hanger. I nurse my daughter,
the hanger, with the blood the field leaves on my fingers.
This is how we christen citizens in the country wherein
the cup of my wound is consulate. I pick a scar
and release a murder. I take this as an order to build
a new tower. I have no other real ideas.

# Faith in Science

Let me begin (scientifically) with a definition of faith: belief in things we cannot prove. Common illustrations include faith in the existence of God, faith in the goodness of God, faith in the fairness of the world, faith that individual people will have certain qualities, such as integrity and morality and decency.

Limits of faith come about when we are confronted with situations that challenge our belief so much that we are tempted to abandon it. For example, we might question our belief in a loving and caring God after witnessing events of great human destruction, such as World War II or the Indian Ocean tsunami of 2004. We might question our belief in the fairness of society after learning that the gap between rich and poor has been drastically widening in the United States, Europe, Japan, and Australia, with the richest ten percent of those populations now earning nearly ten times as much as the poorest ten percent.

A kind of faith not usually discussed is faith in the logical workings of nature, embodied by the so-called "laws of nature." Nevertheless, most of us do indeed exhibit such faith, albeit at a subconscious level, every time we get into a hundred-ton machine called an airplane and allow ourselves to be lifted a couple of miles above the ground and catapulted through space, suspended in the air by Bernoulli's principles of fluid dynamics.

## Alan Lightman

Even scientists are sometimes not conscious of their faith in the laws of nature. Yet almost every scientist makes a commitment to a belief I will call the Central Doctrine of Science: All properties and events in the physical universe are governed by laws, and those laws are true at every time and place in the universe.

When I was a graduate student in physics, although my thesis advisor never explicitly stated anything equivalent to the Central Doctrine of Science, it was taken for granted in everything we did or talked about.

Without laws of nature, anything could happen. Wheelbarrows might suddenly float. Day might change to night and back to day again at random moments. The entire enterprise of science would fall apart. But the Central Doctrine of Science cannot be proven. If a hundred days in a row we observe that a lead weight dropped into a pond sinks straight to the bottom, we cannot be absolutely certain that it will do so on the hundred and first day. We trust that it will, because we trust in the consistent workings of nature. More to the point, we cannot prove that the same laws of physics operating now also operated in identical form fourteen billion years ago at the Big Bang, as required by the Doctrine. Scientists accept the Central Doctrine of Science as a matter of faith.

Over the years, science has experienced various crises of faith. A spectacular example is the ghostly subatomic particle called the neutrino, which, for decades before its discovery, sorely challenged the long-standing belief in the conservation of energy. A major law of nature, the conservation of energy states that the total energy in an isolated box is constant. Energy may change forms in the box, as when the chemical energy in the head of a match changes into heat and light. But if the chemical energy of the unstruck match was eleven units, the total energy in the subsequent heat and light is also eleven units. That's the conservation of energy. For a century and a half, the law of the conservation of energy has been observed to hold true. It is a sacred cow of physics, believed inviolable. It is the example par excellence of the logic and consistency of nature.

Now, the crisis of faith: In the early 1920s, physicists discovered that the energies did not add up in the radioactive emissions of certain atoms.

Such atoms were found to spit out "beta particles." According to the law of the conservation of energy, the energy of the atom before the emission should equal the atom's energy after the emission plus the energy of the emitted beta particle, just as the difference in bank balances at two different times should be equaled by the net expenditure of money during that period. Against these expectations, the energy of the emitted beta particle was less than it should have been—sometimes a little less, sometimes a lot less. Experimental physicists repeated the measurements and got the same upsetting results. Some physicists, including the pioneering Danish physicist Niels Bohr, reluctantly proposed that the conservation of energy might be valid in an average sense but not for each individual event in each individual atom. The great physicist Paul Dirac wrote back to Bohr that he "should prefer to keep rigorous conservation of energy at all costs."

Then in late 1930, physicist Wolfgang Pauli wrote a letter to his colleagues about the troubling dilemma of beta emission: "Dear Radioactive Ladies and Gentlemen . . . I have hit upon a desperate remedy to save . . . the law of conservation of energy." Pauli then went on to propose that when a radioactive atom emits a beta particle, it also emits another kind of particle, previously unknown and now called a neutrino, and the sum of the energies of the neutrino and the beta particle correctly equal the difference in atomic bank balances.

Physicists who had faith in the law of the conservation of energy jumped at Pauli's invisible neutrino and began building it into new theories of radioactive atoms. Others remained skeptical and surrendered their faith. Then, in 1956, the neutrino was discovered in a nuclear reactor in South Carolina.

Today, the faith of physicists is garishly displayed in their belief in a multitude of other universes, most very different from our own. This so-called "multiverse" is predicted by current theories, and even needed to make sense of some phenomena in our universe, but there is little chance we will be able to prove the idea right or wrong.

# Club Zeus

When Zeus knocked up Leto and Hera found out about it, she forbid the slutty girlfriend from birthing her twin babies on land. Leto rowed the seas until she finally settled on a floating island, which the resort where I'm working claims as our own spit of land, and where I am six weeks into an eight week summer job before I return to the US for my last year of high school. There are ruins in the cliffs above the resort, grand columned things in honor of Leto, goddess of motherhood, but here at Club Zeus, we choose to commemorate all those gods and goddesses differently—not that we don't have columns. We have plenty. We commemorate instead with a statue of a big-titted woman in the middle of the huge pool. We commemorate with a make-out pad full of pillows floating in the bay and held up by concrete swans called "Delos," after the island where Leto gave birth to Apollo and Artemis. Mostly we commemorate with as many beverages as you can suck back.

## Ramona Ausubel

Our guests are Russians and Brits who are fat and white when they arrive and fatter and red when they leave six nights, seven days later. Most of the staff is Ukrainian but I'm from California. My job is to be the Wizened Storyteller. I wear a distressed robe, rope sandals, and a fake beard. I sit in a hut all day and tell Greek myths to whoever comes in. It's kids in the morning, almost exclusively. The afternoon hour is a mixed bag of people who have been in the sun too long, people who have been at Club Zeus too long in general and have exhausted all the other activities, and more kids. Some people just nap. At night I get drunks.

I can tell whatever story I want, so I tailor it to my audience. The drunks get the sexier stories: Odysseus trapped on Calypso's island, the sirens. They tip very well if things get hot. At the end of the hour I pass around a burlap satchel, hoping that guests will drop in some of their Leto Liras, which they can use for any of the extra-cost items, like fake tattoos or sunscreen rubdowns by the roving belly dancers, and which I will trade in for postage stamps, gum, and phone cards.

I came here to escape but so far the pleasure has eluded me.

My route to Club Zeus began with my mother's recent midlife swan dive into the pool of Faith. When she discovered spirituality her whole person sprouted as if there had been nothing there before. As if she had been an empty suitcase, waiting to be packed. I was fifteen.

I had never noticed anything about our home's furnishings until they were replaced: a flowered sofa was traded for a low Indonesian bench with throw pillows; white curtains were given away for brightly colored ones. The kitchen counter became populated with an army of spice jars: star anise, cumin, coriander, fenugreek, sumac, saffron. Mom purchased a meditation cushion and various beads to slip mindfully through her fingers. She wanted her awakening to be inclusive, all-encompassing, so there were rosary beads as well as Hindu prayer beads. She had a book of Sufi stories on top of a book of Zen koans. St. Francis, his arms beleaguered with birds, looked down upon a singing crystal bowl meant to cleanse the soul. My mother was happy. This cocktail of religions calmed her loneliness as if by prescription.

Before this, Mom had been normal—the same hair and makeup as all the other moms, the same clothes, the mid-forties divorce, stucco fake-fancy house, ambient depression. She had the same three-to-five glasses of white wine at dinner, the stream of dates with tanned faces and yachts and shitty work hours and insufficient capacities for commitment. This is what it is to grow up in white Orange County; variation is a nonexistent principle.

I did the taking-care-of in our house. I was the one to scramble the eggs and clean the hair out of the drain and Mom was grateful, always grateful. She told me every day that I would grow up to be the kind of man who knew how to treat a woman, that I would be the one good specimen in a state full of assholes. I was happy because I was needed.

Then an unreasonably good-looking blond guy with orange robes and a necklace of marigolds rented what used to be an ice cream shop and hung fabric on the walls and an OPEN sign on the door and pretty soon Mom started going for morning meditation and then afternoon meditation and then evening meditation and then she went to church too, and we lit candles on Friday nights and ate challah and she did sage purification ceremonies and got a guy who said he was Cherokee to put a sweat lodge in our backyard. And Mom was suddenly able to take care of herself. She did the dishes, she cooked, she swept the floors. She had been saved and I had been made obsolete.

> My route to Club Zeus began with my mother's recent midlife swan dive into the pool of Faith.

The deeper Mom went into her spiritual seas, the lonelier I got. One day in November of my junior year, in my fifth semester of the washboard scrape of high school, the geography teacher told us that high school is the stepping stone to college and college is the stepping stone to a good job and a good job is the stepping stone to wealth and isn't that the point of life, isn't that the great dream? It was clear to me that what high school really is is a holding pen: we were too young to be trusted and too old to be cute. The teacher unfurled a map of the US and opened a box of red-headed pins, which he would press to our dreamed-of college towns. "University of Kansas," said Ethan Peters and the teacher pinned and said, "Lawrence. Lovely town."

"Harvard," said Jessica Stride, who was pretty enough to risk being smart, and the teacher stabbed Cambridge. Everyone spouted their list of reach schools and safety schools. They were believers. They were on the path.

The teacher came to me and I stared at that map and all I could see was the Pacific. All I could see was the edge, a place to leap off and escape and it struck me, brick-like. All that ocean, all that land, the entire rolling globe, and I just beat a path from my unremarkable front door to this yellow-walled school, gum stuck under every desk, so that I can go somewhere in state so that I can get a job so that I can raise my kids to do the same? The best we can hope for, the very utmost dream, is to be naked with someone our own age or a little older and muck around with them in the dark? And I thought: *The ocean, the whole entire ocean is right there, walking distance from where I sit.* That day was the day of open eyes, of open roads, and my map included everywhere, just everywhere.

"I have to go to the bathroom," I said.

From point A, which was room 203 of Newport High School, there was a very obvious path: Coast Highway, Bayshore, stop for a few sandwiches to hold me for a day or two and as much cash I could withdraw, across the bridge to the little cottage-riddled island, wade into the Bay to the most seaworthy-looking dinghy I could find, oars in oarlocks, and out. The destination hardly mattered—there were other cities, other towns, islands a few miles offshore, another country not far south—what mattered was the departure.

> The warm feeling that had filled my chest, the feeling that maybe I would live a whole life after all, had cooled to ash.

I rowed past the gigantic houses with their columns and statues, the big as-if of them. I rowed past sea lions fatted out on the decks of yachts despite the netting the owners had installed. The yachts bowed water-ward under all that amphibious weight. I glanced over my shoulder to keep a straight path, then turned and rowed hard.

Within fifteen minutes a police boat zipped in, flipped its lights on. I looked at my sandwiches in the hull, mayonnaise yellowing against the plastic, and I stopped dipping the oars. My big world shrank back down to the size of a postcard.

The arrest was a surprise. I had never done anything bad or wrong, had always associated police uniforms with the Fourth of July parade. They were nice to me, sort of, not mean anyway. No handcuffs, but they put me in the back of their car and read me my rights and the jail cell smelled like microwave popcorn and wet concrete. I thought, *Shit. Oh, well.* But still: *Shit.* My hope turned pocket-sized, and then I couldn't even find it anymore. The warm feeling that had filled my chest, the feeling that maybe I would live a whole life after all, had cooled to ash.

My mother brought me a Zuni fetish when she bailed me out. It was a little beaver the size of a fingernail, carved out of jasper. It had a tiny real stick in its mouth. "Because you are so industrious," she said. "Don't stop being that way." She never asked me why I stole the boat or where I thought I was going. It was as if she already knew, had waited for this day to come, as if she had done it once too. At home, she made me a sandwich since mine had all been confiscated. It was dark by then, and we sat at the table together. She drowned and saved her tea bag over and over.

"You want to go somewhere?" she asked.

"God, yes."

"Okay." So, as a gift for the first time I had ever gotten in trouble—and that's just how my mother put it—she would send me to Turkey for the summer. She had a friend who had an aunt who had a room to rent and they were sure they could find me a summer job. I promised to finish the school year, not to try to run away, not to steal anything. She promised to find me the keys out of Orange County.

Flying into the quaint coastal town made me sick in two ways: the choppy air rolled the plane back and forth, and the color of the sea was so rich it almost ached. The land was pine-scrubby and dry, and I could make out wooden ships floating on the water.

My mother's friend's old auntie lived in a little wooden house at the edge of town, which I walked to wearing my backpack, following a hand-drawn map. Jet lag felt like a wool coat I couldn't take off. I was sweating and hungry and overjoyed. The old woman met me at her iron gate, which had been devoured by bougainvillea. She showed me my room—a single bed, a dresser—and then sat me down in the kitchen and poured me a cup of deep red-brown tea in a delicate tulip-shaped glass. She put out a plate of sliced tomatoes, cucumbers, apricots, and a piece of crumbly white cheese along with a basket of baguette slices and a jar of sour cherry jam. It was the best meal I had eaten in my life. I looked up at her, and she looked fuzzy, almost not real, like a half ghost. "What *time* is it?" I asked, suddenly aware that I had no idea when I was.

I was woken a few hours later by an announcement over loudspeakers, say-ing what, I did not know. I joined the old woman on her small porch, and she made me another cup of tea, the second of ten thousand I would drink in the coming weeks. The tiny deck looked out over first the cemetery, then the roof of the corner store, then the road, then the harbor. Most people would try to ignore the foreground filled with human remains and enjoy the sea in the distance. The old woman seemed to do the opposite.

After they repeated the broadcast on the PA, I asked her what they were saying. I wondered if she spoke more English than she let on because she answered right away. "Some man, he died," she said.

"Do they always announce that?" I asked. She looked at me blankly. Then she trained her eyes on the cemetery again, like a dog waiting for its dinner. By the time the funeral party arrived an hour later, she had made some syrupy pastries and arranged the brightly colored gummies of Turkish delight into a box and pressed her black dress before heading back out to the balcony to observe the grieving.

We watched together. A pack of strays was circling the sparse crowd. I had been studying up on the myths in preparation for my job and I thought of Hades, god of the underworld, and his three-headed dog. After the coffin was lowered into the rectangular hole the old woman sent me down to the funeral party with the sweets she had prepared. I didn't know who to give it to. I stood, stupid, for a long few minutes before she yelled something in Turkish and one of the older ladies came and took them from me. I said thank you and she patted me on the head. Then, remembering a contraption I had built for my tree house back home, I went inside and rigged up a basket on a string tied to the balcony so that the old woman could lower her offering herself and I could stay safely out of other people's funerals. Her face brightened when I showed it to her.

"How do you pronounce your name?" I asked. I pointed at myself and said, "David." Then I pointed at her with a question mark in my eyes. She made a series of sounds beginning with a G, but when I tried to make them back, I spit out an ugly knot. She raised her eyebrows and gave me a look that said, *Do not do that to my name.* So I said, "I'll call you 'Grams.' It's a term of endearment. It's nice."

She gazed out at the cemetery. She must have known which dead got fake flowers and which ones got real. Which dead got tears and which ones got a guilty kneel in the dirt for a second or two and then a fast exit.

My first day at work was fun because I had never been to an all-inclusive resort and I'd had no idea how absurd it would be. My boss, Emir, was Turkish but spoke good English. He told me I was better looking than my photo and then slapped me on the back of the head. The second day was exactly the same as the first, and less fun because of it. The third day I felt a small weight in my stomach, as if a stone had buried itself in the soft muck. The rest of the staff was oblivious to me and the summer-camp camaraderie I had hoped for did not surface. I had imagined that my US passport would get me laid, if nothing else. I could lead a foreign girl to think she might marry me and my long American dollars. But my country's mystique seems to have faded. The Ukrainians hang out together in their dorms at night, the Turks go home to their families, and I go back to Grams and sit on the porch, watching over the dead.

For six weeks I have repeated the pattern: tea and bread with Grams, beard and myths in the tent, meals alone in the staff cafeteria, tea with Grams above hundreds of graves, sleep. The only pleasurable part of the day is when I swim in the sea, cold and wine-dark. Each week, from the other side of the world, my mother asks, "Have you been to a mosque yet?" and each week I have not.

I sit in the story tent, waiting for customers. I tell one straggler how Cronus, believing he would be overthrown by a son, swallowed his first five children. "How bloody fun," the straggler says in a British drawl. I try to think of something lighter but the

> He told me I was better looking than my photo and then slapped me on the back of the head.

only myth that comes to mind is about Hera forbidding all the gods, goddesses, and nymphs to allow Leto to given birth on land, forcing the laboring woman to row across the sea for days until she found a rootless, drifting island surrounded by swans.

The straggler falls asleep. My beard is hot and itchy. What kind of escape is this? In two weeks I will go home with nothing but a handful of odd details to show for my summer. I imagine the other kids coming back from summers spent surfing every day. I imagine Ethan Peters and Jessica Stride lying side by side on his surfboard, floating out past the break, their skin salty and freckled. They'd kiss—they'd have to, it's the perfect teenage moment for kissing. The long casts of their friends' voices would reel them slowly in, but they'd remember the waves rolling under them, their bodies pressed together trying not to tip the board, their warm lips, and paddling back, each using one arm.

Madeleine Reagan is in Italy studying Shakespeare's plays and sketching marble statues with missing anatomy. I imagine a fly landing in those empty penis holes, buzzing around. I already know that Madeleine will come back feeling changed, that she will have had a crush on an American boy in her group who paid no attention to her and that she will have slept with an Italian without meaning to, and that she will be a little carved out by this but also a little proud. It will be a story she continues to tell in college, a small badge of adult credibility. Marcello would be his name, and he will become a conveniently unknowable person, someone she can change depending on her current needs—he can be a tool to make another boy jealous, he can be the partner in sex acts she pretends to have practiced.

Everyone, it seems, will have had a summer that means something. I can already hear the buzz on the first day of school, five hundred teenagers with stories to tell.

And me? I won't know how to explain anything. I spent the summer at an all-inclusive resort on the Turkish coast with a slew of sunburned Ukrainians. I'll have to explain where both Turkey and Ukraine are to everyone, including the teachers. I lived with an old woman above a cemetery, and I ate a lot of olives, I'll say. And I kissed no one. I fell in love with no one. I told Greek myths to people who spent the whole time joking about yanking off my beard. Evidently I have traveled eleven thousand miles and still found a way to fail at my escape.

> Before the late-afternoon donut rush, someone notices a fat man facedown in the pool.

"Mom," I say into my phone. It is evening and I can hear Grams outside thwacking wet laundry against a pole. "Honeypie," my mother says. Her voice on the other end sounds falsely close. Right in my ear. "I've been calling all week," I tell her.

"I know you have. I ended up going on a silent retreat at the last minute. I just needed it. It felt so good, it was just, it was wonderful. One of the dharma talks really reminded me of you."

I do not wonder aloud why it didn't remind her enough of me to call back. To remember that I was real, not just the idea of a son but a fleshy body. "Yeah?" I say instead.

"It was about forgiveness. About forgiving yourself. It was beautiful." She has forgiven herself. It doesn't matter whether I join her or not.

It rains for three days in a row. There is almost nothing to do indoors at Club Zeus. I am swamped with restless kids and asked to schedule three extra sessions. I'm talking six hours a day in a scratchy old man voice and running out of myths. "Tell one about love," a drunk man says and I tell the one about Hades trapping Persephone in the underworld with a single pomegranate seed. "Tell a better one about love," says the drunk man's wife and I tell her about how Achilles met Queen Penthesilea in battle, how he saw her courage and fell instantly and deeply in love with her at the same moment he delivered the fatal stab to her neck. The couple leaves without tipping.

At my break the rain has quieted for a moment, so I walk out to the water. An older blond woman is lying in the rain in a tiny pink bikini. She is tanning. *This*, I think, *this is commitment*.

Zeus's Kebab Shack has been turned into a playpen with constant belly dancing contests, indoor bocce ball, and trivia. The British tabloids have sold out completely from the newsstand, even at the three times' markup. There are chubby ladies huddled around the hookah bar looking cold in shorts and tank tops, their faces in the papers. "Everybody Thought I Was Pregnant but It Wasn't a Baby—It Was a 22-Pound Cyst!" Emir is making the rounds, as if a little flirtation can distract the women from their ruined holiday. Sudoku grids are being filled in at incredible speed, and the booze is pouring.

And then, after lunch and before the late-afternoon donut rush, someone notices a fat man facedown in the pool. He is bobbing against the topless goddess statue. Five feet of water, right in the middle of the resort, no splash. His countrymen are all around, with oversweet cocktails in plastic cups, angry sunburns beneath their all-access wrist bracelets. The body is gathered by Emir—suddenly serious, suddenly silent—with the help of two leaf-collecting nets. He, the man who isn't anymore, is given a piggyback ride on the shoulders of a solemn Russian giant of a woman. I watch her eyes as she lumbers toward the medical center. His skin is scattered with small moles. Relief at not being the carrier burns off the people who follow her, like steam.

I am standing in front of the story tent, feeling belly-up. My fingers graze the buttons on my phone. I keep patterning the US country code. I calculate the time difference in my head: it's the middle of the night in Orange County, and my mother is too far away to save me.

A woman runs to the pool and stands there, searching. It is the woman I saw tanning in the rain, I realize. Her hair is white-blond and wet and her face is Russian, without question, firm and resolved, as if it has always known that this would come. His wife. She looks straight at me.

"He's dead," she says, before anyone else says the words. What is there to say to a woman whose husband has just drowned in a pool he easily could have stood up in?

"I'm sorry," I say.

She does not blame me or any of the other people who should have been watching. "Thank you. We will also die someday." She reaches behind the bar and takes a huge bottle of vodka, pours a plastic cupful.

The bartender says, "Take the whole thing, please. Take anything you want."

No one does any work the rest of the day. We wander around, gathering wet towels or picking up empty cups, but it's just movement for movement's sake. I am thinking about Grams and the cemetery, how she sits on her porch with a fan blowing straight into her face and watches the graves, some dry and hard, some still soft and round, as though a large animal has recently burrowed in and built a nest there. I wonder if they bother to announce the death of a foreigner. Maybe they do so with a little spark of glee—even white people with disposable income can die here, in this place they flock to to snap photos of the blue-black sea, the bay where sunken columns mark the spot where Cleopatra once bathed. They come here to marvel, but sometimes they find out what the people who live here already know: no amount of beauty will keep you alive forever.

I pull my beard down because I'm feeling hot and faint and I don't at this moment care if I get fired. The fat Russian man did not even exist to me this morning. He was one of hundreds of resort guests who I may or may not have laid eyes on, but now, by afternoon, he is singular, and he will be in my life forever. I will bring him to bed with me tonight,, his face-down form floating in the pool of my mind. He will come to my last year of high school, maybe appear in my college essay, will be one of the stories I tell a beautiful girl I have a crush on to make her love me. I'll bring him home with me, give him to my mother to share with me—though it would be kind to spare her, to tell her only the easy stories of sun and sea, of kebabs and soft breads, I will poison her with this death and upset her peace, because sometimes a person deserves company.

I find myself looking at each person who passes and thinking, "That guy is going to die," and "That woman is going to die," and "That little girl in the buttery pigtails is going to die." I understand Grams's interest in the cemetery, in the underworld. She is there to check the names off a list of everyone in town, as diligent as a scientist proving a hypothesis—even the pretty young thing with the baby, even the woman so old it seemed she might just forget to pass on, even the Imam, even the politician's daughter. She does not tire of the proof. She survives by it, waiting to hear her own name on the loudspeaker, to hover as a ghost on her porch to see her own box lowered into the good earth, to measure, finally, the love she has accrued. I almost look forward to going home tonight and telling her

about what I have seen. I imagine being on the receiving end of her offer-
ings—the tulip glass of tea, sugar cubes, sweets.

I think about the dead man and his wife and wonder who is waiting
for them in Russia. There must be children, grandchildren even, brothers
and sisters, a whole root system beneath that fallen tree. There must be a
lot of paperwork involved in transporting a body back home to be buried.
Until it is completed, the wife will have to stay in the fake cheer of Club
Zeus, trapped on our merry-go-round. Kids perpetually flinging them-
selves down the waterslide, men revving the Jet Skis so that the vibration
jiggles their aging testicles, women sliding the strings of their bikinis to
check on the progress of their bronzing,
everyone pouring drinks down their gul-
lets, too much to eat at every meal. This is
the last place where a person should have
to mourn.

> Sometimes they find out what the people who live here already know: no amount of beauty will keep you alive forever.

The pool has to be drained. There is no
yellow police tape in Turkey, I guess, but
people do not need to be told to stay away.
The guests make wide circles to avoid the empty blue hole, which is at the
center of the complex, and impossible to avoid. They have taken on an
animal skittishness; their eyes dart and they take short, nervous steps. The
hookah bar near the pool gets no customers; the alcohol bar, equally close,
is full.

Fact I now know: when one of your fellow holidaymakers dies in your
midst, you do not stop drinking the bottomless drinks. Your wristband is
paid up for the whole week; it's only Tuesday and there is no possibility for
a refund. You ask for an extra maraschino cherry, raise your plastic glass to
the dead man. You admire the female Ukrainian butts all around, perfectly
sized and golden brown, the peek of white skin where the thongs shift as the
women high-heel saunter. You burn and peel.

The higher-ups have asked that everyone stay late in case the police want
to question us. I try to call Grams to tell her that I won't be back for din-
ner but she does not answer the phone. When the sky finally darkens, I go
out to the swan-supported island, hoping I will be alone. In the corner is
a statue of Leto, half-clothed, holding her newly born twins on a drifting
island. They look happy. They are a family and maybe that is enough. They

know who they love. I lie on the tile floor listening to the water lob itself into the pilings. Finally, I dial the number.

"Mom," I say, as if I am prompting her to be that person.

"Oh, hi, sweetheart."

When I tell her about the fat man, there is a thick silence. I hope the story hurts her. I want her to share what I am feeling because my pain is part of her job. "Love," she says. "Oh, love." But she sounds proud of me. As though she is congratulating me for achieving a long-held goal.

I try again to capture her, to drag her into my sadness. I say, "He was just floating there. His *dead body* was just floating there."

There is a pause and I think I may have succeeded. Then she tells me, "My friend Ashtar was over today and he saw that picture of you when you were five, with the tractor. He said you have an old soul. You are stronger than you know."

None of this is real, says the fucked-up history of her country.

What she means is that I am on my own. What she means is that tragedy is also currency. That enlightenment depends on grief. That love grows in soil that has been tilled. For a moment, I wonder if she planned this whole thing, if she prayed to all her gods not for my safety or for my happiness but for me to be deepened, opened, undone so that I might begin to blossom into my truest self.

The water continues to roll into the pilings. The god of the sea must be hungry and sorry. The pilings are stoic and disinterested. After a long time I fall asleep, and sure enough, the fat man joins me there, lying next to me facedown, as if he is waiting for someone to rub sunscreen onto his big freckled back.

A handful of fingers are in my hair, waking me. They are thin and curious, and I jerk away. A woman is kneeling beside me. There is enough light to see that it is the dead man's wife. Her face is hollow, as if she is wearing a mask. Beneath, what could she look like? What dark cavern would I find?

"I must love somebody," she says.

"I'm sure you do," I answer, thinking her statement is an existential one.

"No, now." And she falls into me, her lips on mine, suctioned. I try to pull away, to turn, but she has a hold on me that I can't break. I am the dock and she is the snail. The dead man's wife's tongue is in my mouth now, slipping and searching, and then she has rolled on top of me, and the air goes out of my chest. I am just a place, a heat source, and that is enough for her. Keeping my arms pinned to the floor, she kisses up and down my neck, her tongue in my ear is incredibly loud, like a sudden storm. I can still feel the fat man nearby, floating, and I think maybe the woman can feel him too. Maybe I am him right now, to her.

I notice that I have sustained a small wound for the dead man's wife. Like a paper cut somewhere inside me, sharp-edged and very distinct. It reminds me of when my mother would forget to pick me up at school on time, how I'd stand in the semicircle driveway watching the sun sink and worrying that she was dead or trapped someplace, until her car finally glinted into view and my sadness shifted through relief and into trying to soothe her guilt. "Don't feel bad," I'd say. "It's okay. It's not cold out."

And then I kiss the dead man's wife back. Out of resignation? Out of kindness? Because I felt a flutter somewhere deep? Sensing me agree, she lets my arms go and I wrap her up, feather my fingers over the folds of her neck. Her skin and my skin are as different as paper and rubber. I imagine what I know about the Soviet Union and Siberian prisons and Chernobyl crashing up against the dullness of my life like a battering ram. Bread lines, the KGB and nuclear disaster, the endless sunny emptiness of being a teen-ager in Orange County—they bust open the frozen-banana-stand summers, the pack of blond children learning to sail, the Ferris wheel handholding, the failed marriages, the less-than-perfect mothers, the kids who return after the first year of college and everything they wear, head to toe, is branded UCSB, Harvard, Texas A&M. Gloriously, my life is torn to shreds by the dead man's wife. None of this is real, says the fucked-up history of her country, her brand-new widowhood. Nothing, it says, has truly ever happened to you.

I kiss the dead man's wife and let my hands go up her shirt, cup the soft egg sack of her breast. It is the wrongness that feels the best, the fact that I cannot justify this night. I am doing someone a disgusting favor, inadvisable in every way. She is doing me a favor, too. A simple physical pleasure rolls through me.

She does not take my clothes off, maybe because she knows my skinny half-grown body would be ruinous to her fantasy. I keep pushing my shirt up and she gently smooths it back down. I have sunk far enough into this warm wrongness to want it to go all the way, for us both to come up gasping at the end, to not even be able to look each other in the eye. I want to walk around for the rest of the week knowing what I've done.

As I am getting ready to dip my hand below the waistband of her denim miniskirt, I hear something shuffle. The dead man's wife sits up, hears what I hear. She pulls her tank top down but not before I see the tanned folds of her stomach in the moonlight. She has the same stretch marks as my mother, a white roadmap on her sides. I remember pulling at my mother's skin, asking her why she was tracked like that. "You did that to me," she told me. "You grew and grew and grew and I had to stretch and stretch and stretch."

Someone appears on the steps nearby. It's my boss. I try to gather myself. The blood leaves my crotch.

"The woman has been calling and calling," Emir says.

"My mother?"

"No, no. Here. Where you are staying."

I think of Grams on her porch, waiting for someone living or someone dead to appear. She was worried—it never occurred to me that she would miss me. I wish I were on the porch with her, looking out over the graves, the night sea just a shadow in the distance.

Neither the widow nor I explain why we are here on this floating island in the sea. Why we are alone. Maybe I'll be fired. It's almost the end anyway. I am leaving in two weeks and Turkey is very far from my home and Grams is old and we are unlikely to ever see each other again. Emir's hair, thick with gel, shines in the moonlight. He gives me a little headshake as if he knows every terrible thing I will ever do. He must be used to bad holiday behavior, but this is of another order.

The widow turns to me and puts her palm on my forehead as if I am sick. She looks at Emir and her eyes are soft. "Good boy," she says, coming to my defense.

I wish that I were younger, that I could feel the feeling of being a child with a person who knows how to take care of me. Out of habit, I close my eyes. Her skin is cool and cooler still is the metal of her wedding band. I imagine its counterpart on the finger of the drowned man, his skin swollen around that bright promise. My mother was right: pain is an enzyme and I am softened. A year from now, when a girl asks me if I've ever been in love, I will lie and tell her no, but only because I will not know how to explain this night. Love, I want to say to the widow, to Emir, love is an island. But when I open my mouth, the words get tangled. It begins to rain. Emir clears his throat, trying to prompt us all to return to our separate lives. But when I lean into the widow's hand, she holds my head up. Below us: all the world's water. 🔶

R&B

The old songs teach you to cry
and when.
The new ones are pumping
your blood to the sky.

More moans than cries.
A blue note is waving
itself into a melisma.

So much feeling
spun out of flesh
into air.

The lobes in the throat
are the globe in the club
in your mind.

Late style nearly obscures
the god hidden in a tabernacle
beseeched by the seeker
for joy.

So much obligatory crying
and everything wrong
in this song.

# AGAINST THE PROMISE OF A VIEW

A difficult climb
to a beautiful view—
I don't like it.
I don't like the way
you make me go
positively Protestant
all this deferral
up to a future
only you've seen
the ascent always leveraged
against an alien payoff
already prescripted.
When we get there
I'll be dead
tired too tired to view
the view the way
I wanted. I wanted
the way to be beautiful
as a stroll in the hanging
gardens of Babylon
or the wisteria-laden
lanes of the rose garden
in the Bois du Boulogne
as beautiful as a jammed

Sixth Avenue crosswalk
in midtown. I wanted
to be going nowhere
nowhere we know
not to have to breathe
so hard into a future
someone else promised.
I know
reputable studies show
the capacity
to delay
gratification
makes for a happy
person & nation
but oh
I just want
& want now
a perpetual
beautiful stroll
nowhere
I don't want
to look back
& say ah
that was so

worth it
because even
if it was
it wasn't.
I don't want
to keep my head down
for miles alert
for insurgent roots
a falling branch
my legs punctured
by stinging flies
who harry the way
only to be able to say
at some notional
top however beautiful
*how beautiful*
*—& see, no insects here*
*& why not lunch—*
Somehow
it was just
the glorious sun
and twelve islands
inlaid in a lake

& the distant silent
powerboats.
Somehow it was a vision
of all as dust.
If I go
on pilgrimage
I want every age
to be a stage
one can look around
and say how interesting
& yes a cup of coffee
would be nice.
I'm not going anywhere
fast but where
we're all going

# THE
# IN-BETWEENS

## Mira Ptacin

*Knockin' on heaven's door*

They believed they would live forever.

That once they'd departed, they weren't gone. That death was when life really began. After our bodies were stiff and buried under rosebushes, we humans—in fact, all creatures—would awake as more advanced beings. In the afterlife, our souls would gain not only the ability but also the inclination to provide truths for the living, clues and insights into all their quandaries. Once we were dead, we would finally understand life, and God. This had always been possible and always would be. Those left breathing just had to listen.

Despite the eternity of it all, they set the date of March 31, 1848, as their beginning. A Friday. It began with a sound: tapping. A coded conversation between two sisters and an unknown third party: a ghost in a wall. "Mr. Splitfoot," the sisters called him. The three talked. Folks witnessed. Word spread. Next came the chin-waggers and the believers, the opportunists and the newspapermen. This led to more demonstrations, conversations—séances, if you will—that unearthed glimmers of hope. Faith that there was more to it than *this*. That we would be for always.

The turbulent decade about to unfold—the railways unfurling across the continent, the glittering promise of gold in the west, the slow hurtle toward a war that would rend the country—made the timing just right; an ancient longing was released into the air and blown like a thousand seeds soon to take root in a thousand candlelit living rooms across the country. It would grow into a cultural revolution that challenged then changed the established American institutions of patriarchal authority and the church. It was the conception of a religion that by 1897 would spread across the United States and Europe, sprouting more than eight million disciples. And dead center of all those believers were these two sisters, Kate and Margaret.

Allow me to back up and slow down.

In the town of Hydesville, a small hamlet in upstate New York, Kate and Margaret Fox, ages twelve and fifteen, lived in a house that had always felt sinister, even before their family had moved to town. One night, their parents started hearing things. First some soft taps, then harder knocks that sounded like apples dropping off the dresser in the girls' room. Soon, those noises grew more sophisticated, stronger, like the scrape of a bed being dragged across the plank floor. But when Kate and Margaret's mother would rush upstairs and fling open the door to their room, her daughters would both be deep asleep. Finally, after much confusion and questioning, the sisters called their mother into the room.

*Mother, watch.*

Margaret, the eldest, snapped her fingers once—*tik*—and was immediately answered by a tap in response. She snapped twice, and something tapped twice. Little Kate's hands were on her lap, unwavering. There was something in that room.

*I asked the noise to rap my different children's ages, successively. Instantly, each one of my children's ages was given correctly, pausing between them sufficiently long to individualize them until the seventh, at which a longer pause was made, and then three more emphatic raps were given, corresponding to the age of the little one that died, which was my youngest child.*

*I then asked: 'Is this a human that answers my questions so correctly?' There was no rap. I asked: 'Is it a spirit? If it is, make two raps.' Two sounds were given as soon as the request was made. I then said: 'If it was an injured spirit, make two raps,' which were instantly made, causing the house to tremble. I asked: 'Were you injured in this house?' The answer was given as before. 'Is the person living that injured you?' Answered by raps in the same manner. I ascertained by the same method that it was a man, aged thirty-one years, that he had been murdered in this*

The girls became the talk of antebellum New York and were drafted to serve as clairvoyants for rich believers.

*house, and his remains were buried in the cellar. . . . I asked: 'Will you continue to rap if I call my neighbors that they may hear it too?' The raps were loud in the affirmative . . .*

—*SIGNED, MRS. MARGARET FOX 1848.*
[Mother of the girls]

Two days later, the evening before April Fools' Day, Kate and Margaret, in long pearl-colored nightgowns and bouncy hair, dangled their feet from the edge of their unmade bed, surrounded by huddling neighbors and flickering candlelight. All eyes were on Margaret when she spoke up. *One tap means "yes." Two taps, "no."* The neighbors left the Fox girls' bedroom believing they'd spent a night with an apparition and two girls with mystical powers, and by the end of the next evening, the night of April Fools', they were excavating the Fox family's cellar, digging and digging and digging until water pooled in the hole.

The story might have ended then, or maybe right after the sisters were sent to Rochester by their parents to protect them from a witch-hunt. There, they could live under the eye of their older and more responsible sister, Leah, and move on from their shenanigans. But the ghost seemed to follow them, and Leah was more opportunistic than she was reliable. She booked her younger sisters as the headliners in a four-hundred-seat theater in the city, where they accepted questions from the audience to ask the dead. Thus Kate and Margaret Fox emerged as mediums.

Within a few years, the girls became the talk of antebellum New York and were drafted to serve as clairvoyants for rich believers. The Fox sisters booked a suite on the corner of Broadway and Maiden Lane and began showcasing their work in a parlor at Barnum's, a hotel owned by a cousin of the famed showman and huckster P. T. Preeminent New Yorkers of the time frequented the scene, mostly inquiring about "the state of railway stocks or the issue of love affairs," which soon brought forth the attention of other notables and luminaries: William Cullen Bryant. Mary Todd Lincoln. George Bancroft. Sojourner Truth. James Fenimore Cooper. Elizabeth Cady Stanton. Nathaniel Parker Willis. Susan B. Anthony. Even William Lloyd Garrison, an eminent abolitionist of the time, sat through a Fox sisters session, one in which the spirits rapped in time to a popular song and spelled out a message: *Spiritualism will work miracles in the cause of reform.*

In the girls' hotel parlor, séances were held daily, starting in the morning at ten, then in the evening at five and eight, each session packing thirty deep, humid and breathy, the audience pregnant with expectation or maybe disbelief, their gaping eyes on the two girls at the head of an egg-shaped table. Admission was a dollar.

Dollars added up. Soon, Kate and Maggie were wealthy and famous, touring like rock stars, filling auditoriums to thirty times a hundred. People swarmed from mansions and flophouses, waiting for hours for the chance to hear a simple yes or no answer through the in-betweens.

*Did you die peacefully.*
*Will you forgive me.*
*Do you love me.*
*Are you at peace.*

Some believed. But for many, the sisters were a diversion, a curiosity of the times: There were no televisions, no movies or recorded music. Entertainment wasn't as ubiquitous as it eventually became; these mystics were the reality show. And the girls were captivating. Pretty to look at. Dullness evaporated in their presence. On top of that, even if their audiences didn't believe in ghosts, this was the first time they'd ever witnessed a female, let alone two, speak in public, not just with permission but by popular demand. People were transfixed.

Kate and Maggie's exhibition struck at something vital in a certain kind of seeker. For those who felt shackled by the mores of the times, the very being of the teen-aged Fox sisters was revolutionary. While seeking a higher power was nothing new, the Fox sisters' message rode on the American impulse not only to challenge authority but also to go at it alone. To live one's life without the leadership, permission, and interference of the church or any other institution. Each time the sisters addressed a crowd, they were also shedding their Victorian sensibilities and their assigned gender roles, breaking the ossified boundaries between classes, ages, sexes. Each time they stepped onto the stage, they were inspiring a nation that was hungry for change and for someone to start it, someone who would change the status quo rather than

believe and behave. As they dazzled the crowd, they were also channeling the long-neglected impulses to listen to individual instinct. Before either had even kissed a boy, Kate and Maggie Fox had not only birthed a movement, they'd also launched a religion—Spiritualism—kindling the individual's quest for truth and the permission to believe it with a fearless tenacity.

Around the same moment in time, another group of radical American reformers was gaining momentum. Down the road from where the Fox sisters first publicly demonstrated their séance with Mr. Splitfoot, the very first women's rights convention had just been held in Seneca Falls, New York. Many of those who attended the Seneca Falls Convention caught wind of the Fox sisters and began joining their séances and Spiritualist meetings. They praised the girls for their bravery and progressiveness, for defying their roles as politically, financially, sexually, and socially repressed second-class citizens. These girls were not powerless, mute observers, and this convinced the feminists of their genuineness. They quickly joined forces with the girls, laying the foundations of the bridge that linked Spiritualists and suffragettes.

The collaboration wasn't just limited to protofeminists. In fact, it was a small group of abolitionists who first took the Fox sisters seriously. They helped organize and promote the girls' public séances for smaller crowds before their fame reached its stride. Many of these abolitionists were also Quakers. Quakers don't have much use for religious authority. They believe in self-sovereignty, that no human should rule over another. When a white man controlled the life of a black man, he usurped the place of God. When a husband exercised authority over his wife, he usurped the place of God. The women's rights movement, the abolitionists, and the Fox sisters, guided by their common credo, merged like railroad cars coupling, hitched to a locomotive belief that each human being has the capacity to do good and right the world's wrongs, in whatever shape, form, or plane they may appear. And that's when Spiritualism as an act of feminism began to take off.

By the mid-1850s, Americans weren't just watching the Fox sisters but imitating them, holding séances like we hold potlucks. Female mediums were breaking away from the bounds of Victorian propriety by speaking out, albeit in trance voices, and soon they took their practices to entrepreneurial levels, becoming financially independent and encouraging others to follow suit. Before long, Spiritualism formed its own denominations, rules, principles, and codes of conduct for spirit communication, séances, and table tipping. The basic tenets:

*The belief in spirit communication*

*The belief that the soul continues to exist after the death of the physical body*

*A personal responsibility for life circumstances*

*Continued personal growth, even after death*

*The belief in a God, or Infinite Intelligence, and that the natural world is an expression of said intelligence*

Women, unable to assert leadership publicly in traditional church or governmental roles, could be lay leaders in the movement. Practitioners met in private homes for séances or at lecture halls for trance lectures, which grew in size to state and national conventions. They met at summer camps attended by tens of thousands, all working without canonical texts, attaining cohesion through periodicals, tours by trance lecturers, and the missionary activities of accomplished mediums. By 1897, more than eight million people in the United States and Europe were said to be followers of Spiritualism. Belief was at an all-time high. All was well.

All was not well.

Across her neck I could see a faint liquid blue shadow cast by the small glass angel perched on the windowsill. Behind the figurine, the sun streamed through the window, cooking the uncooled room enough to bring forth the ancient smells of the timeworn rug and the musty odors

> These girls were not powerless, mute observers, and this convinced the feminists of their genuineness.

from a piano's keys. The smell of old fingertips. I could hear my husband outside, wrestling with my son in the grass. Inside, I was following the direction of Janice, president of the board of the Camp Etna Spiritualist Association, to my seat.

Janice had given me permission to visit after I'd found her on Facebook; composed an email with just the right amounts of professionalism and sincerity, distance and submission; and invited myself to explore her camp. Voluptuous and red-haired, Janice blotted the beige foundation on her forehead with a tissue, took a deep breath, and pointed to where I should sit. Soon, the presentation would begin. I knew it was the start of something, but I hadn't yet decided if "it" was an answer or a question.

Earlier that morning, my husband and I, toddler in tow, left our home on Peaks Island, Maine, rode the ferry into town, strapped our little one into his car seat, picked up two coffees, and drove north. I was on some type of grand mission, perhaps a pilgrimage, my husband riding shotgun. We passed the Blackstrap Hill Preserve, bayberries and grass, the Androscoggin River and Cobbosseecontee Stream, slanted abandoned farms, until we finally reached the sleepy town of Etna, Maine. At 77 Stage Road, we turned onto the same gravel driveway as so many wanderers before us. Like me, they had their questions. And I like to imagine that they, too, paused for a moment and drew in a deep breath when they crossed through the wrought-iron arched gates of the Camp Etna Spiritualist Community in search of something larger than themselves.

Three years ago, before I became a mother, my husband and I semi-spontaneously left New York and moved to Maine. I was tired of being stuck. Partially committed. We'd gotten to the point where our options were to slow down or fall apart. We chose Maine for its nature and quiet, its mellow tempo and wholesome lifestyle. It helped that the state's mottos are "Vacationland" and "The Way Life Should Be." Now, we were settled. The stress-fueled arguments evaporated, the worry of divorce became something to chuckle at. And then we became parents, and were peaceful. We had the jobs we'd worked all our younger years for, had fought in New York for, and we'd just purchased our first home—a fixer-upper from a recently deceased woman with a reputation on the island for having been a gardener, an alcoholic, and as bitter as a crab apple. Our home is just down the street from the island's library/fire station/police station; the entire island is less than twice the size of Brooklyn's Prospect Park, with a population around eight hundred, though it feels like forty-five. I was thirty-four, and I finally felt like I had the status and permission to call myself a woman.

> I wasn't here for a headline. I don't write to entertain; I write to understand.

Yet despite this checklist of quasi-adult accomplishments, something still felt off. I felt stirrings, as if I was holding something in, and tightly. The thing felt primitive. And the thing wanted out.

"For those of you who are new here, welcome to Camp Etna."

Janice stood facing our small group, all seated in a half circle of rocking chairs, love seats, and one prickly couch in the main room of a building called the Inn. The ground floor smelled like an attic. It was as cluttered as a small-town secondhand store with an orange velour couch, random furniture and coffee tables, an old piano, some storage boxes, and a coffeepot brewing Folgers coffee.

"Camp Etna was formed over 135 years ago as a Spiritualist meeting camp. We continue to hold that tradition and have a small community of Spiritualists, mediums, and healers practicing on our twenty-seven acres here, living in cottages centered around the common green."

Behind Janice, brown walls were speckled with a handful of paintings with no distinct pattern or theme: sketches of dream catchers, pastel angels, oceans, and waterfalls that looked like they'd been made in a middle schooler's art class. Human profiles (with eyes that could possibly move) that looked like they'd been painted by a professional. I could feel their tenacious gaze. The whole place felt not exactly haunted, but not quite not, either.

"Right now, we have a handful of residents living in the cottages on the grounds.

And we host workshops and programs and each summer have an international week, which we welcome you to participate in. Spiritualists come from all over the country to visit and practice."

It seemed as if I was the only one who hadn't been to Camp Etna before, that everyone knew the speech but still played along. Janice added: "We have a reporter in our presence today who will be taking notes for a newspaper article about our camp."

A newspaper reporter? I was far from one. A friend of mine had mentioned Camp Etna to me months back, suggesting it would make a good story, and the more I looked into it, the more something inside me was triggered. A camp for women to tap into their instinct? Sign me up. Sure, I was here as a writer exploring a curiosity, a possible story, but this was personal. I wasn't here for a headline. I don't write to entertain; I write to understand. Camp Etna offered the chance to dig into something deeper.

With Janice's introduction, I'd been detached from the group, or it from me, and I became the outsider, a position I'd hoped to avoid. The awkward attention that had landed on me sucked up any breeze left in the humid air. I started to sweat. I didn't want the others to think I was a fraud, though I wasn't sure myself if I was. But I didn't want to catch them faking it; I wanted to *believe*. Shaking off my discomfort, I tried to stay as open as possible, to avoid any separation or cynicism. *Anything is possible*, I told myself. *You just never know.*

After a brief overview of the camp's purpose, our group migrated to the building's other tour-able room—a petite cove adjacent to the living room that also served as a kitchen and storage space for all Camp Etna's books, magazines, stationery, and ephemera. The Camp Etna residents were converting it into a museum. The place was as intriguing as an estate sale: framed photographs, hanging crystals, random knickknacks. What felt like the remnants of a massive Rolodex, or the explosion of someone's office junk drawer: notes and addresses, handkerchiefs and small leather diaries, old Victorian jewelry, embroidered banners, hand-stitched dolls, postcards and handwritten letters, some from past presidents, notorious abolitionists, even Sir Arthur Conan Doyle. Most preserved, many in Ziploc bags. The room's belongings, scattered and entropic, gave off the feeling that they were hibernating. Some of them were over a century and a half old and had survived two fires. I snooped around the room like a teenage boy in a panty drawer and soon came upon a framed and faded picture, an old pastel-colored photograph of a young woman with the face of a Native American and the hairdo of an upper-class white girl. The bows on her head were enormous.

"That's Bright Eyes," I heard Janice say. Her hand reached from behind me and touched the photo affectionately. She told me that the young girl in the picture was the spirit guide to the late Mary Scannell, Camp Etna's most famous medium. One night, during a séance when Mary was a little girl, her long-deceased mother's name was spelled out, letter by letter. Next, a clear and strong message came through that the spirit of a dead little Indian girl by the name of Bright Eyes desired to speak through Mary, which Bright Eyes continued to do for the rest of Mary's life.

The rest of the group was now poking through the Jenga puzzle–stacked trinkets, too. There were about nine of us. Considering the randomness of the place, the town, the location, the event, I was impressed by the turnout. Now, Camp Etna is nearly void of humans. But it used to be otherwise. In 1876 it was home to a vibrant and colossal community. Spiritualists made pilgrimages from across the country to pitch their tents and set up shop within Camp Etna's massive woodland acres, like a months-long Burning Man. And Etna wasn't alone—all over the country, as Spiritualism flourished, so did the camps. They were like summer soccer or basketball camps—people attended with the purpose of focusing all their attention, energy, and time on the pursuit of developing a certain set of skills. Back in the day, Spiritualist camps played a pivotal role in the study and promotion of physical phenomena and past-life communication, improving clairvoyance through lectures and demonstrations, tutoring and coaching, prayer and trances, table-tippings and séances (complete with ectoplasm and photographic documentation).

In the early 1900s, Camp Etna was at its peak. Believers traveled from New York and Boston, Hartford and Providence, by train or carriage or horse or, if they had to, on foot. Camp Etna soon had more than just a grassy knoll for people to set up tents. Meeting halls were built; a temple was erected. A dining hall, burial ground, library, and grocery store sprouted up. Soon there were 130 cottages, then plumbing, flush toilets. There was a boat landing, a meat cart, a barbershop, and a photograph saloon. Camp Etna became a fully fledged function-ing community; it even had its own ice-cream room. Among the liv-ing, a democratic system coalesced: an elected president, vice president, secretary. Rules were established. A camp flag was created. The sun-flower was adopted as the symbol of the place, and soon the camp's art clubs plastered sunflowers all over. Next came the Camp Etna Pollyanna Club and the Camp Etna Success Club. Along with trance circles, there were story circles. Sing-alongs. Whistle-alongs. For an establishment whose foundation was based on communication with the dead, Etna was pulsating with life. It was blithe, accepting, cheerful. In its heyday, Camp Etna was more than a religious gather-ing—it was a living organism. Now there were only about ten people at most living at the camp.

"Does anyone know who the first medi-ums were?"

Our tour guide had arrived. She was tardy and was giving us a pop quiz. Her name was Diane: a perky woman, healthy, maybe in her early fifties. She had curly gray locks that rested on her sculpted gym-nast's shoulders, and when she acknowl-edged our group, she did so with the enthusiasm and rapidity of a Jack Russell terrier. Her wrists were bangled, and she wore a long flowy skirt and no shoes.

Diane tried us again. "Any brave soul care to take a guess?" I wanted to raise my hand and answer, proving to the others that I was not some neophyte or impos-tor, but someone else piped up before I could.

"The Fox sisters," he answered confidently, but was promptly shot down by Diane.

"WRONG," said Diane, making the sound of an exaggerated game-show buzzer. "Sorry. Anyone else want to take a stab? Because the answer is the Native Americans. The Native Americans were the first mediums."

Diane walked to the back of the room and stuck her head under the sink while continuing to talk.

"Surprised? Because the history of Spir-itualism is beautiful, delicious, vast, and I've been working on this timeline, which I'm about to . . ." She emerged with a bag, reached inside, and pulled out a large roll of construction paper, then unfurled a hand-made paper scroll containing her rendering of the history of Spiritualism. It was in the form of a timeline, written in purple, black,

> For an establishment whose foundation was based on communication with the dead, Etna was pulsating with life.

and orange Crayola-marker script. Easy to read. Earnest. Cheerful. For the most part, this was the tone of the room, too.

"The Native Americans, or the first Spiritualists, believed that the thoughts coming into our heads were not our own. That they came from spirits." One man nodded, listening intently as if Diane was repeating a shared secret knowledge. I was learning something new, but things still felt ordinary. I was still waiting to tap into something greater.

She raced through her chart: There were the Native Americans, then something about the Thessalonians; Corinthians I, verse 8; and Mother Anne Lee speaking in tongues. Then Martin Luther. Swedenborg, and Mesmer. I couldn't write or connect the dots fast enough. Andrew Jackson Davis and Nelly Holt. A mention of Joan of Arc and the Shakers. Abe Lincoln and Mary Todd. All of this and more and we had barely reached the point in history when the Fox sisters made their appearance. Diane continued all the way through the early 1900s, then put down the timeline and came to a sudden halt. What about what happened between then and now? Diane didn't just skip the explanation of how it unfolded and fell apart; she avoided the century altogether. I began to raise my hand to ask, then thought better of it.

"If there are no further questions," said Diane, "then we can now head outside for the walking portion of our tour."

> My understanding of death was one-dimensional and unimaginative.

We strolled down a lane of cottages under repair, Diane pulling up weeds and pointing out the cottage she'd just moved into with her husband, Don. They were newlyweds, and Don wasn't Diane's first husband. Or her second. As we walked, I asked Diane how a person comes to live at Camp Etna. What would compel a person, compel Diane, to pack up her life and move to a cabin in the woods, shutting out media and modernity and replacing them with pine trees, unrushed hours, and just a few other cabins with just a few other expats? Was she born nearby? Diane's answer was short: it was because of death. She told me a story about the night everything changed. She was making love to her late husband, a musician called "Fiddlin' Red," and as he came inside her, he died. She said that she could feel his "essence" and soul inhabit her body, that his spirit literally moved her. From then on, Diane knew that Fiddlin' Red wasn't completely gone. She would help Red's family, friends, and fans to mourn his sudden departure, but she'd also continue on her mystic path and become a healer.

Halfway up the driveway to the Inn, Diane turned to our group and raised her voice. "If you would all please take a look to your right." We turned toward an overgrown grassy patch of land enclosed by an ornate black wrought-iron fence.

"Throughout its history, Camp Etna has hosted many local and national notables," Diane continued, "from Harrison D. Barrett to C. Harrison Engel. But our most beloved and well-known member was the medium Mary Scannell Pepper Vanderbilt, whose soul left her body in 1919." It was the same Mary I'd heard about inside the Inn. The sidekick to Bright Eyes.

"Mary is buried here below this chestnut tree, and this large boulder, said to weigh twelve tons, marks her resting place."

Diane turned to me to wrap up her response to my question. How did she get here? She landed at Camp Etna because her intuition had led her here, same as everyone else at Etna.

I looked around for my family. I saw my husband and son down the knoll, stretching out in the grass, protected by the shade of a tree. All this made me wonder how I should explain death to my son. How had death been explained to me? I couldn't remember. My understanding of death was one-dimensional and unimaginative, not much different than that of most grown-ups I knew. This struck me as absurd and sad, considering death is so huge and yet something we are comfortable knowing nothing about. And I'd accepted that.

Despite the heat and the humidity and my inner struggle with skepticism, I hadn't lost hope yet. I was waiting to be moved, and I wasn't giving up. I wanted to be convinced, the way a sucker getting a palm reading in a New York storefront wants to believe more than he wants to challenge. I was seeking a quick portal for some kind of freedom, from constraints or church or gender roles or the ordinary or reality. I wanted to have my mind blown, and to have it happen without my help. But despite wanting to fit in here, I felt too distant from it all. Too far from believing. I was so normal, so antibacterial. I was into routines. I vaccinated my child, I owned an iPhone, I didn't howl at the moon, and I didn't have that sixth sense I'd had as a youth anymore. I was married to a mechanical engineer, and we had bedtimes. Still, something in me, I knew for a fact, was still wild.

Just past my boys, a church. The next destination on our tour, with a list of the week's activities posted out front:

Monday 10–2 PM *Radiant Health and Happiness* presented by Julie Griffith $40

Monday 7 PM *Message Circle* with Rev. Jason McCuish $15

Tuesday 7–9 PM *Healing with Stones* presented by Robin Gillette $25

Wednesday 10–12:30 PM *ABCs of Mediumship* presented by Rev Jason McCuish $10

Thursday 1–4 PM *Sacred Geometry Alignment for Body and the Earth* presented by Lea Hill $45

Thursday 7–9 PM *The Millionaire Mindset & Growing Rich Prosperity* presented by Julie Griffin $25

Friday 10–3 PM *Trace with Me—A Channeling Workshop* presented by Graham Connelly and Ann Gallagher $50 Limited to 12 people

*Inquire in person about the week-long past-life regression workshops.

Inside, the building was bare and hot. I was hungry. Tired. Outside, my son was nearing his naptime and my husband was getting fidgety, frustrated. They were ready to go home. But there was one last stop on the tour, and I still wasn't satisfied.

It was time to visit the healing rock. I didn't think to question what the healing rock was. We continued walking down the pebble path into the woods. Trees provided cool shade. Mosquitoes chased our scents. We were distracted by the smell of pines and beach water ahead. I was excited about the rock, tenaciously hopeful but cranky and cautious enough to temper my enthusiasm. We were all seeking. We were all doing this, nearly skipping through the woods and toward the rock, ready to pull back the curtains of the cosmos on our own.

"Now where is that rock?" Diane mumbled as she pulled back shrubs and ducked into the woods. She tromped around a bit in the bushes, then let out a bit of a squeal. "Aha!" A large gray boulder sat behind some bushes like a sleeping dinosaur, and Diane invited us all to touch it. The contact between the rock and each of us was entirely our own. What we felt was what we felt. To me, the rock represented possibility. The rock was my last chance. It

wasn't a human; it couldn't fake anything. I wanted that rock to be clarifying—to wipe my slate clean, let me see things fresh again. It would give me my answer, send a lightning bolt of an impulse into me that was beyond me. The rock would enlighten me, heal me, and, finally, it would reveal to me my truth. This was my whole reason for coming to Maine; this was what had, oddly, led me to be on this path with this group of strangers.

We'd left New York to get back to our more natural states, but we were still yuppies, just living on a smaller island. What would happen if we hightailed it again, going more off the map, living off the grid and in a place populated by just a few women, perhaps some ghosts, little technology, and a whole lot of woods? Would I become sharper? Would I remember who I was?

I was a mother now, and while being a mother was one of the most natural things for my body to do, I had some questions. Stirrings. Worries. I felt out of place in my role. Motherhood was high jumps and hurdles, and cultural expectations became a senseless obstacle course that had nothing to do with the basic love and care between a mother and a child. This had produced an anxiety that became difficult to control. It took over. And then came the day, just a few weeks before our trip to Camp Etna, when I snapped—a simple criticism or maybe just a difference of opinion between my husband and me had revealed my inability to cope. A few tiny, insubstantial, disagreeable words pushed me over the edge, and suddenly I found myself running barefoot and furious to a forest preserve on the island, where I stayed for hours, a grown woman in her swimsuit and jean shorts barefoot in the woods, pacing like a wolf. But for the first time since I'd given birth, I felt at ease. I became primitive, feral, and it felt right, even if it didn't make any sense.

And now, as we approached the healing rock, I couldn't deny that that's what had led me here. Something was revealed to me, and I was trying to make my next move. Make things right for myself. In other words, I came to Camp Etna to pull myself together. At least that's what I'd hoped. And if that failed, if all this proved to be a hoax, at least a good story might come out of it—and if not that, at least an interesting family road trip.

"Come touch the rock! Come now!" called Diane, so we bushwhacked through the overgrown shrubs and made our way to the rock. Diane put her hand on it first, moaning in joy immediately upon impact. Others followed suit. "Can you feel that? Doesn't it feel great?" Yes, they agreed. Yes, it feels wonderful. I waited for a lull in the touching, then cautiously approached the rock. I was nervous. This was it.

I lifted my arm, spread my fingers, touched the rock. I closed my eyes and waited. I could here the "ooooohs" and "ahhhhs" of the others around me. They

I became primitive, feral, and it felt right, even if it didn't make any sense.

sounded so giddy. I paused for a few more seconds, motionless and sensitive, eyes still closed, and waited some more. And then a funny thing happened: Nothing. I felt nothing. Or, thinking back on it now, what I felt was something like a thin film, like a piece of Scotch tape, taped over what, I wasn't sure. I held on to that feeling a little while longer, welcoming the arrival of something deep and faint like a whisper, but all I heard was the sound of my own brain.

The sun low, we pulled onto the interstate, and our son immediately fell asleep. I felt a little dumb and embarrassed, but mostly baffled.

"If Camp Etna was so legit, if it was so magical, why is no one living there now?" I asked my husband, planting my feet onto the dashboard. "If they were immortal, where did everyone go?" I asked, but it wasn't really a question.

One explanation: because it was total bullshit. After the Fox sisters peaked, the child stars fell victim to alcoholism and eventually confessed publicly that they'd made their entire story up. The rappings from Mr. Splitfoot were really the sisters cracking their toes. It was a miserable ending. They died penniless and ostracized. But none of that really mattered, because Spiritualism continued to sweep the nation, even without the sisters who lit the fire.

Another possibility: Maybe our culture has circled back to a place were we don't take women as seriously as we used to. Maybe misogyny is too deeply ingrained for us to hear or sense something quiet and delicate. Maybe Camp Etna is more progressive than it is outdated.

Or maybe intuition wasn't shut down by patriarchy; it was displaced by hand-held devices. Media replaced mediums, and a cheap flood of information replaced intuition. We aren't living in a natural world anymore. We've forgotten how to slow down and listen. How could I be moved by touching a rock when I'd grown accustomed to a daily onslaught of images of brutal deaths, violence, war, racism, images I scroll through at the breakfast table while slurping my milk and cereal? Maybe Camp Etna isn't total bullshit. Maybe the women there aren't asking anyone to put doubt to rest.

Earlier in the day, when I'd brought up the Fox sisters to Diane, I asked her if she thought they'd always been telling the truth about Mr. Splitfoot. I asked if she believed in them, and she said she did. "They were broke and desperate," she said. The sisters had spent their money on alcohol and drugs to drown their anxieties and pressures, went broke, needed money, so accepted payment to say they'd made it all up. Men hated them and wanted to take them down. So when a man offered Margaret a large sum of money to read a simple statement that she'd concocted the whole thing, she took the offer. It was not until fifty-six years after the initial watery excavation that a further excavation was made in the Fox household in Hydesville, and it proved beyond all doubt that someone was buried in the house. In 1904, the skeleton of a man was found beneath a plank, below charcoal and limestone, just a smattering of hair and bones buried deep in the cellar of the Fox sisters' childhood home. "To look is to find," Diane said, as she stepped away from my questioning.

As the sun went down, we stepped off the ferry and walked home, exhausted, my son draped over my shoulders and snoring. I opened the door to my house and petted my happy dogs, little angels. Plopped down on my solid couch and reached for the solid hand of my solid husband. The small warm foot of my son, my own flesh and blood, rubbed against my side, and I felt grateful. But something still felt foggy. That piece of Scotch tape. I opened my purse to check my phone for calls I'd missed and texts awaiting responses, and beside it I saw a bottle of my medicine, little pills prescribed by my doctor the day after I'd disappeared into the woods. Antidepressants. The morning after I'd run through the woods, my husband, shaken and unsure what to do, took me to our family doctor, afraid that I was going to hurt myself. I told the doctor what I'd done, and she told me the symptoms I'd been experiencing before I even told her about them. She was so accurate, as if she'd been inside my body, felt what I had, experienced it too. She convinced me to try the pills. That I hadn't done anything wrong, something was just off and I needed a little extra help setting it straight. Physically. Chemically. No one blames you, she said. This isn't your fault. No one expects you to be able to balance all these things, to do it all. So I took the pills. And I'd been steady since then. The edge had been taken off, the intensity dulled, everything was less sharp. But it wasn't until I was sitting on our couch, looking down at those pills, that it occurred to me that perhaps those pills were dulling valuable things. My compass. Instincts. Intuition. My inner voice, not the ridiculous world outside of it.

There is something deeply American to it. The pragmatism. The dogged endurance. The collective witch-hunt is as American as the Fox sisters' bold challenge of the status quo had been. It's bureaucratic and empirical, not mystical. It's a group activity. But when we go it alone, it gets tricky. There is no one to tell us whether our beliefs are true, and we always want something tangible. We can send messages instantaneously and not be there with our bodies, and we're told that this is "real." What is the spirit? And can love really reach across eternity? What leaves us, what remains? What is the truth and how will we ever find out? Who knows? But there is something I have faith in: that we can believe anything if we want. And we should believe anything we want. Because belief and faith are just as real as anything else we can hold by the shoulders or wrap our arms around, all the things we can see, touch, taste, smell, hear, and feel. Maybe within and beyond this there really is something to it all. 🕯

# A WITCH IS A WITCH
# IS A WITCH

## Alex Mar

*A restless spirit on an endless flight*

A particular image of Doreen Valiente tells two unresolvable stories at once. In this black-and-white portrait, perhaps taken in the fifties at her home in Brighton, she is, at first glance, a suburban wife seated before a pale curtain, wearing a patterned cocktail dress, a string of stones around her neck. (She was in her thirties then, her jet-black hair cut short in a wavy bob, her lips and brows painted in.) But then the photograph becomes complicated: spread before her on a table is an altar laid out with a crystal ball, a bowl, rope, candles, and incense; in one hand she holds up a large bell, in the other a ritual knife. Her eyes peer at the viewer from behind large librarian's eyeglasses—she looks dead into the camera, not in a confrontational way, but smiling a strong, tight-lipped smile. Propped on her elbows, leaning toward us (her audience a half-century into the future), she exudes all the confidence that comes with a hard-earned outsider identity, forged in small-town England in a rigid time. She is vibrant. She is the face of every woman with a secret life. She is the Nerd Queen, a person of rare esoteric knowledge. She is Doreen Valiente, the Mother of Modern Witchcraft.

Though a definitive biography of her life has yet to be published—both scholarship and her own writings have focused on her magical career—we know the basics. She was born Doreen Dominy in 1922 in Surrey, outside London. Her parents were conservative Christians; her father was a civil engineer; but Doreen felt marked for a different life. When she was still a child, she had her first mystical experience one night while staring up at the moon. By thirteen, she believed she was having psychic episodes, and she began experimenting with magic. Doreen made a poppet to protect her mother from a local woman who'd been bothering her, and she believed the spell had worked. Hoping to cure their daughter of her interest in witchcraft, her parents decided to send Doreen to a convent school. But before her second year was up, she walked out the door and never returned.

Doreen was seventeen when World War II broke out, and she soon signed up for a secretarial position in Wales. There she met and married a Greek seaman in the merchant navy—only to have him go missing during the war, eventually presumed dead.

Three years later, she married again—a Spaniard who'd escaped the Spanish Civil War and fought with the Free French Forces. The couple settled in Bournemouth in the south of England, where she took an office job and he found work as a chef. Doreen, who already saw herself as an outsider because of her occult interests, became even more set apart from the mainstream for having married a foreigner in a time of desperate national pride.

She began researching magic more seriously, reading up on the practices of the nineteenth-century occult society the Hermetic Order of the Golden Dawn and studying Hebrew, a language useful in many rituals. Proving that libraries are dangerous places, she also read up on the century-old Spiritualist movement, which held that both women and men had the natural ability to become present-day mystics; and when a major biography of Aleister Crowley was published, she was thrilled to read, for the first time, the life story of a notorious, unrepentant magician. Finally, in the fall of 1952, she came across a magazine article that mentioned the recent opening of a place called the Folklore Centre of Superstition and Witchcraft, on the Isle of Man. In the story, the owner, Cecil Williamson, spoke of witchcraft as "the Old Religion" and plugged the center's "resident witch," a man named Gerald Gardner.

The Witchcraft Act of 1735 had finally been repealed just a year earlier, making it legal for someone to publicly claim he worked with magic or communed with

In a candlelit cottage on the grounds of a nudist club, she took part in rituals with Gerald's Bricket Wood coven.

spirits—and Cecil Williamson had jumped at the chance to capitalize on the situation. Partnering with Gerald, who had been practicing witchcraft in the New Forest region, Cecil immediately launched a publicity campaign for his new museum, which led to headlines like "CALLING ALL COVENS" and the equally exuberant "HE PLANS A JAMBOREE FOR THE WITCHES OF THE WORLD." For Doreen, the possibility of contact with real-life witches was irresistible. She immediately wrote a letter to Cecil, who in turn connected her with his resident expert.

And what came next was a revelation: lessons in how to practice a living, present-day incarnation of witchcraft.

Through Gerald Gardner, Doreen learned the principles of the Craft: nature is sacred, and our lives follow the changing of the seasons; the universe is equally male and female; there is no such thing as sin—sexuality is a source of power. In a candlelit cottage on the grounds of a nudist club, she took part in rituals with Gerald's Bricket Wood coven—its latest incarnation still practices today—and learned how to gather in a magical circle, to chant, to worship "skyclad" (or naked), and to use bondage and the scourge (not for pain, but to enter into an ecstatic state). These were some of the rites of the religion soon to be known as Wicca.

Within about two years, Doreen was ready for initiation. She writes of that evening in one of her books: In the cottage, Gerald stood "tall, stark naked, with wild white hair, a suntanned body, and arms which bore tattoos and a heavy bronze bracelet. In one hand he brandished 'Old Dorothy's' sword while in the other he held the handwritten *Book of Shadows* as he read the ritual by which I was formally made a priestess and witch." That night, Doreen took the magical name Ameth. At the age of thirty-two, she'd finally discovered her true nature. As she would often say: "To paraphrase Gertrude Stein, 'A witch is a witch is a witch is a witch.'"

Gerald invited her to meet the rest of his coven (about ten people) at his London apartment, where they practiced magic together skyclad. "I had never felt any objection to working in the nude," she writes. "On the contrary, it was fun to be free and to dance out the circle in freedom."

She trained with them for the traditional year and a day, learning to feel the change of the seasons in her life and in her body; learning to join with the others in "raising energy," and to call the "Guardians of each direction," those forces of nature. She built an altar in her home, and lived with the musky smell of incense and the ring of the bell she used to call the gods. She grew accustomed to talking to the dead. She earned her first degree, and then her second and her third. The coven "made me welcome, and I felt that a whole new life had opened up before me." She soon worked her way up to become their new high priestess.

For a good while, Doreen remained closeted in her practice, not wanting her Christian mother to discover that her daughter had become a Pagan priestess. She was initiated during a time when the Craft was still very secretive—"in the broom closet," as they say. This was also, of course, pre-feminism: empowered female mystics were an even harder concept to swallow then than today. Women (especially unmarried women) were not supposed to seek out or know anything about sex; nudity was considered obscene; religion was supposed to be a corrective, separate from anything that gave a person pleasure, and certainly not "sex-positive." Someone who declared herself a witch could lose her job, be made a social outcast, or have her children taken away.

At the same time, Doreen began actively shaping both Wicca and the slow-building Pagan movement. While Gerald claimed that the rites he was teaching had been handed to him directly by a centuries-old coven he'd discovered in the New Forest, Doreen realized that several elements of his *Book of Shadows* (the coven's master book of spells and practices) had actually been copied from historical spell compilations: from *Aradia*, a witches' "gospel" published by a turn-of-the-century American folklorist; from Masonic ceremonies; from Crowley's writings; and even from a poem by Rudyard Kipling. When challenged, Gerald explained that he'd used existing sources to embellish what few fragments of written text he'd inherited from the New Forest group. In a bold move, Doreen pushed to rewrite much of the *Book of Shadows*, removing the most obvious derivative material and creating a new version

of "The Charge of the Goddess" (the text read to a Wiccan once she received her first-degree initiation). Still popular sixty years later, across the many strains of Wicca that have developed, "the Charge" is often used in circle to evoke the presence of the Goddess. The dramatic opening, in Doreen's original verse form, reads:

> *Mother darksome and divine,*
> *Mine the scourge and mine the kiss.*
> *Five-point star of life and bliss,*
> *Here I charge ye in this sign*

But Doreen's life with Gerald would be short-lived. Eager to spread word of the Old Religion, Gerald published his book *Witchcraft Today* in 1954, announcing Wicca to the world. Over the next few years, Doreen, uncomfortable with the increasing level of exposure, rallied several coven members to her side, insisting that they outline clearer rules for their actions moving forward. Without missing a beat, Gerald replied that there *were* rules, passed down across the centuries—he'd simply forgotten to mention them. Conveniently, the rules required that he now replace her with a new, younger high priestess.

Doreen called bullshit. She left, moved to Brighton, and, though she continued practicing the "Gardnerian" style of Wicca, formed her *own* coven (she brought another of Gerald's coven members with her, as her high priest).

In 1962, she published her first book, *Where Witchcraft Lives*, about historical witchcraft in her home county of Sussex. She remained in the closet, however, "for personal reasons," writing the book as a "student" rather than an initiate of witchcraft. (When later asked about England's Christian majority, she would say with a smile, "They seem remarkably short on Christian charity when it comes to witches!")

Shortly after the publication of *Where Witchcraft Lives*, Doreen's conservative Christian mother died; and by the late, liberal sixties, new, much freer ideas about spirituality and sexuality were on the rise. Doreen was finally ready to out herself as a full-fledged high priestess.

In 1971, she took part in the BBC documentary *The Power of the Witch*. The film opens with an image of a sunlit field. In the distance, coming slowly into focus as she walks toward the viewer, is a witch in a red cape. This is Doreen, striding toward the camera, completely self-assured in her signature bob and sizable eyeglasses. A few minutes later, smiling her half smile, she talks about the heart of the Craft in her West Country accent: "I'd say to a person who really wanted to know what was the spirit of witchcraft that they'll learn more by, say, going out on the Downs at midnight and listening to the wind in the trees and looking at the full moon. They'll learn more about the spirit of witchcraft, the *real* spirit of witchcraft, in that way than they will by reading any amount of books."

This was also, of course, pre-feminism: empowered female mystics were an even harder concept to swallow then than today.

That said, Doreen continued writing—this time as a Pagan priestess, going on to publish a string of seminal books on the history and practice of the Craft, including *An ABC of Witchcraft* (1973) and *Witchcraft for Tomorrow* (1978). In *ABC*, she writes about the pleasure of her magical life: "I have danced at the witches' Sabbat on many occasions, and found carefree enjoyment in it. I have stood under the stars at midnight and invoked the Old Gods; and I have found in such invocations of the most primeval powers, those of Life, Love and Death, an uplifting of consciousness that no orthodox religious service has ever given me."

Throughout the seventies, Doreen campaigned for the religious rights of Pagans, helping to found the Pagan Front advocacy group and laying the groundwork, through her writings and press, for an international Pagan movement. (Today in the United States, perhaps as many as one million Americans consider themselves Pagan.) With the rise of second-wave feminism, she also pushed for stronger, more active roles for women in the Craft: in spite of pioneering "Goddess" worship in the West, Paganism had been dominated (at least on the surface) by its male practitioners. In 1989, she wrote *The Rebirth of Witchcraft*, in which she traces some of the Pagan movement's history while also coming down strongly against the culturally conscribed roles of Western women. She uses heated words about how female bodies are viewed, contorted, and abused, and she blames Christianity for plenty of it: "One of the chief weapons used against women has been the Christian Bible, heavily censored as it has been over the years until the references in the Old Testament to goddess-worship have been almost, though not entirely, obliterated. God, we have always been told, is masculine; from which it naturally followed that the male was somehow superior."

In her later years, Doreen cut the figure of a very cool older lady, in severe, straight-across bangs and a formidable collection of sweater vests. More importantly, ever the iconoclast, she advocated for maximum personal freedom—even among the witches themselves, who had a range of views on secrecy and the right to initiate. In an interview she gave to a fellow witch in the late eighties, she warned against limiting access to Craft practices that could have a greater positive influence if more people were able to discover them. Why shouldn't normal folks have a chance to learn to cast a magical circle? To make offerings to the gods? To draw energy up through the earth and into their own bodies? She also admitted that she'd grown conflicted, decades after being initiated by Gerald, about what exactly was required for a person to call herself a serious witch. "I don't like this idea that has started to spring up in some quarters that some people have got a way of saying, 'Well, but we

are the only genuine article, and if you've not been initiated by us, then you can't be a witch,'" she said. "I don't *like* this sort of power hierarchy. I don't see why people need somebody's permission to follow the Old Religion and follow the old gods."

After her second husband died in the early seventies, Doreen moved into a non-descript block of Brighton council apartments, where she fell for a man who also became her magical partner (he would die two years before her). She started working at a local pharmacy and, rarely seen by neighbors, continued writing in her small upstairs flat on an old word processor, surrounded by her collection of some two thousand books.

There, early on a fall morning in 1999, she died of pancreatic cancer. Her body was taken to a barn for an all-night vigil, and then her remains were cremated.

Her obituary in the *New York Times* carried the headline "Doreen Valiente, 77, Dies; Advocated Positive Witchcraft"; and the *Times of London* called her the "mother of modern paganism." In the summer of 2013, she became the first witch in British history to be awarded a blue plaque (used to mark the places where significant Brits lived), unveiled by the mayor. This was a year before Gerald's home would receive one.

But the Doreen of legend has less to do with historical consensus and everything to do with a kind of radical individualism. "It is important for people not to slavishly follow *anyone's* lead, I think. I hope witchcraft never sees any gurus." The Craft, she said, was about helping people "to develop their own powers"—the first thing Gerald had taught her. Witchcraft "isn't some sort of gift which people are given by some supernatural force," she said. "All the trappings of the circle, the magical tools, and so on, are simply there to enable you to do that, to create the atmosphere for you to bring out your own power—which is natural, which is latent in *everybody*."

Doreen didn't need Gerald Gardner to tell her this. Just look to her earliest days: she was raised in a string of smaller English towns by conventional parents; the only unique episodes in her life were experiences she was convinced had taken place deep inside her. Her appetite for the occult, the psychic episodes, her communion with the moon—this was the welling-up of abilities that were her very own, not handed down. What is it, this quality that makes a young girl believe she is so wholly different from everyone around her? What is the place this secret confidence comes from? How does a person know in her heart, before she understands the word, that she is a witch? 🜚

**James Gendron**

## *from* WEIRDE SISTER

Now my thoughts wander sexfully
Toward the image of Satan
Sumptuous dark angel
His voice a white root
His voice a river of onyx and venom
His velvet wing brushing the velvet rat
His visage reflecting & refracting
Along the tortured surface of the waters
Sometimes I think I am in lava with him
Upon the windswept & majestic heights
Of Sex Cliff he calls my secret name
His castle jiggles in the air
Due to being made of human gelatin
He wears a shawl of knit-together stars
His bed is a venomous tongue
His flames are dark but they glow in the dark
His hands very warm from the flames
His skin brightly lit by the flames
A supervisible radioactive mirror
The boundary of God's love in the world
Satan poofIs into the village of Fisherton Anger
There is rancor there
It's like oxygen to him
He takes a whiff
His lungs are tongues

His skeleton comprises one bone
From every species of dinosaur
Satan brushes a hand through his hair
All of his hair is pubic
His horns rise & throb like cocks
His sense of humor is perfect
He drapes insane black fungus on the fields of rye
He takes the form of a lettuce eaten by a nun
A portrait of Satan jotting down ideas for STDs
One that turns your genitals to clowns
One that, when you contract it, it kills your best friend
One that cancels your parents' influence in your life
He invented chocolate
He is the one who first thought up drugs
One day he doodled in his notebook a rough draft
Of the outline for speaking disrespectfully to officers of the law
He has many fingers
I would even say too many
He soaked & burst a planet by crying into it
He fishes whalesongs from the sea to do self-pleasure with
His eyes tangled in stars
What we see is a kaleidoscope compared to what he sees
In a locked cabinet in his library is an autographed copy
Of a creature's book of space-numbers
He actually cries when he sees a rainbow

It reminds him of the beauty of being gay
It reminds him of literature
Which he cries when he reads it
His tears fall on the page and light it on fire
It reminds him of his imprisonment
Ensconced within a vast bouquet
Of history's warmest flames
In his world the flames have names
And names burst into flames
Green ghosts wiggle all around the cake
He lovingly has prepped for the birthday of alcohol
Green cats follow his scent
Of a rotting mule carcass touched with milk
Everywhere his pawprints are available to lick
Satan sits in a cavern and reflects
His teeth are scary
He has scary teeth
Scary, scary teeth
Boo! they seem to say
I mean
Somebody needs to care about us
Even if they only care to the extent
That they want to make sure we suffer
So thank you, Satan
You alone have recognized me
Of all the deities you fly solo
In that you take an interest in my life

# The Hand Has Twenty-Seven Bones

*Whatsoever your hand finds to do, do it with your might; for there is no work, nor device, nor knowledge, nor wisdom, in the grave, where you go.*

~ECCLESIASTES 9:10

1. I make my faith in my hands. A writer can declare faith in nothing but must bear faith in her hands. Hands are the inventors of language. We make words for what we must do. Our words are made of hands. 2. The pen isn't separate from the hand but like all instruments it is an extension of the hand. Pen becomes hand. 3. Written letters, *manuscripts*, are drawn like threads from the *manus*, are connected to the *manus*. *Manus* as puppeteer—bowing the *n* in supplication, lifting then lowering the leg of the *h* as it breaks into a run, opening the mouth of the *v* to its white teeth, making a cup of the *u* then drinking from it. 4. We press our hands into the page until the page becomes our body. We are an ouroboros—writing ourselves onto ourselves. 5. Consider your hand in its moment of making. Hold your fingers and thumb together so there is no space between them. In this pose it's easy to remember your hand as it was in the beginning, before it

## Natalie Diaz

became itself—a paddle, a fin, a solid clayed thing. This was before we were finished. 6. To be finished, the hand had to be broken. Lessened before it became more, split four times, crafting the fingers and thumb—our handsome hydra. 7. Georgia O'Keefe called lover Alfred Stieglitz, *my hand*. She wrote, *Greetings—my hand—It's Sunday night 9:30—* 8. I once had a lover I called *my hand*. 9. I had another lover whom I also called *my hand*. 10. Both lovers are gone. My hands remain. 11. My hands are an archive. 12. Some linguists believe *masturbate* is derived from the words *manus* (hand) and *stuprare* (defile). 13. A year ago, my mind and body wrecked. I had to find a new way. My doctor prescribed medicine I didn't want to take. I talked about this worry to a friend, who is also a poet and doctor. He said, *You need to masturbate.* I laughed. He said, *You need to masturbate a lot.* 14. The scientific explanation: orgasm releases oxytocin and lowers cortisol. (Midwives once masturbated women suffering hysteria as a type of treatment.) I took my medicine and my friend's advice. 15. *My hands wanted to touch your hands / because we had hands*, wrote Frank Bidart. It's a *mise en abyme*—he wrote about his hands with his own hands. To touch a lover's hands with our hands, to know our hands in a new way through hands not ours, to become them as they are becoming you, is to be *placed into the abyss* of touch. 16. Physics say we never truly touch anything. Electrons in our hands repel electrons in the object we think we are touching. Touch is the brain's interpretation of the repulsion taking place between our body's electrons and the object's electromagnetic field. 17. The feeling of touch is just luck. 18. In alchemy, the Hand of Mysteries represents the transformation of man into god. The symbols above each finger signify the formula for physicorum, a red ethereal fluid that can turn any substance into gold. 19. There are twenty-seven bones in the hand and twenty-seven protons in the nucleus of an atom of cobalt. Cobalt blue. Our hands are the masters of our blues. How many times have I given up my head for them to hold? 20. Are the acts my hands act on my behalf, the tasks I set them to upon her body, different than what our creators did when they molded our bodies? When I am behind her, my hands pressing her hips and shoulders, she pushing back into me, doesn't it seem as if my hands have conjured her? From this position, if you looked upon us, would you believe she is leaping brand-new from my rib? 21. *A hand lying on the shoulder or thigh of another body no longer belongs completely to the one it came from*, wrote Rilke. I don't know if he wrote this before or after he pushed his wife down the stairs. *Pushed* implying hands—perhaps there was a moment when they were not his hands fully but half hers. Did he believe she shared the blame? 22. In Florence I saw the hand of David. Like the way Athena was born from the axed-open head of Zeus, David's body must have escaped from this soft marble hand. Michelangelo's hand again and again upon the hand of David—the bend of his fingers and his own smooth veins. A hand giving birth to a hand. 23. Cheiromancy divines the future by studying lines of the hand. To know my hands is to know me—they *are* my thoughts. Their wishes become mine. Read my hands, can't you tell they will soon reach to touch her? 24. My hands—my body's gates of tenderness, the tools of my wonders. The things I reach out with—toward her wrist, toward the orange and the stone alike, into every darkness before me. Strikers of flame to the lantern wick, looseners of the laces of my shoes. 25. Again and again they command the copper button of her pants back through the button loop and each time it is no different than leaping a bright tiger through a fiery hoop to the applause and whistles of the crowd of blood dizzying my head—all this, the circus of love, the lighting of dark, the Father, Son, and Holy Ghost, at the tips of my fingers. My little makers, my ringmasters, my revelers of joy. 26. Without the hand, the lamp would stay cold. 27. I'm an artist because of my hands. They are two artists building things with me. My hands, me—we are three in one. 🛡️

## REV. VALENTINE RATHBURN MEETS THE SHAKERS

*Niskayuna, New York, 1780*

Hard to say whose throat
it started from, the tune
that tests the length
of the wooden, high-windowed room,
an unknown mutter mixed with English
sliding like static
among their prone spirits
until, without apparent sign
or rule, all fall in,
dancing, hopping,
the so-called Believers bound together
only in their bodies'
tensions, their coiled
distinctions from each other:
one jigs, one drops
face-first on the floor,
one clings to the wall in prayer,
one stands and claps,
defiantly bored.
Wind fills the fastest dresses,

sprays them up, like wood hoops,
when the Mother changes time,
from deep in her bones
digging out notes.
This the company calls
the worship of God, which stops
oddly as it began,
and one by one
they break off, trailing laughter,
for a spell of smoking.

# AUGUSTINE ON TIME

*after Book X of the* Confessions

Where is it that you go
when I say I've found you,
my mind tricked the right way to look?

Without you, in my lack,
you must've been ahead there, too—
but there is no place like that!

Before my mind learned you,
where else would you have been
but leading me to find you,

moving forward, and then back?
It could have been it was
my mind, tricked the right way to look,

but leading me to find you
without you. In my lack,
when I say I've found you,

where is it that you go?
You must've been ahead, there, too;
where else would you have been

before? My mind learned *you*.
Moving forward, and then back—
it could have been. It was.

But there is no place like that.

# GRACE

Not that anyone actually changes—that the small charge
of a green change can't help but stumble,

on its own time, among no particular

people, feeling nothing, nothing different,
close faces craned toward another's phone, or, alone,

toward some point through the glass at tracks' end

perhaps, in the dark the unstill ground
hiding and giving us where we are going.

# AFTER FORTUNE

## Alexis Knapp

*Down on luck*

Three weeks before my first pregnancy ended in a miscarriage, my friend Sarah asked the table if we thought we were lucky. It was ladies' poker night and the four of us were gathered in Lucy's dining room. There was a bowl of fancy olives, some cheese and crackers, a bar of expensive chocolate. Wine I was pretending to drink. We hadn't yet played a hand, but not playing poker was part of the pleasure of ladies' poker night. We'd get caught up in conversation, lose track of bets, forget whose turn it was to deal. At the same time, poker, or at least the pretense of poker, was an essential ingredient in these nights' success. It was like the distraction that finally lets your subconscious work out the answer to a problem you've been wrestling with, or like one of those optical puzzles from which you have

to look away before you can see the hidden image. We'd all met through our husbands or boyfriends and didn't share a long history; but somehow, with cards in our hands and chips on the table, we'd slip into the easy intimacy of old friends.

I was the only one who answered "yes" to Sarah's question, though I added, "sort of." Lucy and Erika didn't feel especially lucky, although Erika mentioned that she'd once won a TV at a car dealership. Before I could explain my "yes, sort of," the conversation moved on to a different topic. This, too, was common at ladies' poker night—the way our talk would follow one track for a while before hitting an invisible switch and shooting off in another direction. It was always twisting and turning and looping back on itself, never following a straight line. You had to let it flow like that, you couldn't try to control it. If you did, you'd spoil things.

I won that night, once we finally got around to playing, but that wasn't exactly what I meant when I said I was lucky. I don't really believe that kind of luck exists— the kind that puts two aces in your hand instead of someone else's, or that whispers the winning lotto numbers in your ear. Faith in that sort of luck seems foolish, even frivolous, like believing in unicorns or a god who controls the weather.

And yet, when I won, I had the dizzy-ing sense that by *declaring* myself lucky, I had made it so. Why not? During the brief weeks of my pregnancy, I felt unusually potent. I had the sense that I was a part of nature now in a way I hadn't been before. In that time, summer had given way to fall, and I felt intimately connected to the trees that flared golden and ochre and crimson as they pre-pared to shed their leaves. The same ancient magic that painted the hills around me was, I believed, at work inside of me. Each day was now charged with meaning, and even time felt different. It became slower, denser—so much so that when, just six weeks after get-ting a positive pregnancy test, I learned that the embryo had died, it seemed to me that I had already been pregnant for months.

Emily Dickinson wrote, "Luck is not chance— / It's Toil—." We create our own luck, in other words, through hard, unceas-ing labor. I'm almost always in Dickinson's corner, but this strikes me as a pretty lim-ited way of looking at things. In fact, the line itself, with its distinctly puritanical bent, seems to undermine its own authority,

as it reminds us that while Dickinson was without doubt a true original, she was also very much a product of her society—of the world into which she *happened* to be born. She forged her art through toil, yes, and unrelenting dedication, too. But it's hard to imagine that her work would exist, or exist in the same form, if she had lived in a different time or place, or under differ-ent circumstances. How fortunate for us all, for instance, that her family was wealthy enough to support her, liberal enough to educate her, and smart enough to leave her more or less alone. And what would her poems have been without the hymn meter that she heard so often in her youth? Or if the Civil War had never happened? The four dark years of the war formed Dickin-son's most intensely productive period; she wrote nearly a thousand poems in that span, more than half the number she produced throughout her entire lifetime. And then of course there's the luck of being born at all: not so easy as it seems, it turns out.

Today, I count Dickinson's poems among my top reasons for living, but I almost missed her entirely. Despite majoring in English and creative writing, I somehow made it through six years of higher edu-cation without encountering more than a handful of her poems, and those that I did read hardly made an impression. It wasn't until after graduate school, when I was teaching part-time at a local com-munity college, that I took another look. Usually adjuncts like me taught only com-position, but through a stroke of luck, a twist of fate—something—I was offered the opportunity to teach a nineteenth-century American literature course. While designing the syllabus for that class, I picked up a collection of Dickinson's poems that had sat untouched on my bookshelf for years, opened it to a random page, and fell swiftly and deeply in love.

Montaigne speculated that inspiration is a form of luck. He wrote, "Why should we not attribute to good luck those poetic sallies which catch an author away and ravish him outside himself?" I love that phrase, *catch an author away and ravish him outside himself*. How different this is from Dickinson's earthly "toil," which by comparison feels like a pair of sensible brown loafers. And Montaigne's idea seems right to me on an intuitive level. On the few occasions when I have written something that really pleased me, the process of creation didn't feel effortful at all. It felt like the opposite of effort, like being led in a dance by a masterful partner. The work you labor over the most often feels contorted, stretched. It bears the scars of your efforts. Whereas the best stuff comes easily, in the end.

My favorite Dickinson lines hover on the edge of literal sense, in a way that tells me no amount of *thinking* could have yielded this result. It's magic, or luck, or genius, maybe even a kind of grace. Take the final couplet from poem 315: "When Winds take Forests in their paws— / The Universe—is still—." There's something slightly off-kilter about

*I had the sense that I was a part of nature now in a way I hadn't been before.*

these lines, some way in which they resist any single interpretation. They're bottomless. Their power comes from the particular music their syllables create together and from the tension between the ways we can penetrate them and the ways we can't. To write lines like that requires something more, or other, than hard work. To write lines like that, you have to forget yourself, forget that you're writing, forget whatever it is you're *trying* to do.

Still, you have to put the time in. You have to be there, at the ready, when luck flits by. And maybe you have to write the wrong word a hundred times before you finally "catch" the right one, or the right one catches you. An earlier version of poem 315 ends with "When Winds hold Forests in their paws— / The Firmaments—are still—." Later, Dickinson rewrote the poem, replacing "hold" with "take," "Firmaments" with "Universe." And what a difference those two small edits make! Now, instead of calm winds that bring a sense of harmony by gently *holding* forests, we have the strange and thrilling dissonance between violent winds that *take* forests in their paws (I picture a cat batting around a bloodied mouse) and a universe that's somehow rendered peaceful, "still," by that act of aggression. And do I even have to point out how awkward "Firmaments" sounds in place of "Universe"?

My own concept of luck involved toil and trust and chance all braided together.

When I told Sarah that I thought I was lucky, "sort of," I didn't mean I'd always win at cards or that good things would simply fall into my lap. But I felt fairly confident that when I really wanted something, and I went after it with all the focus and will I could muster, my efforts would not be in vain. I thought of it kind of like riding a bicycle, the way you have to use your own strength and balance and belief to get things going, but then after a certain point other forces—gravity, speed, momentum—kick in and help carry you. I guess you could say I believed that I carried around with me my own little gravity.

I had, as evidence, a life that seemed to me not extraordinary but uncommonly *good*. Eight years earlier I'd moved to Portland, Oregon, on little more than a whim. Now I owned a handsome old house there with big windows and a wide front porch overlooking the leafy street. My husband moved to the city around the same time as I did but from the opposite side of the country. Somehow, out of all the people in the world, we found each other. Then we both found the kinds of jobs that hardly exist anymore: Cheston became an editor at a literary journal, while my part-time teaching turned into what felt like the world's last tenure-track position. How astonishing they were, all these pieces of my life, things that I had worked at but

*On important days, I always find it reassuring to think that I've selected the right outfit.*

that had also just *worked out*. I couldn't help taking them as proof that I was, in some small way, charmed.

My pregnancy had felt like the latest sign. I'd done my share of the work (beyond the obvious), preparing for conception as I would have prepared for a test or a job interview. I took all the right vitamins, cut down on caffeine and booze. At thirty-one years old, I applied myself for the first time to truly learning about what was happening inside my body every month. I noted each twinge, each shift in mood and feeling. And it seemed to me then that a vast store of knowledge opened up to me, and I was like the forests and the seas, intuitive and immortal. When I got pregnant the first month we tried, I was hardly surprised. Yet I knew even then that this wasn't the norm and I believed my good luck had something to do with it.

Everything about this pregnancy was perfect. According to my due date calculator, the baby would be born on June 20, the longest and brightest day of the year. Spring term would have just ended, so I'd be able to spend the entire summer—the baby's first three months—at home without missing any work or losing any pay. And I loved the idea of a summer baby. I imagined that with such a special birthday, whatever luck I possessed would be redoubled in her. (I couldn't help hoping for a girl, though I suspected that my luck might not extend that far, and began resigning myself to the idea of a boy.)

I had no nausea, plenty of energy, and instead of dramatic mood swings, a pervading feeling of calm. This, too, I took as evidence of my good luck. I thought ahead to the birth; though I told myself I wouldn't feel bad about taking drugs if I wanted them or having a C-section if I needed one, I secretly treasured the idea that when the time came I would be brave and strong, and that my labor would proceed as smoothly and easily as my pregnancy so far had. Only as the day of our first doctor's visit drew near did I begin to worry that my lack of symptoms might be a sign of something else, an omen rather than a promise. Like silence on the line, a signal that something was wrong.

• • •

When the morning of my appointment finally arrived, I dressed carefully, as though I was headed for one of my tenure meetings or starting a new semester. On important days, I always find it reassuring to think that I've selected the right outfit. That morning, I was especially heartened by my choice of socks, since I figured I would be removing my shoes before climbing onto the examination table and liked the idea of looking down to see that small, unexpected, but pleasant detail. They were black ankle socks with tiny white polka dots, and they were brand new.

But I was nervous. Or maybe not nervous, exactly, but unsettled. As Cheston and I passed through the sliding glass doors of the hospital, I seemed to leave my body for a brief moment and, watching myself from above, I thought, *This isn't happening.* I suddenly felt like an imposter, like someone only playing the role of a pregnant woman. I couldn't quite believe that any of this would ever actually lead to a baby, *my* baby. This surreal feeling followed me into the elevator, up to the third floor, down a featureless hallway, and into my doctor's office. What was happening to me was at once enormous and pedestrian in a way I couldn't quite sort out, and nothing drove the strange mundanity of it all home like my doctor's waiting room, with its functional furniture, generic artwork, and months-old parenting magazines.

But then a receptionist gave me some forms to fill out, and this brought me back into the world. It soothed me to tick "no" in response to all the questions about prior illnesses and chronic health conditions: *Ever suffered from amnesia, blood clots, cancer, convulsions? Do you, or the baby's father, have a birth defect, a genetic disorder, a chromosomal abnormality?* Later, in the examination room, I cheerfully rolled up my sleeve to have my blood pressure taken. I was used to nurses following their readings of my numbers with exclamations of "That's excellent" or even "Perfect," and that day was no different. And though I knew my good health was at least partly due to genetics, or youth, or other factors unknowable to me and outside my control, I received the nurse's positive remarks on my chart as I'd once received gold stars from my elementary school teachers, as though I had earned them.

Then I was lying on the examination table and Cheston was behind me, his fingers resting lightly on my shoulders. My OB, Dr. Reilly, was an elfin woman in her forties who cocked her head and squinted her green eyes whenever I asked a question, I guess to show that she was really listening. She had positioned Cheston at the head of the table so that we'd both be able to see the baby's heartbeat on the ultrasound screen. She covered my belly with a thin layer of jelly that was surprisingly warm. Then she slid the ultrasound wand across my abdomen and focused on the screen, her sharp little chin angled toward it.

We waited for her to turn the screen in our direction, to show us our baby. We waited for the tiny black-and-white fluttering of life, the eager gallop of the heart. Mother and Father looking back and forth between the screen and each other. Smiles, gasps, eyes brimming. Would it be like that for us? Would it feel real? Though typically a major sap, I often find it difficult to experience powerful emotions when I know I'm supposed to. I remained completely dry-eyed throughout my wedding vows. Delivering my grandmother's eulogy, I felt more like a cheesy nightclub performer than a grief-stricken mourner. I wondered if this was a deficiency of mine alone, or something other people feel too. I worried that it meant I was less deep, less genuine, less adept at living in the moment than others. I even worried that I might not feel profoundly enough for my baby, or that

becoming a mother would alter only the surface of my life, without ruffling my soul.

Dr. Reilly removed the wand from my belly. She wanted to try using a different machine, she explained, one that would "give her a better look."

In came the new machine. Again Dr. Reilly searched the screen. Again she kept it angled away from us. On the wall to my left hung a framed photograph of twin greyhounds that I assumed belong to Dr. Reilly. With their narrow faces and green eyes, they even looked a little bit like her. I stared at the dogs' gleaming coats and grinning muzzles, their lolling pink tongues. Then I felt my husband's hands leave my shoulders.

"I'm sorry," he said somewhere behind me, "I just have to sit down for a minute."

When I turned toward him, Cheston's face had gone gray and filmy, like old soapy dishwater. I'd never seen anyone look like that before, only heard the expression: *The blood drained from his face.* But that was just what had happened. Fear or dread had drawn the blood away from his extremities, pumping it into his muscles and core, preparing his body for fight or flight. Seconds before Dr. Reilly confirmed it, before I understood it, Cheston had known—there was no heartbeat.

Later he would tell me that he'd had a premonition. A "vision," I think he called it. He'd seen it all, or at least anticipated it somehow, just before it actually happened. Dr. Reilly's apologetic expression as she pointed to the ultrasound screen. The fuzzy white lump that, she explained, would never develop into a healthy baby. The door clicking shut behind her as she left us to digest the news on our own. Although the blood had mostly returned to Cheston's face by then, sweat dripped from his temples. His shirt and sweater were both soaked through. Now, looking back, I picture these early moments of our grief like the dark hole in the center of a storm, the eye of loss: when the pain is so fresh and encompassing that, for a short time, nothing else exists. *When Winds take Forests in their paws— / The Universe—is still—*.

Leaving moments like this behind, returning to the ordinary flow of everyday life, can feel impossible. And yet, somehow, it never is. Cheston and I let go of each other. I got dressed, slipped my feet in their polka-dotted socks back into my shoes. We had "options" to discuss now—what to do about the thing that had failed to grow. Dr. Reilly advised waiting a week to see if my body would catch on to the fact that the pregnancy wasn't viable and initiate a miscarriage on its own. If that didn't happen, there were pills I could take or, as a last resort, surgery.

We agreed to the "wait and see" option, scheduled a follow-up appointment, and then left the office through a side door. This was for my protection, I understood, so that I wouldn't have to confront any newborn babies or round-bellied women in the waiting room. But it also seemed to me that I should avoid that waiting room so as to not risk contaminating it, and the women who sat there, with my bad luck. I had landed on the wrong side of a statistic, and already I was learning what a lonely and shameful place that is to be.

•  •  •

Here is a story about luck I tell my American literature students.

On New Year's Eve, 1896, the writer Stephen Crane boarded the *S.S. Commodore* in Jacksonville, Florida. Crane was only twenty-six years old but already a respected novelist. Now he was headed for Cuba as a war correspondent, covering the Cuban rebellion against Spain. In images from around this time, he is handsome, even dashing. He has dark, tousled hair and an impressive mustache, a strong profile, ocean-gray eyes. Watching the shore recede from the deck of the *Commodore* that night, young and attractive and newly famous, bound now for paid adventure, he must have felt excited and optimistic about the future. He must have felt lucky.

But the *Commodore* never made it to Cuba, and neither did Crane. Damaged in a storm two miles off the Florida coast, the ship began taking on water. Most of its crew clambered into lifeboats, while the first mate and a few others stayed behind and struggled to right the ship.

> I suddenly felt like an imposter, like someone only playing the role of a pregnant woman.

In the rough waves, nearly all of the life-boats sank. Soon, only one remained. In it were the ship's captain, its cook, its oiler, and Crane. Together, they watched the *Commodore* lurch forward, then backward, then forward again, before it quietly disappeared beneath the bucking surface of the sea.

The four men spent the next thirty hours desperately rowing toward land. In the end, Crane survived, as did the captain and the cook. But in the journey's final moments, as the men swam for shore, the oiler, Billy Higgins, drowned. The surf tumbled his lifeless body onto the beach.

For most of the *Commodore*'s crew, this is a story about bad luck, about being in the wrong place at the wrong time, landing on the wrong side of a statistic. But for the four men left afloat in the dinghy, things are a bit more complicated. Are they unlucky to have been on a ship that sank, or lucky to have survived the wreck? Lucky to be in a ten-foot dinghy rather than at the bottom of the sea, or unlucky to be in a dinghy instead of in a yacht or ferry or—even better—on dry land? Poor Billy Higgins asked the captain *at the last minute* if he could join him in the dinghy; he was the final man to leave the ship, which sank without a groan or gurgle soon afterward. What luck for Billy! But after a grueling day and a half aboard the miserable little boat, Billy is the only one

There are no answers for the men's questions, no reasons why—only the next wave coming at them.

of the four men to end up facedown in the sand. Ultimately, the fact that he made it so far only adds absurdity to tragedy, and by this strange arithmetic Billy Higgins becomes unluckier even than all the faceless crewmen who drowned with the ship.

And Crane? He failed to reach Cuba, failed to write his story about the Cuban rebels. Instead he wrote about the *Commodore*, the wreck, his escape and survival. If he'd had a bit of a gallant air before, now he became a hero. Later, he wrote of the ordeal again, this time as fiction. "The Open Boat"—which my students and countless others read every year—is a gorgeous and enduring story, one that lives by its own rules and offers up sentences that demand and deserve a special kind of attention. All this might suggest that Crane was lucky after all to have boarded the doomed ship. But then consider that his health began to decline soon afterward, his body weakened by his adventures as a war correspondent; that he became burdened with debts he couldn't pay; that he died of pulmonary tuberculosis at the age of twenty-eight. In the end, there's one statistic that none of us escapes, though it snatched Crane earlier than most. In the end, we all outrun whatever luck we may possess.

I found myself thinking about this story in the days following my appointment with Dr. Reilly. As the men struggle up

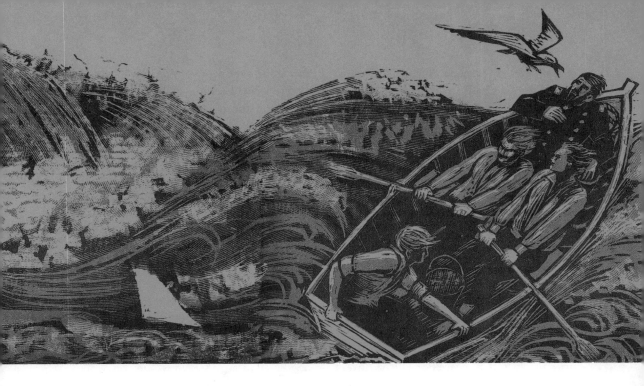

WOODCUT © ROBERT QUACKENBUSH

and over one wave after another in their bathtub-sized boat—so vulnerable, so tiny in all that wide water!—they continually ask themselves *why*. Why them? Why this, why now? Why were they allowed to survive the sinking of the ship only to find themselves here, teetering on the brink of disaster? It just wouldn't be fair, they reason with no one in particular, if they were to die now. "Other people had drowned at sea since galleys swarmed with painted sails," they acknowledge, "but still—."

How I love that "but still—." The way the sentence remains unfinished. That "but still—" is the men's feverish belief in their own significance, and they cling to it like a buoy as they cast about for someone or something to blame for their predicament. They curse the sea, the gods, even a seagull that has the audacity to briefly alight on the captain's head. But there isn't anyone to blame, and when they survive (most of them, that is) there will be no one to thank. There are no answers for the men's questions, no reasons why—only the next wave coming at them.

My students struggle fiercely with this idea. The insignificance of the men and their plight is as puzzling to them as it is to the men themselves. So they say, "Nature is cruel," or "The sea wants to kill the men." They write, "The oiler, Billy Higgins, drowns because he is a working-class man and this is a story about how hard life is for the working class," or "Billy drowns because he is the only character to whom the author has given a name." No, I tell them. Billy drowns because Billy drowns.

Billy drowns because meaninglessness, randomness, chaos. He drowns because for most of history everyone agreed that the gods or just one God controlled everything, and then artists like Crane began to ask, What if it isn't God but chance that rules our lives? What if shit just *happens*?

I'd always taken a kind of perverse delight in insisting to my students that the message of "The Open Boat" is that there is no message. But now some shit had happened to me, and I wanted to know why. Why me? Why this, why now? Why had I been allowed to get pregnant so quickly, only to miscarry? It seemed unfair, even cruel—but whom could I blame for what was happening, who had authored this cruelty? If I had been born in a different era or raised with different beliefs, I might have sought some sort of deeper spiritual significance, or resigned myself to that odious cliché, "God works in mysterious ways." Instead, modern that I am, I put my faith in science. Surely I'd find a cogent medical explanation for what had happened, one that would give me the knowledge I needed to make sure it never happened again.

Instead, the only explanation I was offered was "bad luck." Most early miscarriages occur, I learned, because of a faulty collision of chromosomes at conception—in other words, a random accident of nature. Only after three or more miscarriages in a row do most doctors even bother looking for an underlying cause or condition. Even when they do look, I was told, they may never find anything. Yet none of this information penetrated my heart. As easy as it had been for me to believe that I was lucky, the opposite was impossible to accept. The thought that something like this could happen to me for no reason at all, or that I just as easily could have left Dr. Reilly's office in one piece, with all my hopeful visions of the future intact—how could that ever make sense? How could it *not* make me feel like I was drowning?

• • •

In the days before my follow-up appointment, it remained remotely possible that there might have been a mistake, that at my next ultrasound, Dr. Reilly would shake her head in wonder and Cheston would tenderly squeeze my hand: *A miracle*. But despite what Cheston and I whispered to each other in bed at night, despite the fact that I continued not to bleed, despite all the confidence I'd once had in my own good fortune, I did not really believe that anything incredible would happen to me now. In truth, I felt with leaden certainty that my body was not a source of life and light after all, that it—that *I*—had failed.

The appointment confirmed this. My pregnancy had stopped progressing at about six weeks, though it had now been nearly two months since I'd gotten a positive result on a home pregnancy test. That afternoon, I left Dr. Reilly's office with three prescriptions: one for Misoprostol, which would induce a miscarriage; one to ease the pain that the miscarriage would cause; and a third for the nausea that the pain pills would bring on. "A chemically induced chain reaction of bummers," I joked lamely.

The next day, as soon as I finished teaching my classes, I took the first dose of Misoprostol. I'd heard that it could take anywhere from two to twenty-four hours to finish its job. "Your doctor will tell you that the pain will be like a heavy period, but DON'T believe that," I'd read on some Internet discussion board. "It's actually much, much worse." So I lay on the couch with my pain meds and a heating pad at my side and binge-watched a few episodes of *Project Runway*. Soon after Cheston got home from work, around six o'clock, the cramping began. It wasn't all that bad, at least not yet. I think a part of me welcomed the pain, although I was also afraid.

But the cramps died down just a couple of hours after they began. Only a few drops of blood accompanied them. Over the phone, a nurse instructed me to take the second dose of Misoprostol. Just one pill was supposed to be ninety percent effective; two would undoubtedly do the trick. And yet, the second dose had even less effect than the first. By the following afternoon, it was clear to me that my body couldn't even get this part right. Or maybe the scales of fortune had tipped against me, and from now on everything that could go wrong, would. In the end, strung

> Or maybe the scales of fortune had tipped against me, and from now on everything that could go wrong, would.

out by all the waiting and anticipation, I opted for surgery.

The procedure used to clear the womb of a failed pregnancy is called a dilation and curettage, or D&C for short. It involves dilating the cervix and using a slender metal instrument called a curette to gently scrape the walls of the uterus and remove its contents. It is over quickly. It hurts, but not too bad. You're given pain pills beforehand—good ones that make you calm and strangely grateful. Afterward comes a sense of relief: maybe now you can move on, put this behind you.

But the healing process turns out to be much longer and knottier than you would have guessed. It involves countless ups and downs, and milestones that are actually just the beginnings of new phases in your grieving, not the end points they looked like back when they were still ahead of you. A few days after the procedure, for instance, there's the hormone crash: tears and anxiety and migraine and sleeplessness, a kind of postpartum depression without the partum. There's the first time you get your period again—half-reassuring, half-devastating. Then there's every other time it comes after that, and the disappointment and frustration that arrives with it, the loss made new again. There's realizing your friends are tired of hearing about your sadness and your longing, and that to protect your marriage you have to find a way to talk about something else. There's the haunting sense that instead of helping you grow, this stretch of suffering, this bout of bad luck, has only made you smaller and harder. Less open and giving. More afraid.

. . .

Time felt different after the miscarriage. Inside of me, it barely budged. I dragged myself through the days, always waiting and waiting and waiting for a change that seemed less likely to come with each month that passed. I felt immobile, stuck. On the outside, though, time was moving much too quickly. Weeks and then months and then entire seasons dropped *like Flakes / . . . like Stars, / Like Petals from a Rose*. Meanwhile, one after another, friends of mine announced *their* pregnancies, and those pregnancies seemed to progress with the speed of time-lapse photographs. I watched these friends refuse drinks with sly smiles one moment (my heart silently flopping about like a fish), and the next moment they were swollen, "showing," their distended bellies never ceasing to amaze me, as they offered undeniable evidence that these other pregnancies were real, were *happening*, while mine was only a memory that might have been a dream, a white smudge on a screen that I'd looked at for less than a minute, two pink lines on a stick that I sometimes wanted to bury and sometimes wanted to sew onto my sleeve but always just ended up shoving back into my messy nightstand drawer.

It wasn't just my perception. Time really was playing strange tricks. The winter after my miscarriage was the shortest I'd experienced in Portland. Normally it grinds on and on; sometimes even into June the rain remains relentless, the sky heavy and low. But this year, as early as February brought cheerful yellow daffodils, baby-pink cherry blossoms, cloudless blue skies, and practically balmy temperatures. In the past, such sights had caused Dickinson's line "I cannot meet the Spring unmoved" to leap spontaneously to mind, but now they struck me as sure signs that everything was falling apart—the world heating up, weather patterns becoming increasingly volatile, storms gathering out at sea. All around me, people reveled—naively, I felt—in this surprise early spring. My students in particular, dressed in tank tops and sundresses, seemed to think nothing of it beyond how lucky they were to enjoy it, as though they'd been put on this earth for no other reason, or as though nature had no purpose but to please them.

There is always a certain smugness, I realize now, to those who refer to themselves as lucky. The words may be "I'm so fortunate" or, worse yet, "blessed," but the subtext is something more like "I *deserve* this." I've been guilty of this myself, just as I've been guilty of using magical thinking to find meaning in coincidence or to see wonder and affirmation in a perfectly predictable chain of cause and effect. I remember quite clearly that night at ladies' poker, the image that came to mind as I said yes, I was lucky: a bright yellow sunbeam shining down on me like a spotlight. How nice it was to see myself that way, to imagine that the sunbeam would follow me wherever I went.

But if we believe, on some level, that we deserve our good fortune, what are we to think when bad luck finds us? That we deserve *it*, too? Some people do seem to have a knack for drawing unfortunate events toward them, and certain negative outcomes can be easily traced back to bad decisions. But what about the parents who toil endlessly for their families without being rewarded? The man who takes a freak fall, or the lung cancer patient who never smoked a day in her life? What about the thousands every year who miscarry or deal with unexplained infertility (or both), while all around them babies appear as effortlessly as dandelion seeds are blown about by the wind?

Long gone are the days when a woman who couldn't conceive or who suffered recurrent miscarriages would be accused of having the devil in her womb, or even of being a witch herself. But we have our own subtle ways of implying there's something other than pure chance at work. Suggestions abound for women trying to conceive, for foods to eat and avoid, exercise regimens to adopt, supplements to take, alternative therapies to try. On the other hand, you might be overthinking things, stressing yourself out, "trying too hard"—one must remember to try only an appropriate amount! It's impolite to blame the victim, but maybe we can't help but feel a little suspicious of the unlucky. Human beings excel at pattern recognition. It's one of the skills that sets us apart as a species, allowing us to anticipate, to reason, to see connections and draw conclusions. We're hardwired to resist the idea of randomness, and so we find endless ways to create the illusion of control. Some lock themselves away at home; others run full speed at every opportunity to confront danger and chaos, as though the risks meant nothing at all. Still others search for signs that fortune favors them, or else assume the opposite, as though by expecting the worst we could insulate ourselves against the pain of disappointment.

Yet for all we resist it, randomness is fundamental to our existence: atoms and molecules bopping around in constant, random motion; the diversity of life that surrounds us the result of accidental genetic changes; the universe itself emerging spontaneously 13.8 billion years ago from a sudden fluctuation in whatever nothingness there was just before that. And somehow, from that distant moment comes this present: in which I find myself visiting specialists and taking tests and diligently swallowing my supplements, grateful for the love of a good man, aching for the gift and the burden of a child, as bewildered now when things go right as I once was when they didn't. ⬡

# Conversation with the Sacred

*Faith* and *religion* are neither synonyms nor antonyms. The religious can be in a state of hopeful doubt about the depth and authenticity of their faith. Those who have faith can feel that it is aligned very inexactly with the doctrines and practices that are meant to express it, and to govern it. And *faith* is not another word for belief. Belief is invested in certain tenets that take the form of factual statements—the Bible is inerrant, the pope is the successor of Peter. Faith, on the other hand, can and must doubt and interrogate. This is true because it exists before and apart from doctrine, and also beside it, pondering its difficulties and its richnesses. It is very Protestant of me, I know, to say faith creates dissent. But faith, in my experience as well as my tradition, has all the potency of conscience. It cannot be excused from its loyalty to itself.

This loyalty is deeper than individual judgment, resting finally on a sense that there is a divine nature attentive to matters of generosity and justice, the things that make the human world beautiful and thriving where they are honored, and a desolation where they are flouted. Faith is not an entitlement, a guarantor of eternal reward. It is a boundless and inexhaustible obligation, sensitive to its own failures and instructed by them, and grateful for the instruction. It opens experience to an awareness that encounter, thought, and perception are always, in the deepest

## Marilynne Robinson

sense, meaningful, and that to be engaged in experience, to be human, is an inestimable privilege. Individually and as a species we are honored by the special character of our participation in experience, which is some part of our likeness to God. This is a statement of faith, of course, which is also faithful to the brilliance and dignity of humankind.

I am a Christian. This means that, for me, the Christian narrative has the authority of great beauty, beauty of the kind whose convergence with truth is absolute. For this reason it has as much influence as I can give it on how I think and how I write. Beauty encodes meaning more richly than doctrine, which is paraphrase, or exegesis, which is also paraphrase, can ever do. This is not to say that these things are not a help to faith, only that they are always tentative, partial, and inexhaustible. They are insufficient to the magnificence of Being itself, which they celebrate in the very fact of falling short.

Every brilliant human work is a celebration of the same kind. But faith can love the failure of the most strenuous thought because it is one side of a conversation with the sacred, and the reply that comes is the wonderful assurance that there is much more, so much more, sacred like the mind that yearns toward it. 🜂

# DREAM TRANSLATIONS FROM THE EARLY HASIDIC AND ELSEWHERE

## Joshua Cohen

*Tell a dream, gain a reader?*

Nachman of Breslov, born in Medzhybizh, present-day Ukraine, in 1772, was the founder of Breslov Hasidism and despite his death, in Uman in 1810, remains the movement's leader. This is why Breslovers have been called, have called themselves, the "Dead Hasidim." Fittingly, their essential principle is what Rebbe Nachman referred to as *hitbodedut*: "self-seclusion," "auto-isolation"—a lone contemplative state to be sought not in a sanctuary but in nature, for the purpose of inspiring spontaneous personal prayer, not necessarily in Hebrew, but in one's most fluent tongue. Breslov, then, can be considered a sect only inasmuch as it's considered a sect of individuals, each of whom pursues a direct and utterly private dialogue with God. The Rebbe's chosen setting for *hitbodedut* was in the woods or fields. His chosen time was in the middle of the night—the time of dreaming. Psychoanalysis defined dream as wish fulfillment, and so allied it with prayer. If it follows that a collective prayer can express a collective dream, then the Breslovers' rejection of community worship might express an unfulfilled wish for extinction: their own, or their people's, the world's.

In 2014, due to a variety of factors too traumatic and banal to recount, I found myself suffering from insomnia and immobilized by depression, and sought psychiatric treatment. I would go to school and deliver my lectures in the mornings, then have two hours to kill—to thought-murder—before my afternoon appointments. I had no appetite for lunch, home was too far. I considered joining a minyan, I considered suicide. Instead, I wound up sitting on a bench in Bryant Park in Manhattan and reading and translating Hasidic texts, which led to my reading and translating texts from elsewhere and earlier in the Jewish tradition (the languages were Hebrew, Yiddish, German, and Aramaic). The following selections are from two of the spiralbounds I was spiraling through at the time—call them wishful dream journals, unfulfilled prayer books: solaces for sleepless yearning.

. . .

Once, in 1802, in the woods outside Breslov, a young Hasid was troubled—about an upcoming marriage? or his sister's infirmity?—and wandered among the trees mumbling a prayer. Another young Hasid was also troubled—perhaps he too had a marriage? or sister?—and, at the same time, was doing the same, wandering and mumbling. Though they were unable to see each other, due to the density of greenery, it is said that they were able to hear each other, and, indeed, not only were their practices the same, their prayers were the same as well. Their individual spontaneous prayers were identical, verbatim.

*Chayey Moharan*, the book's title, means *Life of the Rebbe*. "Moharan" is an acronym: "Morenu, HaRav Nachman," "Our Teacher, Rebbe Nachman." It was compiled, or written, by a disciple called Reb Noson, and contains, amid homiletics and practical advice, numerous accounts of the Rebbe's dreaming. The Rebbe himself features in many of his dreams, and in not a few he importunes another dream-character—to demand an explanation, to demand an interpretation.

Rabbinic opinion differs as to how to interpret the interpretation of a dream that's presented in a dream, but it's significant that even the Rebbe's oneiric interlocutors seem to doubt the endeavor—to doubt the Rebbe's capacities, or intentions. After a particularly wild dream (#83), about twin palaces and swords with multiple blades (one that brings death, one that brings penury, one that brings physical afflictions, etc.), and disciples who swallow sparks that seed strange creatures in their guts, the Rebbe begs "an old man" for his thoughts, and the old man grabs his beard and says, "My beard is the explanation."

Another time, in 1868, a goy merchant from Kiev (or Lvov), was in Lvov (or Kiev), and strolling past a bank, from which an ornament, or the scaffold for the workers installing an ornament, fell—fell on his head—and knocked him into a coma. The goy merchant was kept in hospital, where he babbled in a language suspiciously Hebraic. Brought to interpret was Reb Nachman Chazan, or, in other tellings, one or both of the Lubarsky brothers (Reb Moshe and/or Reb Zanvil). The merchant, despite never being a Jew, was pronouncing a perfect rendition of Ma Tovu, a common Jewish prayer that, when he emerged from his coma, he was unable to remember or even recognize.

Another of the Rebbe's dreams (#85) seems too explicitly didactic. In it, a man is flying one moment, and home the next—he's in a valley, and home again—he's atop a mountain, and home—he's picking golden vessels from a golden tree, home. Is this possible? How is this possible? These are the questions the Rebbe's somniloquous surrogate—"the host"—asks a man, who turns out to be an angel—"the guest." The angel's answer is—like the dream itself—too long, and too intricate with references and puns, but basically he says: "You've been reading."

. . .

The Rebbe had a dream: I was sitting in my room [he said]. No one was around. I got up, went to the other room. No one was around. I went into the house of study, went into the shul, but no one was anywhere. I went outside. People stood around whispering. One laughed at me, another provoked me. Arrogant stares all around. Even my own followers had turned against me. Insolent stares. Whispers around.

I called to one of my followers: *What's going on?* He replied: *How could you have done such a thing?*

I had no idea what he meant and asked him to explain, but he left me. So I traveled to another country, but when I got there, people stood around whispering. Even there, my sin was known. Everyone knew my sin but me. So I went to live with the trees. They became my followers.

We lived together, and whenever I required food, or water, or a book, one of my trees would uproot itself and go scampering into the city to fetch it. When the tree would return, I'd ask: *Has the commotion died down?* to which the tree would reply: *No, the rumor is stronger than ever.*

—*CHAYEY MOHARAN*, REB NOSON, AKA NATHAN STERNHARTZ (1780–44)

Once there was a turkey that dwelled beneath a table, pecking at flecks and bones. The king quit, the doctors and nurses quit, the Rebbe was called for, came. The Rebbe took off his robes, sat under the table, pecked at flecks and bones. The turkey asked: *What are you doing here?* The Rebbe asked: *What are YOU doing here?* The turkey replied: *I'm a turkey*, the Rebbe replied: *So I'm a turkey too.*

They sat together through many meals, the king feasting his queens, orgies of doctors and nurses. Then the Rebbe gave the signal for his shirt, which was tossed to him. He said to the turkey: *What—a turkey can't wear a shirt?* So another shirt was tossed, and both their breasts were covered. Many meals, orgies, and so on. Then the Rebbe gave the signal for his pants. He said to the turkey: *What—a turkey can't wear pants?* And so on, until both were dressed from top to bottom and human foodstuffs—delicacies not yet partaken of above—were hurled.

*One can eat what humans eat and still be a turkey, I assure you,* said the Rebbe, *and what's more—one can rise to sit as humans sit, not under the table, but at the table, in the laps of the feet around us, more commonly referred to as chairs.*

And so they rose, and so they chaired. (The turkey once again became a prince.)

—*KOCHAVEY OR*, REB ABRAHAM CHAZAN (1849–17)

A king once told his vizier: *The stars tell me that he who will eat from this year's grain harvest will go insane—what is to be done?*

The vizier said: *We must set aside a stock of foreign grain, for ourselves, so as to not become tainted.*

But the king objected: *We do not have enough foreign grain for everyone in the kingdom, and if we set aside a foreign stock for just us two,*

*we will be the only ones in the kingdom with intact minds. Everyone else will be insane and yet will come to regard US as insane.*

*It is better, then, for us two to eat from this year's grain harvest, but we will each put a cut on our foreheads, so I will look at your forehead, and you will look at my forehead, and when we see the cuts, at least we will be reminded of our insanities.*

—*SIPURIM NEFLAIM*, REB SHMUEL HOROWITZ (1903–73)

> This world compares to the next world as sleeping does to wakefulness.

One Sabbath a man came to the Rebbe and said, *I am lonely,* and the Rebbe gave him counsel: *Take a wife.*

The man did as instructed, but returned the next Sabbath and said, *Even with a wife I am lonely.* The Rebbe said, *Have children.*

The man did as instructed, but months—even years—later, his complaint remained: *Even with children I am lonely.*

The Rebbe said, *Sleep.*

What does this mean?

It means that one is never lonely in a dream.

—*MAAMARIM YEKARIM*, REB YISROEL DOV BER ODESSER (ca. 1888–94)

• • •

This world compares to the next world as sleeping does to wakefulness. In a dream you are never ashamed. For if you were ashamed, you would never dream of sleeping with a woman—sex would never occur to you. You would never commit acts in your dreams that you would be ashamed of committing awake. The reason for this is that dreams at night stem from the day-time's imaginings.

Once a certain Hasid, who commanded his son not to enjoy this world more than necessary, and not to let more than thirty days pass without a fast, died. But then it transpired that rivals had his corpse disin-terred, and flogged, which grieved all his adepts deeply. He appeared to one of his adepts in a dream and said, *This befell me because I used to live among tattered books with their leaves all shredded and I took no initiative to reassemble and protect them.*

—SEFER HASIDIM

. . .

*in which three things require God's mercy*
Rav Yehudah said in the name of Rav, "Three are the things that require God's mercy: a good king, a good year, a good dream."

*in which sufficiency is its own interpretation*
Rav Hisda said: "Any dream but that of a fast." R. Hisda also: "A dream not inter-preted is like a letter not read." R. Hisda also: "Neither a good dream nor a bad dream is ever completely fulfilled." R. Hisda also: "A bad dream is better than a good dream." R. Hisda also: "The sad-ness of a bad dream is sufficient [in lieu of interpretation] and the happiness of a good dream sufficient too [in lieu of inter-pretation]." R. Yosef: "For me, even the happiness of a good dream nullifies."

*in which sense is derived from grain*
What does chaff have to do with wheat? wondered the Lord—or, better, what's the connection between chaff/wheat and dreaming? "No wheat without chaff," said R. Yochanan in the name of R. Shimon bar Yochai, "just like no dream without nonsense."

*in which something might come to be*
R. Berechyah said, "A dream that seems to tell the future: even though some of it might come to be, not all of it will come to be." How do we know this? From Joseph. As it's written in Torah, Joseph dreamed that the sun and moon and eleven stars were bowing to him, and the sun and moon were to be understood as his parents, and the eleven stars were to be understood as his eleven brothers—yet at the time that Joseph dreamed this, his mother was dead, and the dead do not bow.

*in which is stressed the importance of counting*
R. Levi said: "A man should await the fulfillment of a good dream for as much as twenty-two years—we know this from where? From Joseph. As it's written in Torah: 'These are the generations of Jacob. Joseph being seventeen years old,' and as it's further written in Torah, 'And Joseph was thirty years old when he stood before Pharaoh.' How many years is it from

seventeen to thirty? Thirteen. Add to that the seven years of plenty and the two years of famine, for a sum total of twenty-two."

*in which everybody or nobody gets what he deserves*
R. Huna said, "A good dream is not shown to a good man, an evil dream is not shown to an evil man."

*in which memory lasts not a week*
Though he does not see an evil dream, others see one around him. Is this not seeing evil to be considered an advantage? Hasn't R. Zeira said: "If a man goes seven days without a dream he's called evil, since it says, 'He shall abide satisfied, he shall not be visited by evil?'—Read not *save'a* [satisfied] but *sheva* [seven]." What he means is: A righteous man can see evil in his sleep, but won't remember what he's seen.

*in which it is recommended to combat sadness with rereading*
R. Huna b. Ammi said in the name of R. Pedath who had it from R. Yochanan: If you have a dream that saddens you, you should go and have it interpreted thrice. Hasn't R. Hisda said: A dream uninterpreted is like a letter unread?

*in which a prayer is formulated, the right nostril neglected, and a contradiction is itself contradicted*
Amemar, Mar Zutra, and R. Ashi once sat. They said: "Let each of us say a thing that the others haven't heard." One began: "If one has seen a dream and does not remember what he saw, let him stand before the priests at the time when they spread their hands, and repeat after me: 'Lord my God, I am Thine and my dreams are Thine. I have dreamt a dream incomprehensible. Whether I have dreamt about myself or my companions have dreamt about me, or whether I have dreamt about others, regardless, only if the dreams are good, confirm them like the dreams of Joseph were confirmed, and if they require a remedy, heal them, as the waters of Marah were purified by Moses, as Miriam was cured of her rash and Hezekiah of his boils, as the waters of Jericho were, by Elisha, repristinated. As Thou didst turn the curse of the wicked Balaam into a blessing, so turn all my dreams to good.' He should conclude his prayer along with the priests, so that the congregation may answer, 'Amen.' If he cannot manage this, he should say: 'Thou Who art majestic on high, Who abidest in might, Thou art peace and Thy name is peace— May it be Thy will to bestow peace on us.'" The second commenced: "If a man on venturing into a city is afraid of the evil eye, let him take the thumb of his right hand in his left and the thumb of his left hand in his right, and say: 'I, INSERT NAME, am of the seed of Joseph over which the evil eye has no power, as Torah says: Joseph is a fruitful vine by a fountain.' [. . .] Though if he is afraid of his own evil eye, he must examine his left nostril." The third commenced: "If a man falls infirm, the first day he should not tell anyone, so that he should not have bad luck, but after that he may tell anyone. When Raba fell infirm, on the first day he did not tell, but after that he said to his attendant: 'Go and tell that Raba is wasting. Whoever

loves him, let him pray, and whoever hates him, let him rejoice' [. . .]. When Samuel had a bad dream, he said, 'Dreams speak falsely.' When he had a good dream, he said, 'Do dreams speak falsely?' as it's written in Torah, 'I [God] speak with him in a dream?' It was Raba who pointed out the contradiction. Torah says both 'I [God] speak with him in a dream' and 'dreams speak falsely.' But there isn't any contradiction—in the one case it was communicated through an angel, in the other through a demon."

### in which psychoanalysis is invented

R. Bizna b. Zabda said in the name of R. Akiva who had it from R. Panda who had it from R. Nahum, who had it from R. Biryam reporting a certain elder—and who was this? R. Banaah: "There were twenty-four interpreters of dreams in Jerusalem. Once I dreamt a dream and I went round to all of them and they all gave different interpretations and all were fulfilled, thus confirming that which is said: 'All dreams follow the mouth.'" Is this statement supported by Torah? Yes, according to R. Eleazar. For R. Eleazar said: "From where do we know this, that all dreams follow the mouth? From where Torah says, 'And it came to pass, as he interpreted to us, so it was.'" Raba said: "This is only if the interpretation corresponds to the content of the dream: for it says, 'To each man according to his dream Joseph did

interpret.' The verse continues, 'When the chief baker saw that the interpretation was good'—but how did he know it was good?" R. Eleazar says: "This verse tells us that each of Pharaoh's stewards—the chief baker, the chief cupbearer—was shown not only his own personal dream but also the interpretation of the other's dream."

### in which your dream of a friend goes unmentioned

R. Yochanan: "If one rises early and a Torah verse rises to the lips, this is minor prophecy." R. Yochanan also: "Three kinds of dreams are fulfilled: a predawn dream, a friend's dream of you, and a dream interpreted in the midst of a dream." Some add also, "A recurring dream," as Torah says, "And for that the dream was doubled unto Pharaoh."

### in which an elephant serves as a camel

R. Samuel b. Nachmani said in the name of R. Yonatan: "A man is shown in a dream only what is suggested by his own thoughts, as Torah says, 'As for thee, O King, thy thoughts came into thy mind upon thy bed.' Or if you like, I can derive it from this verse: 'That thou mayest know the thoughts of the heart.'" Raba said: "This is proved by the fact that a man is never shown in a dream a date palm of gold, or an elephant passing through the eye of a needle."

—TALMUD, BERACHOS 55A-B

*If you have a dream that saddens you, you should go and have it interpreted thrice.*

. . .

A legend is told (because the chronology does not fit), of Der Heiliger Ruzhiner, "The Vaunt of Ruzhin," Israel Friedman. He, who knew all, is said to have asked toward his old age for a refreshment of the laws of inheritance. It was thought that he was considering the succession of his schools, but, truly, after bathing clean in his children's murkiest commentaries, he shocked them by dismissing them and inquiring for a secular expert, to relate to him everything of the new sciences of the passage from body, and of the passage from mind.

An evolutionist called at court and spoke and his speech was translated, as so: "What you are, in your characteristics, you transfer to your progeny, Rabbi: not necessarily the exactitudes of your height and weight, or even of your coloration, but only what has allowed you to survive will survive, what is transferred is exactly what is necessary for existence."

Then a psychoanalyst called at court and spoke and his speech was translated, likewise: "What you are, in your characteristics, you transmit to your progeny, Rabbi: both your wisdom and your wickedness, your disappointment and your hope, but in the transmission they will become confused, and your progeny will spend their lives striving after the original definitions."

The Vaunt of Ruzhin, Israel Friedman, nodded.

Only when the scientists were dismissed did he deliver his verdict:

"For such laws not even a fool can be credited: What the evolutionist said, I knew already from my sons. What the psychoanalyst said, I knew already from my daughters."

The legend has been told alternately as having been revealed to the Vaunt of Ruzhin's children—all ten given to him by his first wife, Sarah, daughter of Reb Moshe Ha-Levi Efrati of Berdichev—in a common dream. That very same night, the eve of Passover, the two children of the Vaunt of Ruzhin's second wife, Malka—the boy and girl she had by her first husband, Reb Tzvi Hirsch of Rimanov—also had dreams, but individually.

The boy dreamt that a certain type of cart, a droshky, which normally had four wheels, had been outfitted with twelve, and was being dragged through the market square of Zhitomir by an ancient gray dray horse with a single leg, whose hoof was a human fist. The girl dreamt also of the market square of Zhitomir, but where a goy merchant accosted her, pressed her against a bank, and unbuttoned his coat, though all that was exposed was a samovar, with, instead of a navel, a rusty spigot. The goy forced her hand to turn it, but when nothing flowed, he laughed. She woke up clutching a ruble. 🛡

# Nate Gertzman Draws the Internet

## Daniel Torday

During a particularly easy period for things unrelated to the complicated business of baby-making, a YouTube series I'd started, called *Nate Draws the Internet*, took off. We didn't have happiness, my wife and I, we didn't have certainty—but we had money for the first time. I walked around with David Byrne's voice in my head warbling, *I've got money now, I've got money now*. The money was simple: it arrived weekly in a PayPal account, then was direct deposited into checking so we could spend it on stuff, or on medical bills like the one coming if we had to terminate the pregnancy. The happiness wasn't simple, as I say. It wasn't around yet. It might never find us.

I was teaching a regular slate of classes at a college near our house, where real humans came to sit in real classrooms. I'm a hopeless Luddite and I prohibit technology in my classroom, so whenever it came time for a diatribe on the Internet I had no choice but to draw it. My students and I would find ourselves talking about Facebook. Soon I'd draw a rudimentary box, inside it smaller boxes, and ask, "So what do you have in this space here on your Facebook page?" Then I'd tap my index finger on a box that represented the area where a Facebook user could upload her photograph. Inevitably a student would admit she sometimes put up a picture of Emma Watson or Katy Perry—"All my friends say I look exactly like Katy Perry, and I kinda do I guess," the Katy Perry doppelgänger would say—and admit that, yes, there was something a little odd about that, but.

We talked about books and occasionally smelled each other's breath. That's a thing about being around humans: we sense them, not in some supernatural way, but in an I-can-smell-hear-see/hopefully-not-taste-or-touch-you way. More often than not we didn't like it—who wants to smell even the wintermintiest breath?—but because we were humans sharing physical space this was an unavoidable fact. Sometimes I would ask some-one for a stick of gum. Increasingly what I found myself doing in class-rooms was drawing chalkboard drawings of what we just minutes earlier, before we arrived in class, had all been looking at on our computer screens.

Around this time all the colleges were starting to create things they called MOOCs. M-O-O-C stood for "massive open online course." MOOCs were just video textbooks. These MOOCs would supposedly one day make a lot of money, so people at the college where I taught asked, "Should we make MOOCs?" Everyone said, "No!" The next year instead of asking, "Should we make MOOCs?" someone asked, "Can we afford *not* to make MOOCs?" The physicists said, "Yes," and the philosophers said, "Is this a teleological or an epistemological problem?"

Nothing was decided.

So at the prompting of a student who knew how to produce them, I started shooting segments that were posted online, and were open, but weren't MOOCs; I uploaded them to YouTube: *Nate Draws Facebook. Nate Draws Nate Watching an Episode of The Daily Show on Hulu after Suffering through a Long "Advertising Experience." Nate Draws the Waze Directions from His Recent Zipcar Rental.* Not one of these things was writing a poem, which was the thing I wanted most in life to do, but instead of getting back to that work I set up a camera. I stood in front of a chalkboard and Reader, while there are so many screens we look at it on, I turned my back on it all, and with all my heart and meager skill, I drew the Internet.

> The happiness wasn't simple, as I say. It wasn't around yet. It might never find us.

Soon the number of hits I was receiving suggested I had a thousand viewers, then a hundred thousand, then well into the millions.

Then I looked at my PayPal account.

I got an email from someone at YouTube who said they would like to make me one of a select group of posters who would be put on a special channel, who would receive corporate sponsorship.

I stopped teaching for the year and instead made segments.

Then my wife and I went to look at a different kind of screen, for our twenty-week ultrasound, and our OB said something about the baby maybe didn't look so good.

. . .

This was a rough time for Gillian and me in ways that didn't pertain to my successes drawing the Internet—or to my marked lack of success in my chosen art. For years we'd wanted a baby, but we didn't have money. In order properly to raise a baby you need to have money to spend on food for the baby, then on its care and education, then expensive sneakers. When I was a kid my father took me to buy a pair of David Robinson's Reebok Pumps and those Reebok Pumps cost $129.99 back in the early 1990s, so adjusting for inflation, a pair of sneakers now would cost . . . Well, I'm no quant wizard. I'm more of a qual guy (meaning qualification) if that's a thing (it's not). But a lot. Shoes would cost a lot. And now we finally had money for shoes—and instead the OB said it was possible, not certain but possible, that something about the baby didn't look so good.

I should also pause here to say that when I say "we'd wanted a baby" that is not quite a fully accurate depiction of the truth. Being in a married couple is a miraculous experience of symbiosis. But there are still two separate beings, each with his/her own desires. My half of the organism came around slowly to the baby-making. Or the one-day-baby-having, anyway. I'd grown up with a brother who was born blind and mute. I loved him beyond words, but life was difficult for him in obvious ways, ways that had been tangible to me since before I could remember. I saw the strain it put on my parents. I was scared beyond words of having a kid. For years I pushed against the idea, while being regularly engaged in the physical act that might make it a reality. One day Gillian called and said, "I'm pregnant." The crazy thing? All at once, it was okay. All the Trojans and pullouts and Plan B: vanished. All the anxiety, too.

We were going to have a kid!

Then suddenly maybe we weren't.

. . .

At the end of the week Gillian and I both took off work. We drove along the river to the hospital where we would have another ultrasound. This was four days after the initial one. We were already into Week 21. We didn't say much. Gillian looked out the window at the glittering silver tinsel atop the river to our left, the corners of her mouth drawn down. When

> **We were going to have a kid! Then suddenly maybe we weren't.**

she looked back, where once she would have looked at me, instead she swiped the screen on her phone, tapped the four digits of her PIN, touched things with her fingertips. I imagined myself drawing her on a chalkboard: *Nate Draws a Woman Looking at an iPhone on a Potentially Life-Altering Car Ride.* Not exactly the source material for YouTube clickbait.

"What are you looking at?" I asked. I knew the answer: The Ultrasound. But I asked anyway.

"Nothing," Gillian said. By which she meant: The Ultrasound.

"You know we could talk about it, about how you're feeling," I said.

"I think we should talk about nothing at all right now, Nate. Once we hear what we hear, then there will be something to talk about." She was about to look back down at her screen when she stopped and looked instead at me. "Sorry. It's just so awful, this waiting. I mean, I feel like it would almost be okay if I just knew we needed to terminate. We could do it and start trying again. But this waiting. This waiting."

Then she did look back down at her screen.

The OB's office was on the fourth floor of a building on Market Street, where on every corner an upstart university had planted its flags. This upstart university had existed for a very long time before the advent of the Internet without putting up flags, but they'd put all their eggs in the basket of technology. Good choice of basket. They had hundreds of millions of dollars and more MOOCs than you could count. They'd turned those dollars into the ownership of parcels of land right in the middle of the city. Gillian worked as the editor of the psychology research journal said flag-posting university produced. She got good health benefits, and Fridays to herself.

We waited in an anteroom and then a post-anteroom and then a pre-waiting room, each of which had flat-screen TVs fixed to their walls, blaring the same midday talk show. The OB's medical assistant took Gillian's blood pressure. Then we waited in the waiting room. Then we were finally taken into an examination room. Then the OB came in.

"Well let's get you up there and see what we can see," Dr. Singh said. She pulled up Gillian's T-shirt to reveal the small bump that had arisen there, as though Gillian's stomach was pushing out after too much sushi. She spread clear goop all around and then ran the paddle over and over and over it. I held Gillian's hand and she held mine, but she didn't look at me. One fact about being in a room with actual humans is that in addition to smelling their breath—Gillian's is minty, always fresh, though I've never seen her chew gum—you can hold eye contact or not. Your whole mood might change based on subtle shifts in how long it is held. Gillian didn't hold mine long. On a screen in front of us was the ultrasound, a muddy hash of unreadable lines that Dr. Singh was attempting to read. It looked like trying to tell what spices were in a marinara sauce by sliding a spoon through the cooking murk.

"My son is a big fan," Dr. Singh said.

"Of what?" Gillian said.

Dr. Singh looked over at me. I couldn't help but smile. Then I saw that Gillian still didn't know what we were talking about.

"He wanted me to tell you that you should do *Nate Draws Twenty-four Insane Justin Bieber Fans*. Thinks that one would be funny." Gillian looked up at Dr. Singh with a scowl, then over at the screen. "And telling," Dr. Singh said. "Funny and telling."

Gillian looked at me, then back at her doctor again.

"That stupid show," she said.

Dr. Singh looked into the ultrasound's screen and pushed the paddle over and over my wife's stomach. Her face showed no emotion. What she had to say next was the worst thing I've ever heard in my life. I won't do you the pain of repeating it here. Later that night we sat on our couch and tried to watch television, until at some point Gillian simply stood up and turned it off and said, "We need to at least say goodbye."

So we did. We sat on the couch together and we each put our hands on her stomach, and we said goodbye.

. . .

In the period after the procedure I would have liked to sit down to write a poem about it, to imagine my way into a life with a little bundle of sweet rabbit in our house—sleeplessness punctuated by that calm of entering the home fresh with baby. It's a feeling we'd come to know well. We were in our late thirties, after all. All our friends were baby-making, talking about that sweet fresh smell on their babies' mouths. By dint of present-giving I knew the difference between a BOB jogging stroller and a Bugaboo pram. I knew of the genius of having the happiest baby on the block after reading *The Happiest Baby on the Block*. We'd entered countless homes full of gifted lasagna and bowls the size of bowler hats full of quinoa salads teeming with feta and chocolate heirloom grape tomato goodness.

We wanted that.

We lived instead now in this other space, the space between, the space before or never, where tranquility was something we could taste and hear and somehow feel, but after which we came home to our house to binge watch episodes of *Friends*.

Instead of looking back over a sestina I was working on, I went into the recording studio. Today we were recording an episode of *Nate Draws Last Night's SportsCenter's Web Gems*. I picked up the chalk. I did my best to draw the Kansas City Royals' center fielder outstretched, then tucked like a roly-poly bug after hitting the green field, catching a baseball that should have eluded his grasp. Only this time while I was drawing—and it was on, my chalk skills were becoming something my ability to make a simile had never been—the door opened. Gillian was standing there.

"Am I interrupting?" she said. Her face was white as a frog's belly. Her hand was on the bump at the middle of her body. It had been a week since the procedure. I said of course not.

**What she had to say next was the worst thing I've ever heard in my life.**

We went out to lunch at a nearby pho place. I ordered a killer fried pork banh mi and Gillian sat with a bowl the size of her head full of brothy liquid.

"I had to proofread an awful case history for the journal today," Gillian said. "It was about the mother of a kid who was severely injured. He fell out of a tree. Compound fractures to both arms. For some reason seeing it set the mother off into catatonia. Brought up some past trauma. All I could think was, I wish we had a kid who had fallen out of a tree."

"You don't wish that," I said. Gillian looked up at me. She held the big plastic spoon in her hand, thick white sprouts and mint leaves suspended in thin liquid.

"You know what I mean," she said.

"I know what you mean."

"Are we there now, Nate? Are you ready to try again? Because I'm ready to try again. ASAP."

I told her her body wasn't ready yet.

"I know," she said. "I'm not talking about bodies."

There was a thin white to her skin that made it so you could tell she hadn't slept the night before. The thing about her face, about the real Gillian face on the real Gillian before me, was that there was this subtle pink glow that throbbed and emitted light just beneath the surface. This is what happens if you look at a real person: there are three dimensions, sure. There's also another thing. Light fell across Gillian's face from the picture windows behind us, the sunlight on the street. But light came from *inside* her face, too. It's not a thing you think about every day, it's not a thing you notice if you're not looking hard, but it's a thing. A patina. Human.

It was something that drawing the Internet, or the Internet, or a video on the Internet, would never bring. It was love. It was also something far simpler, the experience of there-being.

"I want to have a kid," I said.

> No one wants to watch a man deal with the very personal pain of attempting to depict an ultrasound on a chalkboard drawing.

"I do, too," she said, and for the first time I felt it—that it would happen, that it would take time but that we would try and try until we had done it. Whatever it took.

The tears that fell down into her pho were of the exact consistency and color of the pho broth. The tears that fell on my fried pork banh mi just made the white-bread roll the slightest bit soggy.

· · ·

There are a lot of facts: a number of weeks. A list of states in which the number of weeks we were into the pregnancy would have made it illegal to do what we did. A number of pieces of legislation proposed in Congress to make that time frame ever smaller. Chromosomes pairing off into gametes through the process of meiosis. Things we said to each other that were kind and things that were hurtful but grimaced at, not taken in, understood to be the product of undigested grief.

Those things are the Internet.

All these words are a drawing of the Internet.

· · ·

The next day I had another installment to shoot. Most of my installments for the YouTube videos had been straightforward: things people did on the Internet already, only I was drawing me doing them. The plan for today was to do a session called *Nate Draws a Google Maps Search of His Block*. I would do two drawings next to each other: On the left, the whole US, so far from where we stood, a perspective so distant it was just an outline and some shading. But then on the right, fingers pinch tight on the screen, bringing us up to our neighborhood in West Philly—lines running vertical and diagonal, street names, landmarks. Maybe I'd even draw our house through Street View. Recognizable. Fixed in time.

But when I got to work, I walked into the production studio and stood in front of the chalkboard and found myself drawing something different. I'd never before drawn a screen that wasn't the Internet, but screens are screens are screens are screens. My crew was there—when I say crew I really just mean a sophomore named Brittany who knows more about DV production at nineteen than entire retirement homes full of teeming senescence, and our technical director, Farah, whose job is to turn the lights on in the classroom. They were set up and ready for me to draw me searching Google Maps.

"This is a different kind of screen," I said. "It's mostly just brown, and you can't really make anything out."

Brittany laughed. Then she could see I wasn't laughing and she stopped.

We shot the rest of the segment though we knew, all of us, from the moment I started drawing—from the moment Farah flipped the light switch—we wouldn't upload it. YouTube has its limits. And what would you draw, anyway? So much of the time the ultrasound screen was just a muddle of brown haze, Google Maps finger-spread so far out you almost couldn't see landmasses. No one wants to watch a man deal with the very personal pain of attempting to depict an ultrasound on a chalkboard drawing. It was hard enough to write down words on a page. Maybe I would go back to writing after all. Maybe Gillian and I would have baby after baby, she could quit her job at the journal and we would populate our own private nursery—a whole city block—with babies who would wake up all night for indecipherable reasons and we would never sleep again, room after infinite room full of the quiet tranquility of infant care, and one day all those infinite babies would grow up to be infinitely loving infinitely caring brothers and sisters.

A friend said the experience of having his second son was the experience, all at once, of seeing his own death and accepting mortality all in one move—I'd just look at my sons, the guy said, and I'd think, One day they'll be fifty-five, hanging out together at a vacation rental in Cape May or Rehoboth or Shelter Island, and I'll be dead, and it makes me honestly truly happy to think of it, to have given up my fear of my own mortality because these two kids, they just make me feel so happy, knowing it—

But for now it was just Nate Gertzman drawing a box on a screen, shading it in with a piece of chalk, recognizing it was a mess, erasing it and doing it again and again until maybe it looks like you can just make out in the mess of chalk a hand, some fingers, the gentle arc of a skull every now and again but really it's just a smear of chalk being smeared and erased over and over and over, etc., ad infinitum, the end.

# Not Even Wrong

One of the most difficult things to outgrow is the need for, the belief in, permanent things. Fixities, finalities, poles on which you can place your hand and say, *This I believe*, like that old Edward R. Murrow radio show from the fifties that asked great men (almost always men) to map their minds for us—that we might map our own.

> To me mankind, a vast family of creatures, is growing inevitably towards a state of civilization.
>
> GEORGE LESLIE STOUDT

> I believe that this hairless embryo with the aching oversized braincase and the opposable thumb—this animal barely up from the apes—will endure, will endure longer than his home planet, will spread out to the other planets—to the stars and beyond—carrying with him his honesty, his insatiable curiosity, his unlimited courage, and his noble essential decency.
>
> ROBERT A. HEINLEIN

You get the idea. It's hard to imagine such confident encompassing sentiments now. (Indeed, when the series was revived briefly in recent years

## Christian Wiman

it was striking just how different it was from the original, relying mostly on the modest observations and easily digestible anecdotes that are the currency of our own atomized time.) The sententious statements from the Murrow program aren't "untrue" exactly. They're not even wrong, as the theoretical physicist Peter Woit has said about string theory. Human intelligence and culture undoubtedly *have* developed over time, as these men predicted, but one of the ways that humans have developed, it turns out, has been an increasingly sophisticated understanding of the limitations of human development. The need for certainties, for "belief," is a symptom of intellectual adolescence, and it can afflict a culture as well as an individual consciousness. (And can express itself as militant atheism. And can recur. Cultures oscillate in and out of different forms of maturity. There is no straight line.) Religion often gets blamed for this addiction to absolutes, and rightly so, insofar as creeds calcify into mere concepts, are dead superstitions rather than the framework for living intuitions. But the religion that doesn't realize this, however lively and thriving it may seem in certain corners of the earth, is feeding on a corpse.

The one place in contemporary intellectual culture where you still find this language of human triumphalism is in science. Stephen Hawking has famously declared philosophy (by which he means all metaphysics) "dead" because it has not—indeed cannot—keep up with modern science. Brian Greene, though he is eloquent and inspiring on his own sense of wonder, believes adamantly that there is no such thing as free will, that even your decision whether or not to read my next sentence has been preordained by the anonymous bits of information in the sleek machine that is your brain. And these are the *physicists*, whose wispy theoretical musings sometimes seem akin to the intuitions of medieval mystics. Turn to the neuroscientists, who every other day publish some article explaining how a blob of mayonnaise causes your brain to "light up" because one of your ancestors was almost eaten by a saber-toothed tiger, or the cognitive scientists (e.g., Daniel Dennett, who believes that consciousness is a benign "user illusion"), and you begin to feel every last bit of intellectual and spiritual oxygen sucked out of existence. There has been some salutary resistance to this totalizing impulse (from the physicist Marcelo Gleiser, for instance), but one would have to be in a monastery or a madhouse not to realize that an austere version of scientific materialism and determinism has permeated the intellectual air so thoroughly that it seems like . . . air.

As it happens, I actually *agree* with some of the assumptions made by some of the scientists who most irritate me. The difference is that I believe they are assumptions, and I disagree with the conclusions. If you assert that we can predict the fundamental nature of human experience from the fundamental laws of physics, then you must admit the element of conjecture therein. Quantum mechanics doesn't somehow salvage the supernatural, but it does introduce quite a weird and seemingly ineradicable wiggle into the natural. More crucially, though, pointing out the physical nature of a metaphysical experience (the brain lighting up, for instance) says nothing about the reality of that experience, nor does a metaphysical experience, no matter how intense and transformative, preclude physical cause. Just as we do not seriously question the reality of physical existence, although we are determining that reality on mathematical calculations of elements that we cannot physically perceive, so we cannot discount the spiritual content of physical reality. "'Exist' may be too strong a verb," says Gleiser of the electrons on which so much of quantum physics is based, although no one has ever actually "seen" one. (Scientists measure their trace.) Well, if "exist" can be too strong a verb, then it can probably sometimes be too weak as well. *I am that I am.*

The idolatry of science that surrounds us now is a symptom of superstition and not, as the scientists argue, a remedy for it. The superstition involves math and matter rather than ghosts and gods, but the leap into belief, which is the refusal of faith, is the same. (By "faith" I mean an admission that our minds cannot know our selves or the universe in any ultimate sense; or, if one is inclined to hold—as many scientists are—that the universe and our place in it are knowable even if such knowledge is in its infancy, then an admission that this position is an act of faith and indistinguishable, in metaphysical terms, from a religious gesture.) Not long ago I sat listening to a brilliant chemist explain the immense existential relief he felt when he realized that every single thing about humans is explained by evolution, including not only our need to have things explained but also our inability ever to understand those explanations at either the macro- or microscopic level. (Richard Dawkins has said much the same thing.) This is the ouroboros, the snake with its tail in its mouth, the circular reasoning from which there is no escape. "No greater clarity should be sought than reality permits." Does it help at all that this quote comes from a renowned physicist? I expect not, for he—John Polkinghorne—is also a renowned believer. This I believe: that we—priests and penitents, geneticists and journalists, physicists and philosophers—will never outgrow our need to say, *This I believe.* 🜨

## SACRED SPRING

Roman
water gods
and the driftwood
and to hike
over islands
to visit
marketplaces
and the food
and the people
the great
ships come
and go
the sky
on fire
cobbled
and crowned
alone
and happy
walking by the surf
and make
fire in
darkness
in the wild grass

I am *Ver Sacrum*
I am sacred spring
everyone no one
blowing
bubbles
everyone no one
throwing
babies in the air
in crunch position
shaking hands
with danger

# BAPTISM

My father
held up his hand
in a square.

It looked
like a slap.

My foot kept
coming up
out of the water.

After the bomb
they made
me write 8.

Over and over.

I drew two circles
joined together.

You start
sinning at 8.

Sinning
is infinity.

The spirit
is supposed
to stay
white.

Go inside
and give
it a scrub.

I was always
dirty.

8 is the beginning
of wisdom.

# PASSOVER,
## A CONVERSATION

### Adam and Jonathan Wilson

*Gut Yontiff, mensches.*

More than any other holiday, Passover is concerned with issues of parenting. Its hero is Moses, the original orphan, raised in the palace of his people's oppressors. Its story climaxes with the tenth plague: the killing of the firstborn. And I'm always strangely moved when, after closing the Red Sea behind the escaping Israelites, and sending the chasing Egyptian army to its watery doom, God chastises the angels for celebrating: the Egyptians, he explains to the angels, are also his children.

The seder is the only ritual I can think of in the Jewish faith that doesn't merely encourage the participation of children but actively demands it. For starters, the group's youngest member is tasked with asking the Four Questions, a series of queries that request explanation for certain aspects of the seder. After the meal, the children search for the Afikomen, a piece of broken-off matzoh that's hidden earlier by an adult. The game's simplicity is deceptive. It's a symbolically loaded ritual in which, according to some scholars, the children are tasked with metaphorically reunifying the diaspora. (This might explain why one of my cousins, a

thirty-eight-year-old PhD in astrophysics, still insists on participating despite being well past the appropriate age.) Even the delaying of the meal until after the first half of the seder seems designed to hold the children's attention. Everywhere there's emphasis on planning for the future, on making sure the next generation understands the burdens and triumphs of its ancestors. Perhaps this makes sense; Passover takes place in spring, and its origins are in pagan rites that celebrated budding and flowering. But I find something distinctly Jewish in the stress on education. Procreation is encouraged, but it's not exactly free. We're constantly reminded of the moral obligations it begets.

I've always found the Haggadah's discussion of the four sons—the Wise Son, the Rebellious Son, the Simple Son, and the Son Who Does Not Even Know How to Ask—to be one of its most compelling and confounding sections. It instructs how each son should be invited to participate in the performance of the exodus. The Wise Son is inducted into the group's collective voice. He is part of the "we" that recall being slaves in Egypt. So is the Simple Son. The implication seems to be that the Son Who Does Not Even Know How to Ask is not old enough for inclusion, but eventually will be. Like the Son Who Does Not Know How to Ask, the Rebellious Son is also excluded, but in his case, there is no

implication that his exclusion is temporary. Rather than treating his insolence as a passing phase, something to extinguish with love and kindness, we are told to reinforce his choice by exiling him to the role of spectator.

I'm not sure I understand why. It seems unnecessarily cruel, and I've always found myself sympathizing with the Rebellious Son because of his maltreatment. Perhaps I relate; in high school, I used to show up to our family's seders stoned and zone out until the food came. It felt like a private act of rebellion, a rejection of what seemed to be a ridiculous and obsolete ritual. More so, perhaps it was an unconscious rejection of my father, who ran the seder with a professorial authority I couldn't help but envy.

My father conducts the seder a bit like a college class: he calls on people to answer questions, and much time is devoted to the free flow of ideas. Digressions and theological debate are encouraged. Though I currently teach in universities, as a teenager I did not thrive in the classroom setting. It wasn't that I was uninterested in studying so much as I'd set my own curriculum, with a heavy emphasis on Joint Rolling 101 and a survey of All-You-Can-Eat Chinese lunch buffets in the metro Boston area.

I later came to love many things about Passover. I love the food, for one. There are the symbolic bitter herbs, which in my family take the form of my aunt Suzi's

> I later came to love many things about Passover. I love the food, for one.

sinus-clearing homemade beet horseradish. There is my mother's chunky and delicious haroseth, a mixture of apples, spices, dried fruit, and crumbled walnuts that symbolizes both the mortar used by the brick-laying slaves and the sweetness of their freedom after the exodus. I love the nonsymbolic items too, like my grandmother's squash soufflé. I recently saw the recipe for the first time and realized why it's so tasty—a full cup of white sugar.

More than the food, though, I love the mix of people that gather around our table each year: family and friends, artists and academics, children and geriatrics. One seder featured a fierce debate between my uncle's militantly Communist Jewish cousin and a friend of mine from college whose parents were Cuban dissidents, and another year my father nearly gave my mother's parents heart attacks by insisting that, according to his research, it seemed unlikely that the Israelites were ever actually in Egypt. The Four Questions have been asked at our table in many languages, including Portuguese and Mandarin (the latter by Ying Han, a Chinese scholar from Beijing and an expert on Isaac Bashevis Singer, and who appeared to know more about seders than anyone else present). And I'd be remiss if I didn't mention my uncle's late father, Sidney Katz, a one-time card-carrying American Communist who was hunted by McCarthy, and who insisted,

each year, that we sing the old African American spiritual "Go Down Moses."

Last year my parents came down from Boston to celebrate the holiday with my fiancée, Sarah, and me and a small group of friends at our Brooklyn apartment. This was the first time I'd hosted a seder. I cooked for two days, making both brisket and chicken, as is family tradition, and Sarah made haroseth and set a beautiful seder plate.

But my father led the seder. I'm not ready yet; I still have much to learn.

In my ongoing effort to embody the Wise Son, I've come up with my own set of Four Questions that I'm hoping my father can answer. I'm interested in his Talmudic commentaries (this is a guy who subscribes to a magazine called *Biblical Archeological Review*), but more so in his own memories of Passover. His most recent book, a memoir about his lifelong obsession with soccer, which in large part documents growing up Jewish in London in the 1950s and 1960s, shed light on aspects of his upbringing I knew nothing about, and now I'm eager for more.

The great Isaac Babel once wrote that the Jew has "spectacles on his nose" and "autumn in his heart." I've never been quite sure what he meant, but I like the description; it seems to speak to a balance between scholarship and emotion, the head and the heart. As I type this, Sarah's out on our patio raking leaves in this

> Aside from the pickles, as a child I found most of the food a little gross.

November's unseasonable warmth. I can see her through the window. I'm wearing glasses.

—ADAM WILSON

## 1.

**ADAM WILSON:** My earliest memories of Passover are culinary: the blandness of *shmurah* matzoh and the burn of home-made horseradish. What jumps out most, weirdly, are pickles. There was always a bowl on the table. They weren't pickles, really, just cut-up cucumbers bathing in white vinegar. But they were the only item we were allowed to eat before the meal—you could nosh on them during the first half of the seder. Aside from the pickles, as a child I found most of the food a little gross. Only years later did I realize this was because my grandmother refused to season her cooking with salt in deference to my grandfather's high cholesterol. Do you remember us searching high and low for a saltshaker one year, then sneaking it to the table? Adding salt to the meal was like the first time I put on a pair of glasses: I could see!

I'm wondering about your earliest memories of Passover, specifically the meal. Were there pickled cucumbers on your seder table? Brisket? Salt? Growing up in England, did the local cuisine have a presence on the seder table?

**JONATHAN WILSON:** At age five, I was obliged, as the youngest in my family, to attempt the Four Questions at our northwest London seder. I already had a library card, so reading the English wouldn't have been a problem, but in our observant Orthodox home, the Haggadah—that wonderful saga with its mishmash of history, legend, short fiction, prayer, Talmudic glosses, blessings, poetry, and song—was recited entirely in Hebrew. Only my father truly understood what he was reading: my two older brothers (who in misery and anarchy had made their way through the occluded world of weeknight and Sunday Hebrew school) could "read" Hebrew but had only negligible powers of translation: to this day the vast majority of Jewish Hebrew "readers" in the diaspora cannot tell "basket" from "bulrushes." I must have somehow stumbled through at least the first sentence, with help, but I did not sing, as seems to be customary in most other parts of the world; in the English tradition, we preferred dramatic soliloquy.

As to the meal itself, it was unwaveringly kosher, and, possibly thanks to the end of fourteen years of war-induced food rationing in the UK, there were enough eggs to go around in their saltwater baths. There was chicken soup and homemade gefilte fish, which was eaten with a dollop of *chrain*, or horseradish. The wine was Palwin, the British equivalent of Manischewitz, so named due to its origins with the nineteenth-century vintners, the Palestine Wine and Trading Company, whose vineyards were in Rishon LeZion. Of the main course, which must have included the staples brisket and potatoes, I remember little, except that it was served on special kosher-for-Passover plates reserved only for this night and placed on a spotless white tablecloth.

The word "cuisine" was not in our vocabulary, but my mother was a good cook and an excellent baker, a skill she probably picked up from her father. (He owned and operated a small bakery in Dalston.) There were indeed sweet-and-sour pickled cucumbers that my mother selected from a barrel in a neighborhood grocery, Brooks, where the floor was covered in sawdust. If, on returning home, she found their consistency inadequate, she returned them.

Seder time was measured in the sliding of individual yarmulkes (called *kappels* in our community) into a partial eclipse of the foreheads of their wearers. In the drowsy hours I turned the pages of my Children's Haggadah, spinning a cardboard wheel of the ten plagues, or pulling a tab at the side of a page to drown the Egyptian army in the Red Sea or bring baby Moses in his basket of reeds down the waters of the Nile. God performed a number of miracles, and Pharaoh learned a lesson about hubris in devastating fashion. While my father led the seder it was my mother who orchestrated the evening in her inimitable fashion, part Virginia Woolf's Mrs. Ramsay and part Deborah, the only female judge mentioned in the Hebrew Bible: either way an equally formidable opponent for Pharaoh.

There was considerable back-and-forth at the table. Despite our family's careful observation of dietary laws and adherence to the text (we didn't skip) we were all freethinkers. The possible exception was my father, a compassionate moral compass whose devotion was genuine and who certainly believed in the power of prayer, the centrality of ritual, and the adherence to code. His position as company secretary in Great Britain's United Synagogue (the governing body of the country's Orthodox synagogues) determined that his family appear devout, but this was a social requirement that had little to do with belief or God. For example, the tenets of Orthodox practice were frequently overruled by my mother: God may have stipulated that matzoh was to be eaten until sundown on the eighth day of Passover, but my mother, her Englishness trumping her Jewishness, insisted it was perfectly okay to have toast and tea at 4:00 PM on the festival's last day.

Precisely what the seder meant to my father is mysterious to me: born in London in 1906, he lost sixty-two Polish relatives in the Holocaust, uncles, aunts (eight of my grandmother's siblings), cousins; adults, children, babies, but we only learned of them decades after my father had died in 1965. The line in the Haggadah "It is not only one that has risen up against us to destroy us but in every generation they rise against us to annihilate us" must have carried a special, and unimaginable, weight for him.

2.

**AW:** I'm pretty sure the first time I got drunk was at a seder. I must have been about ten. I vaguely remember retiring to the living room and watching the Boston Celtics on my grandparents' old TV on which, for some reason, the color green came out as blue. My head spun as I tracked the Celtics' strangely blue uniforms. As far as I know, the only other Jewish ritual at which a child is given wine is at his own bris, when a drop is poured into the infant's mouth during the removal of his foreskin. In a sense, I find this similar to wine's function at Passover in that it is used both to help us celebrate and to remind us of pain—during the reading of the plagues it's meant to symbolize spilt blood. Jews aren't historically thought of as big drinkers. We're known for our temperance. Do you think this has anything to do with the way alcohol is incorporated into our religious rituals? Or is this a recent thing that has more to do with the immigrant work ethos, or persecution paranoia, needing to keep our wits about us? Or is it simply another incarnation of the way guilt rules our lives?

**JW:** The endearingly myth-busting scholar Theodor Gaster long ago explained that the four cups of wine ritual, usually explained as a symbolic replacement for four expressions in Exodus that describe God's deliverance of Israel, is more than likely Roman in origin, a normal Roman dinner (then as now?)

requiring a minimum of three cups for the various libations (Gods, guests, hosts, or emperors). But the seder has come to focus on the number four. Four glasses of wine, four questions, four sons or children: the latter two are fixed in the Haggadah; the first, like a speed limit, is only a suggestion. As the evening progresses and dullness or stupefaction sets in, it is not uncommon for imbibers to push beyond the minimum required.

But it is true that Jews do not have much of a reputation as big drinkers. "If drunk, still only drunk Jews. So far and no further," says Nathan Zuckerman describing himself and the writer E. I. Lonoff as they sip brandy in Philip Roth's *The Ghost Writer*. And yet moderation is not exactly temperance, and reputation is not always reality, and even if it is there are always significant exceptions. Eleven years ago, I was in Dublin interviewing locals for a piece about Bloomsday and the city's declining Jewish community (about nine hundred Jews are left). I asked one member of a dynastic political Irish Jewish family if there was any difference between Irish Jews and Jews in the rest of the world. He lifted his hand toward his mouth and made the traditional gesture for emptying a tumbler of whiskey.

Also, it's probably worth noting that during Prohibition the sale of wine was permitted for religious purposes, a

> While my father led the seder it was my mother who orchestrated the evening in her inimitable fashion.

loophole that opened a straight road to bootlegging for those Jews and Catholics who were inclined to travel it.

## 3.

**AW**: Before he died, Oliver Sacks wrote a moving piece about craving gefilte fish during his final bout with cancer. It was something his mother used to make. He hadn't eaten it in years, but in his weakened state, he developed the craving. I have no love for gefilte fish myself, but at the first sign of flu or head cold I demand matzoh ball soup and pickles. You grew up in the same London neighborhood as Dr. Sacks, and I imagine that if you didn't get your gefilte from the same trough as he did, your trough couldn't have been much different. Was gefilte fish better back then? What do you crave when you're sick? And why do we ultimately find comfort in the foods from our childhood?

**JW**: Sacks was a contemporary of my older brother Geoffrey, and he grew up in an observant Jewish family much like my own in the northwest London suburb of Willesden. His parents owned one of the larger houses in the neighborhood, on Mapesbury Road, a short walk from our semidetached. (For a few years before World War II my mother, newly wed and new to the neighborhood, was a patient of Sacks's father, Dr.

> No matter how much I learn, there's a part of me that still feels like the Rebellious Son.

Samuel Sacks, whom she admired greatly.) I don't know how her gefilte fish shaped up next to Sacks's mother's, but they probably bought their carp at the same fishmonger. I think I avoided eating gefilte fish for as long as I could—the word "gefilte" put me off and the taste was bland, or too fishy, or the carrot slice on top was unappealing, and I didn't like the fish-broth jelly residue—but in the end I grew to like it, or at least began to respect it in the way that Larry David respects wood.

As for those childhood edible delights, and the cravings that persist into adulthood, I think we all know what Dr. Freud would say, or Dr. Roth in *The Anatomy Lesson*, which begins, "When he is sick every man wants his mother; if she's not around, other women must do." When I was ill as a child (I had tonsillitis eleven times) my mother always brought me Lucozade, an early effervescent energy drink, and the latest issues of those superb comic books *The Beano* and *The Dandy*. To be honest, I am not sure which I prefer, four glasses of Lucozade and *The Beano* or four cups of wine and the Haggadah.

## 4.

**AW**: I imagine you'll eventually retire from running the seder, and that my brother or I will inherit the task. If I'm up for it, it's because I've spent years watching you perform the ritual. I know which sections to linger on, and which to skip over if people are getting hungry. I've seen you engage a bored-looking people by having them read passages aloud, or asking them questions you feel they might personally find interesting. I know that a long seder needs a lot of laughter. That said, I'm afraid that my biblical knowledge is still rather limited. No matter how much I learn, there's a part of me that still feels like the Rebellious Son.

It occurs to me that this is not so different from becoming a college professor—unlike schoolteachers, future professors aren't given pedagogical instruction; we figure it out from watching others. It's like cooking too, a skill that's passed down through observation and then honed through trial and error. Or at least that's how it used to be. These days there are classes for everything, and instruction videos on YouTube. I learned to cook mostly from television. I'm curious as to your evolution as a seder leader. How did your father run the seder? When did you first start to do it yourself? How has your approach to the seder changed over the years?

**JW:** I began leading family seders about twenty years ago, after your American grandfather felt that he didn't want, or didn't have the energy, to do it anymore. At first I made use of a Haggadah created by my friend Gabriel Levin's father, Meyer Levin (the author of *Compulsion* and many other novels). Meyer's Haggadah was quirky, disrupted the traditional order of

the narrative, and threw in some poetry from the Song of Songs for good measure. I found it aesthetically appealing. The book had a kind of starlit evanescence and nice pictures of wild flowers, but it tended to confuse everyone else, so at some point I switched to Michael Shire's *The Illuminated Haggadah*, which features images from medieval manuscripts in the British Library and probably assuages my nostalgia for English spelling. These days there are Haggadahs that appeal to every constituency: in progressive versions, almost all of which admirably foreground the theme of political and social freedom, there is a tendency to elide the central fact in the Exodus story that escape from slavery is not so much a virtue as an opportunity. What matters is the acceptance of the yoke of the Torah in Sinai. To cross the Red Sea (a Greek mistranslation of the Hebrew for "Sea of Reeds") is liberating, but without the ensuing covenant at Sinai, no guarantee of the only kind of freedom that matters.

For liberal, egalitarian-minded Jews, the four sons are presently rendered as four children, and the Wicked Son of my childhood is sometimes reincarnated as the "Rebellious Child," which is altogether less loaded, but of course less forceful and enthralling. And while we're on the subject of the four sons it occurs to me that, like you, I identified with one (or in my case, two) as a child. Seated around our family table, it was clear to me that my brother Geoffrey, sixteen years my senior, was the Wise Son, and that in retribution for teasing me, my brother Stephen should be the Wicked Son. Which left two possible openings for me, neither particularly appealing. I am not sure how much psychological damage was done by my playing the role of both a simpleton and someone who isn't even smart enough to ask a question. But I am still in therapy.

As to my approach to the seder, I am not a great scholar, and come at things with the help of some pertinent texts, like Gaster's *Festivals of the Jewish Year* and Yosef Yerushalmi's *Zakhor: Jewish History and Jewish Memory*. Increasingly, I like any clear thing that blinds us with surprise, and that, to my everlasting pleasure, is what the group at the table invariably provides. My questions are not profound, but the answers of family and friends are often both deep and delightful, or just wonderfully comic. Our guest from China, Ying, once told me that after a year in America she realized that when Americans said, "Hmm . . . interesting" what they really meant was "boring."

When the seders become ". . . interesting," it will be time to pass the baton.

•   •   •

Passover always begins on the night of a full moon, and I imagine it floating like a silver dirigible from where it hung over my childhood home in London across the Atlantic to linger above your home in Brooklyn. We are not observant Jews, we do not, for the most part, eat kosher food, we rarely attend synagogue, we ride on the Sabbath. And yet, at the seder table, we sit and lean, as required, in imitation of languid Roman freemen. Your brother sinks deep into a low couch, next to him a friend is precarious on a stool, and the attire is both formal and informal, yarmulkes or inventive headgear for some and nothing for others. We eat unleavened bread that gets stuck in our teeth and we tell an old old story. We continue to sing and talk long into the night, and somehow this enduring conversation makes all that wandering in the desert absolutely worth it.

—JONATHAN WILSON

# Roasted Kosher Sweet Salami

This is an old-ish recipe from my mother's side of the family. It is not served on Passover (the bread rules out that possibility) but is a staple at our Chanukah parties and as a Thanksgiving appetizer. I have never met anyone else who's ever heard of this dish, and my guess is that it was "invented" by someone in my family based on what was in the fridge one night. The alternate version (see below) was almost certainly developed on the fly by someone (most likely my mother) who had run out of mustard.

## INGREDIENTS

1 Hebrew National kosher salami (whole, unsliced)*

1 jar honey mustard

1 mini loaf of rye or pumpernickel bread

## DIRECTIONS

Preheat oven to 300 degrees. Line a cookie sheet with aluminum foil. With a knife, cut four or five half-inch scores in the salami. Slather salami with honey mustard until evenly coated. Roast for 1–2 hours, or until slightly charred and bursting. Serve with rye bread and more mustard.

Variation: Substitute orange marmalade for honey mustard.

*NOTE: This recipe can be made only with Hebrew National brand kosher salami. This has nothing to do with brand loyalty. Hebrew National salami can be difficult to find but I have tried all variation of other products and, for whatever reason, I have never had success with another salami. For the honey mustard, I recommend Honeycup brand, but as long as you use the thick kind that comes in a squat glass jar and has a consistency closer to molasses than mustard, you'll be fine.*

*\*The observant reader will note that despite the earlier discussion of my grandmother's strict no-salt requirement, the rule does not apply to items that have been salted (or otherwise sodium compromised) before purchase, including, but not limited to, deli meats of all variety. My understanding is that the acceptance of these products works on much the same principle as that in play for those members of the Jewish community who try hard to observe the laws of kashrut but cannot resist Chinese food—so long as the offending ingredients are hidden, as in dumplings, what you can't see won't hurt you.*

**Ramona Ausubel** is the author of *No One Is Here Except All of Us*, *A Guide to Being Born*, and *Sons and Daughters of Ease and Plenty*.

**Aimee Bender** is the author of five books. The most recent, *The Color Master*, was a *New York Times* Notable book of 2013.

**James Carse** taught for thirty years at New York University. His books include *Finite and Infinite Games* and *The Religious Case Against Belief*.

**Anne Carson** is a Canadian poet, essayist, translator, and professor of Classics.

**Joshua Cohen**'s most recent novel is *Book of Numbers*.

**Natalie Diaz** was born in the Fort Mojave Indian Village in Needles, California. She splits life between Princeton, New Jersey, and the Mojave Desert.

**Joel Drucker** is the author of *Jimmy Connors Saved My Life*. His work has appeared in *Salon*, *Huffington Post*, the *Tennis Channel* and others.

**James Gendron** is the author of *Sexual Boat (Sex Boats)* and *Weirde Sister*. He lives online at jamesgendron.cool

**Mohsin Hamid** is the author of *Moth Smoke*, *The Reluctant Fundamentalist*, *How to Get Filthy Rich in Rising Asia*, and *Discontent and Its Civilizations*.

**Michael Helm**'s novel, *After James*, will appear in September. He lives in semi-rural Ontario.

**Caoilinn Hughes** is an Irish writer and Assistant Professor at Maastricht University in the Netherlands.

**Ha Poong Kim**, a professor of philosophy emeritus at Eastern Illinois University, recently finished his translation of *Shi Jing*, the anthology of songs in ancient China.

**Nate Klug** is the author of *Rude Woods*, an adaptation of Virgil's *Eclogues*, and *Anyone*, a book of poems. He works as an UCC (Congregational) minister.

**Alexis Knapp**'s essays have appeared in *The Iowa Review*, *The Normal School*, and *Tin House*.

**Cheston Knapp** lives in Portland, Oregon, with the choices he's made.

**Emma Komlos-Hrobsky** has written for *Bookforum*, *Hunger Mountain*, *Web Conjunctions*, and the *Story Collider*.

**Alan Lightman** is a novelist, essayist, and physicist, and Professor of the Practice of the Humanities at MIT. His books include *Einstein's Dreams*.

**Alex Mar** is the author of *Witches of America*. She is also the director of the documentary *American Mystic*.

Maureen N. McLane's most recent book of poems is *This Blue*.

Leigh Newman is the author of *Still Points North*.

Justin Nobel's stories have been published in *Best American Science and Nature Writing 2014* and *Best American Travel Writing 2011*. He lives in New Orleans.

Mira Ptacin is the author of the memoir *Poor Your Soul*. She lives in Maine and dedicates this piece to Olga "Yoga" Kreimer.

Jamie Quatro is the author of a story collection, *I Want to Show You More*. A second collection and novel are forthcoming.

Alicia Jo Rabins is a poet, composer, musician, and performer based in Portland, Oregon. Her book *Divinity School* won the 2015 APR/Honickman First Book Prize.

Marilynne Robinson's most recent books are *Lila*, a novel, and *The Givenness of Things*, a collection of essays.

Sarah V. Schweig's poems have appeared in *BOMB*, *Boston Review*, *Slice* and elsewhere. She lives in New York City with a man and their cats.

Marcus Slease was born in Portadown, Northern Ireland. He lives in the Docklands of East London. His latest book is *Rides*.

Darcey Steinke is, most recently, the author of *Sister Golden Hair*. She lives in Brooklyn and teaches at Columbia, Princeton, and the American University of Paris.

Daniel Torday is the author of the novel *The Last Flight of Poxl West* and the novella *The Sensualist*.

Pauls Toutonghi teaches at Lewis & Clark College. He is an essayist and fiction writer.

Joy Williams is the author, most recently, of *The Visiting Privilege: New & Collected Stories*.

Adam Wilson is the author of *Flatscreen* and *What's Important Is Feeling*. He lives in Brooklyn.

Jonathan Wilson's most recent book is *Kick and Run: Memoir with Soccer Ball*. He is Director of the Center for the Humanities at Tufts University.

Christian Wiman's selected poems will be published next fall.

CREDITS:
FRONT COVER:
*A Hundred Sunsets*, digital illustration, 18" x 18", 2015.
© James R. Eads. www.jamesreads.com.

## A WELL-MADE BED
### A Novel by Abby Frucht & Laurie Alberts

ISBN 978-1-59709-305-7 / $16.95 / March 1ˢᵗ

Nearly fifteen years after the death of her childhood friend in a violent hit-and-run accident, Noor Khan is still in the midst of struggle. With a failing equestrian business and suspicions of an unfaithful husband, her years of physical and psychological therapies have driven her to cross a line that blurs what is law, and what is right. When Noor's home-steading neighbor, Jaycee, gives her the chance to save her business and her marriage through the underground cocaine market, the two fall into a world of murder, copyright infringement, dementia, and one large, Peruvian cheese wheel that has them trapped in the morally ambiguous lifestyle they may have desired all along.

## Praise for *A Well-Made Bed*:

"Brilliant and beautifully written, *A Well-Made Bed* centers around Jaycee and Noor and the unexpected but inevitable predicaments they get themselves into. Soon the interlocking plots and subplots make it impossible to separate character from destiny, humor from sorrow, or truth from lies. *A Well-Made Bed* is deliciously addictive."

—ALICE FOGEL, Poet Laureate of New Hampshire

"Laurie Alberts and Abby Frucht have written a rollicking novel with so many plot twists and surprises I couldn't put it down. Jaycee and Noor are unforgettable characters: funny, flawed, full of hope, and deeply human. *A Well-Made Bed* is a tour de force written by two wildly talented writers."
—CONNIE MAY FOWLER, author of *How Clarissa Burden Learned to Fly* and *Before Woman had Wings*

"*A Well-Made Bed* is a beautifully made story and a modern parable. What happens when good people need money—a bunch of money, and fast? You can guess. Noor and Jaycee are friends from opposite sides of the tracks, but their urgent needs push them to consider what seems like a rather low-grade form of mayhem, a simple plan, and practically foolproof. So begins a story that will make you laugh, and shudder, and identify, whether you want to or not."
—JACQUELYN MITCHARD, author of *The Deep End of the Ocean*

Available from the Chicago Distribution Center
To place an order: (800) 621-2736 / www.redhen.org

## PSYCHOANALYSIS IS BACK
### RICHARD SELDIN

**BELOW THE LINE IN BEIJING**

RICHARD SELDIN

*Richard Seldin packs a lot into his well-written, fast-paced, novel about psychoanalysis, marital love and declining male sexuality. The book's psychoanalytic orientation teems with unusual mental states—psychological muteness, an imagined playmate, a womanizing double and mind/body disturbances. In fact, this is one of the best novels about psychoanalysis I've ever read, and offers readers the pleasure of following a protagonist who thinks in a psychoanalytic way.*

"This compelling novel will hold you in its grip from beginning to end. Part mystery, part psychological thriller, *Below the Line in Beijing* is a terrific read and an auspicious debut by a gifted writer."

—Dr. Theodore Jacobs, psychoanalyst, Clinical Professor of Psychiatry, Albert Einstein College of Medicine, and author.

"Readers of Saul Bellow's literary classics of middle age and diminished powers will quickly appreciate the setting and concerns of this novel. The action in *Below the Line in Beijing* is largely internal and observational, but excels in its tone and approach. Steeped in the cultural atmosphere of China, the special circumstances of the Olympics, and the unique struggles of an aging man, Below the Line in Beijing is a solid recommendation for any who want a novel packed with introspection and cultural analysis."

—D. Donovan, Senior eBook Reviewer, Midwest Book Review.

The novel's plot line is fairly simple, though its structure, which includes dreams and fascinating footnotes, is atypical. When the book begins the narrator, a 61-year old, Federal Government attorney, awakens next to his wife, Sheryl, with an erection pressed against her thigh. Though initially pleased by his desire—he's had little sexual interest in her for some time—he discovers it comes packaged with an inability to speak. This peculiarity further confounds him when he finds that, while mute in English, he can communicate in the foreign languages he knows. Although he can only guess at it, he connects the muteness to three unrelated matters: a quirky stuttering problem; powerful fantasies about hooking-up with young women; and fortuitously running into his friend, Jim, a philanderer and fashionista, after not having seen him for forty years.

As Freud's talking cure requires talking and the narrator's psychoanalyst, Isaac Lutansky, only speaks English, they agree to suspend their work. Soon thereafter the narrator and Jim travel to Beijing for the 2008 Olympics. While the narrator, a proficient Mandarin speaker and expert on things Chinese, expects to dominate their relationship in Beijing, Jim immediately takes over and leads them on a quest for young women.

I won't give the ending away, but will say that it is marvelously written. While the book's most poignant erotic scenes might bring to mind Nabokov's *Lolita*, its larger influence clearly is Freud. And right out of the Freudian book, the narrator's story is one of a not-too abnormal mind gone awry and attempting to heal itself, both with and without Lutansky's help.

*For more of the review, see Richard Seldin's website blog at www.richardseldin.blogspot.com*

*Below the Line in Beijing* was **published by International Psychoanalytic Books - 256 pp. $19.95, paper; $7.99, Kindle.** The book can be purchased at **Politics and Prose**, www.IPBooks.net, www.amazon.com and most retail bookstores

# THE MUSE & THE MARKETPLACE

**APRIL 29TH - MAY 1ST, 2016**
**AT THE BOSTON PARK PLAZA HOTEL**

Write What You Love, Sell What You Write

Intensive writing seminars.

Expert Publishing Advice.

One-on-One Manuscript Consultations.

Networking with Top Literary Agents, Editors, and Authors.

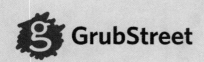

GrubStreet

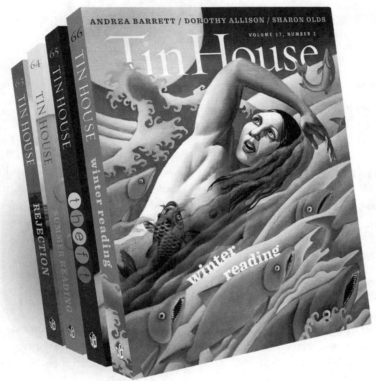

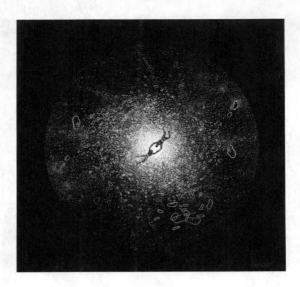

# ABOUT THE COVER

This month's cover art is part of a series concerning past lives and soulmates. Artist James R. Eads says that *A Hundred Sunsets* "is meant to capture the indescribable feeling of being reunited with someone after what feels like thousands of years." He writes further in this companion poem:

*A Hundred Sunsets*

*And then it happened*
*like a hundred sunsets all at once*
*the many secrets of life and death*
*were no longer hidden*
*and we were left alone*
*to bask in the light.*

Though his artistic background is traditional, Eads's work has a distinctly modern feel—the colors and amoeba-like shapes of *A Hundred Sunsets* have a neon, almost psychedelic vibe. An experienced woodcut artist, Eads has translated his knowledge of mark making into the digital medium. These printmaking techniques are evident in his use of negative space, specifically where fine lines of color break up the black silhouettes of his figures. He is also influenced by the Impressionist paintings of Monet and Seurat.

Through his art, Eads expresses complex themes, such as the notion of an eternal soul and the passage of time. He gives the soul a physical form, suggesting "something inside us in between the heart and the mind."

You can see more of his work at www. jamesreads.com

---

Written by *Tin House* designer Jakob Vala, based on an interview with the artist.